KULTUS

A Thaddeus Blaklok Novel

First published 2011 by Solaris
an imprint of Rebellion Publishing Ltd,
Riverside House, Osney Mead,
Oxford, OX2 0ES, UK

www.solarisbooks.com

ISBN: 978-1-907992-27-8

10 9 8 7 6 5 4 3 2 1

A CIP catalogue record for this book is available from the
British Library.

Designed & typeset by Rebellion Publishing

Printed and bound by CPI Group (UK) Ltd, Croydon, CR0 4YY

KULTUS

RICHARD FORD

SOLARIS

For Dad.

CHAPTER
ONE

HE WAS SO very proud of his tower; it was one of the highest in the Spires, and a soaring monument to solitude.

From far below wafted the sounds of the streets, the hustle and bustle of the Manufactory with its pumps and its gears and its engines. The window to his spacious study was kept closed most of the time to guard against the pollution that would ride up on the ether and creep into the sanctity of his domain. He would only open it to vent out the smoke from his calabash pipe, an indulgence he seldom allowed himself. Strangely, he found that the murky stench left by the city's air was far preferable to the pungent miasma left behind by his spicy Latakian weed.

Earl Beuphalus placed his book down on the wide, dark-oak desk and reclined in his worn leather armchair. He ran a finger and thumb up the bridge of his nose, loosening the wire-rimmed spectacles that sat there, and gently rubbed the spot where they pinched his flesh. Damn his eyes for their reliance on eyeglasses, they were a curse to all vain men. He peeled the fragile metal and glass from his face and flung it down on top of his book.

Stretching, he looked around his wood panelled study, glancing in turn at the paintings that hung on every wall, each depicting a key noble of House Westowe. In the corner was great uncle Hannibal, a well-known raconteur and carouser. It was rumoured the old sot had nearly demolished the Westowe fortune before he died. If it had not been for his brother, Duke Cresto, who took over after Hannibal's untimely demise, there would be nothing left. Cresto's image hung on the opposite wall, as far from Hannibal as was possible, and next to Cresto was Earl Beuphalus's father, Gaius, glaring down, red faced and furious as he had been in life. The artist had managed to capture him perfectly; a little too perfectly for Beuphalus's taste.

The Earl could only wonder what his own portrait would look like as it hung in this ancient study. Would he appear regal, or merely pompous? It mattered little, as long as they got his raiment correct. Beuphalus was a man who enjoyed smart dress at all times. Even now, reclining in his private study, he wore a green satin suit, bespoke made by the finest tailor on Kraken Street. His brown waistcoat was moleskin, made from real moles, and his silken shirt and cravat had cost more than the rest of his attire put together. At the moment he wore leather slippers, but the shoes that matched his current accoutrements had been specially imported from the colonies, hand-crafted and polished to a mirror sheen. It was important, nay imperative, to Earl Beuphalus that he looked his best at all times, even when, as now, he was in private repose. Well, one never knew when one might have visitors.

Outside, the sky was beginning to darken and the ambient glow of the gaslights on the streets below would soon permeate upwards, penetrating the thick smog that hung over the Manufactory. The view would be tremendous, as it always was. From his lofty tower, Beuphalus would look down onto the gaseous pall, lit from beneath by a myriad of colours. It never ceased to take his breath away.

But that would be some time yet. For now he would have to content himself with his books. Or perhaps one book in particular.

Rising from his armchair he walked towards the tall shelf that took up most of one wall. It stretched from floor to ceiling, packed with tomes both ancient and modern. There was no rhyme or reason to the order these books were stacked, but Beuphalus knew the location of each one instinctually. He could close his eyes and reach out, knowing that his fingers would easily find his copy of *The Scatological Scientist*, by Castigan, or if he wanted something a little more light hearted he could reach down for *The Torturer's Gambol*, by Shrike. But it was not scientific journals or canonised comedies that the Earl was looking for. He wanted something much more forbidding.

With a slender hand, he reached up to the top shelf. A thin layer of dust had formed across it – the top shelf was reserved for books he seldom spared the time to read – and he gently pressed the spine of *Getty's Almanac of the Bestial* with one long finger. At his tender touch the book slid inwards, just an inch, then sprang back into place with a click.

Beuphalus stood back and waited. After the gentle purring of cogs from behind the shelf, a wood panel on the wall quietly slid open with a whooshing sound reminiscent of a lover's gasp. Almost ceremonially, the Earl reached inside the hidden alcove and reverently retrieved the ancient codex within. Cradling the tome in one hand he pushed the panel back across the small alcove until it clicked into place.

Carrying the book like a newborn baby, Beuphalus returned to his desk, pushing the clutter aside and laying the codex down as though returning it to the cradle. Then he sat and stared at his most precious possession.

The cover was plain and leather bound, though it had faded from years of wear. Round its edge was stitching of fresh cord, where Beuphalus had painstakingly replaced the previous hemp that had grown frayed over the decades.

Tentatively, the Earl reached out and laid his hand on it, feeling it, breathing it in. He knew he shouldn't really open it until the dark hours but he couldn't wait. It was like the book was calling to him, whispering sweet temptations like a back street doxy gently beckoning him from a night-darkened alleyway.

He curled his fingers around the cover and opened up the leather, revealing the crisp yellow pages within. The first page bore a simple sigil; a stylised V. Beuphalus caressed it, tracing the faded ink with his fingertip. He turned another page, cringing slightly as he heard the fragile leaf of the ancient tome crack. The age-worn pages only served to remind him of the book's profane history. It was a reminder that what he was doing was wrong. It was forbidden, his secret vice, but it would be its own reward eventually… he had been promised.

As he reached to turn another page a tremendous banging sound echoed along the hall outside. Beuphalus froze, his eyes suddenly wide with fear. The heart in his chest was pounding and a sudden cold sweat began to bead beneath the cravat at his neck.

He was alone, his retainers had been sent home for the night. Who could possibly be in his tower at this hour? Perhaps a burglar, a footpad off the streets below, come to help himself to the Westowe fortune. Perhaps the Judicature, come to investigate him and his vile 'hobbies', bringing their chains and their billy clubs and their thumbscrews. Perhaps it was something far worse.

Quickly, the Earl concealed his precious tome back in its secret alcove. It almost hurt to hide the codex away so soon after its unveiling but it had to remain secret. He kicked the slippers off his feet and moved towards the door. Beuphalus reached for the handle, noting that his fingers were trembling as he did so, but before he could reach it he had a second thought. After stealing barefoot to the fireplace, he grasped an iron poker, then returned to the door. It creaked noisily as he opened it, revealing the long dark corridor beyond.

On one side of the passage was the same style wooden panelling that adorned the study, on the other was rough-hewn stone, interspersed with high windows that reached to the ceiling. Intermittently the dim grey light of the city encroached on the dark corridor, lighting the Earl's way. He could see nothing ahead but an empty passage stretching out for twenty feet until it turned to the right.

'Hello?' cried Beuphalus. 'Is anyone there? Mrs Rooney, is that you?'

There was no answer. If Mrs Rooney, the cleaner, had decided to work late she was not answering.

There was another sudden bang, this time louder and a lot nearer, and the Earl almost jumped out of his tailor-made attire. It seemed to come from just beyond the turn in the corridor.

Steeling himself against the fear, Beuphalus stepped out into the dark. He was the sixteenth Earl of the House Westowe after all. Besides that, he was guardian of the codex of the President Valac, Lord of the Eighth Gate, Master of Serpents and Keeper of Hidden Secrets. He had seen things that would make an ordinary man shit himself. It was stupid to think he should fear noises in the dark. And yet Beuphalus *was* afraid, there was no getting away from it.

His bare feet made little sound on the wooden floor. Occasionally his soles squeaked on the polished wood, or one of the boards creaked under his weight, but otherwise he moved like a spectre. When he had crept to the end of the corridor he stopped, raising the poker high above his head before peering around the corner.

As soon as he saw the source of the sound, Beuphalus let out a sigh. A window had sprung open, clearly blown inwards by the wind. It must have banged heavily against the stone wall, echoing its sound down the passageway to his study. It was a wonder the glass had not shattered within its frame.

The curtains to either side of the window were billowing in the wind, and the smells of the Manufactory were beginning to waft in on the evening breeze.

The Earl leaned the poker against the mahogany panelled wall and strode forward, his confidence fast returning. He should have felt just a little foolish at being so spooked, but then again he was right to be cautious; any number of intruders would love to encroach on the great tower of the Westowes, and it always paid to be careful, as great uncle Cresto had often said.

Before he shut the window, Beuphalus paused, gazing out onto the Manufactory below. The sun had all but set, and he could see that, far below, different coloured beacons were beginning to wink into life as the lamplighters went about their work. There was the chatter on the streets, and the sounds of engines and horses moving along the vast scribble of roads that entwined the tall towers of the Spires. Above, the droning sound of an airship peeled down as the vast machine cruised between two soaring towers, black smoke billowing from its vents as it went.

He closed the window and fastened the latch. Pausing a second more to look out at the vast metropolis, he suddenly caught sight of his image reflected in the glass. Beuphalus had never been a handsome man but he had always prided himself on personal grooming. Alas, the years were beginning to catch up with him and soon no amount of preening and trimming would be able to halt the onset of age. It was in that moment he saw that his own reflection was not the only one caught in the window. Someone was standing behind him, just visible in the shadows. Someone… or something.

The Earl froze, clutching the curtain that was still in his right hand. As he watched, gripped by sudden terror, the figure moved out of the dark. It was hooded, wearing a long cowl that shadowed the head and ran down a pair of broad shoulders. When it drew closer, Beuphalus could discern more features of the face; bestial, with a long pointed nose and black shadows for eyes.

There was no point trying to confront the thing, he had left the poker behind and, besides, he was no pugilist. With a girlish yelp of terror, the Earl set off at a sprint down the corridor, away from his study and the hooded intruder. As he ran he gave a quick glance over his shoulder. The cloaked figure merely stood, watching him from the darkness as he ran.

Beuphalus turned a corner, then another. If he could get to the entrance hall there were several exits from his lofty rooms. At least if he made it out of his front door he could call for help. But who would there be? This was a tower of House Westowe, there were no neighbours to speak of; he would have to race all the way to the base of the tower before he would see another soul. Silently he cursed himself for his stupidity in not hiring a minder, or five minders, or ten. But it had not seemed necessary at the time, the security of his tower was second to none, it could not be scaled and the locks that barred the great doors were beyond the skill of even the most proficient intruder.

But then obviously not!

When he turned the last corner before the grand staircase, all thoughts of flight became moot. Ahead of him, blocking the corridor, stood another cloaked figure, identical to the first.

Beuphalus stopped dead in his tracks, mouth agape. He thought of talking, of pleading, but it was obvious these infiltrators were not mere housebreakers. As he looked he could see that what he had previously thought was a bestial face was in fact a mask. The robes were designed for ceremony, not concealment. These figures were sinister indeed, sent to scare him, or kill him. Worshippers of a rival to Valac perhaps... or something worse? The powers Beuphalus had been toying with over the years were bound to catch up with him sometime. But he was not about to give in easily.

With a shrill cry of defiance, the Earl threw himself at the nearest window. The heavy glass shattered under his weight, and he felt the stinging pain of fresh cuts upon the flesh of his hands and face.

He lay on the balcony beyond, the stiff evening breeze was blowing strong, and it served to ripen the pain of his cuts.

Beuphalus knew he was hurt, he found it difficult to move, but he still managed to crawl to the balcony's edge, hearing the crunch of glass beneath him. Glancing down he could see that his suit was in tatters, but it mattered little now.

Grasping the balustrade, Beuphalus pulled himself up. Blood covered his hands and left a dark smear on the stonework. He managed to get his head over the top, seeing nothing but clear air between him and the ground, hundreds of feet below.

'Help!' he screamed to the distant earth. 'Help me!'

His second cry turned into a strangled sob, but the Manufactory did not seem to be listening. It was too preoccupied with its own noisome clangour. It was hopeless; there would be no rescue now.

Desperately, Beuphalus lifted one leg, the tattered cloth of his trouser fluttering in the breeze. He almost made it, almost shifted enough of his weight over the balcony for gravity to do the rest, but he was not quick enough.

Firm hands grasped him, with strong fingers that dug into his flesh and held him tight. As he was dragged back across the balcony, through the broken glass and into the darkness of his tower, Earl Beuphalus managed to scream one last time.

CHAPTER
TWO

The room stank.

It was a mix of rotten eggs and dead animal. There was an eviscerated rat on the floor but that wasn't the source of the animal stench. The rat still smelled bad, anyone who thinks that dead rats don't leave an odour should try giving one a sniff, but this was worse; a more intense musk, reminiscent of a well used stable.

Thaddeus Blaklok lifted his head from the bare wood floor of the tiny room. It was fuddled, like a hooch hangover of the worst kind, but with an intense feeling of elation inextricably locked into the nausea. His hands were shaking. Could have been the adrenalin; the buzz of his recent communion. Or was it just fear? No matter how many times he did it, whether the invocation was a minor one or a full-blown hellfire-and-sulphur stink, it took all his willpower not to shit his trousers. Of course, anyone watching would struggle to notice. There was rarely any clue on Thaddeus Blaklok's face as to his thoughts. That was where his power lay. Most of his power, at least. Had he been a card sharp, Blaklok would have been very rich indeed.

He rose to his hands and knees, heaving a large gulp of air into his lungs. A bead of sweat ran across his shaved head and dripped onto the floorboards. It spattered and spread, making a tiny sound as it hit the dry wood, the moisture quickly consumed into the thirsty wooden veins. Thaddeus raised a hand to his moist head and ran his fingers across it, feeling the droplets of perspiration gather into a puddle on his palm. With a deft flick he sent his sweat flying towards the floorboards.

Bending one leg he put an unsteady foot to the floor, trying to lever himself upwards on his powerful limbs, but the going was difficult. He was drained, as though some infernal machine had stripped his musculature of all power, leaving behind only dry and impotent sinew. Every movement sent a tingling pulse through his ligaments and he moved slowly, as though afflicted with a pox.

Thaddeus managed to gain his feet, but the room insisted on spinning like a whirligig. It seemed violently set against him, bent on sending him sprawling to the ground. Quickly he closed his eyes, hoping that by blocking the sight of the room that was shooting past his field of vision in a blur of colour it might somehow allow him to stand straight. It didn't work, and he stumbled all the way to one wall, feeling the pain of a table corner dig sharply into his thigh. Something tumbled from the table, crashing to the wooden floor with a crack and a smash. The pulsing light he could see through his clasped eyelids suddenly dimmed, and Thaddeus realised he had broken a lamp. Never mind; it wasn't his lamp anyway.

Before starting the incantation he had done his best to move all the furniture to the edge of the room. Considering the repercussions there could be from summoning the chthonian creatures of the netherplanes he supposed a broken lamp was a small price to pay.

Thaddeus clung to the wall like a drowning man to a piece of flotsam. There he waited for the spinning to subside, with nothing but the inside of his eyelids for company. It would not have been so bad had the spinning been merely visual, but he could hear it too, whooshing past his ears like the wings of some great bird, sweeping past him, adding to the nausea. But he would not be sick. To puke was to give in to it, to show weakness. That was not Blaklok's way.

The stench of singed wood drifted up to him, the lamp he had smashed must be igniting the floorboards. There was nothing else for it; he would have to open his eyes. If the lamp had leaked oil everywhere it would not take much for it to ignite. If he were set afire when he was already feeling like crap it would not be a great way to end the day.

Tentatively, Thaddeus lifted the lid of one eye. The room was still spinning its merry-go-round waltz, but nowhere near as fast as it had been. He glanced down at the lamp. The glass shade had shattered into several pieces at his feet but it had not yet spilt its cargo of oil. The flame still flickered from the lamp's wick and it was scorching the wooden floor. He knelt gingerly and stood the lamp upright, taking a deep breath and willing the room to slow. It seemed to work, and Thaddeus managed to open his other eye and stand on both feet without the aid of the wall.

The tingling in his limbs was beginning to subside and the shaking lessened. Like a rush of fuel to a combustion engine he felt the strength returning to his taut muscles. There was still nausea, the urge to vomit almost overwhelming, but it was the least of the side effects and the one he could tolerate best.

His skin began to cool, and the moisture that covered his body cooled with it. With a shiver, Blaklok surveyed his room. The chalk pentangle was still intact, a wisp of grey smoke still rising from its centre where the object of his conjuration had so recently debarked. The salt circle he had laid within was now smeared and skewed across the floorboards. Between the two markings was the eviscerated rat. Even now, mere seconds after its demise, jinking flies were beginning to congregate to lay their spawn and feast on the fresh carcass.

It had been a simple invocation. The circle of salt was merely a precaution. After all, the imp he had summoned had entreated *him* for aid, not the other way around. But old habits were hard to shake, and a protective circle of salt was an elementary and requisite aspect of necromancy; any novice knew it.

The encounter had been mercifully brief and Thaddeus was left in no doubt as to the importance of the liaison. Unfortunately, as with all things associated with the demonic, he had been given the most cryptic of clues as to the nature of his task.

Procure the Key for us, Rankpuddle had said, its dog-like muzzle forming the words perfectly. As it spoke its mouth seemed strange, the bestial jaws working just as a man's would. Blaklok didn't know whether the key in question was meant for the imp or for someone else, for the creature always spoke about itself in the third person, and even then not very plainly. *A deluge is coming that must be stopped* continued the imp, *the Key is the way*. Of course Thaddeus had asked which key in particular, to which the answer had been, *look to the dead*. Then, with a flash of blinding light and a whiff of sulphur, the foul creature was gone.

Look to the dead, Blaklok thought. Well, that could mean anything. If the damnable beast demanded his aid then why not just ask for it? Why all the puzzles?

Thaddeus sat himself in the small wooden chair that had been pushed to the room's edge. The shaking in his hands had all but left him now and even the bilious feeling in his gut was beginning to subside.

A sudden rapping at the door set his heart racing once more.

'Mr Blaklok?' It was Mrs Fotheringay, his landlady. Trust her to pick now of all occasions to bother him. 'Is everything all right in there? I heard a terrible loud bang earlier on. And next door is complaining of a peculiar smell.'

Thaddeus opened his mouth to give his usual gruff reply, when he noticed something on the floor. More flies had rushed to join their fellows around the rat, and something black and hairy had crawled from beneath the floorboards to investigate the tiny body. But it was not the carousing of insects that had caught Blaklok's attention. He moved from the chair, crawling on all fours to where the carcass lay, its entrails strewn in what he had originally believed a haphazard manner.

Look to the dead, he thought again with a smile. The rat's innards spelled out a word, the slimy guts spread across the floorboards in an elegant script. *Chronicle,* they said, bold as brass.

Thaddeus jumped to his feet, feeling the sudden elation of triumph. Mrs Fotheringay bashed on the door once more, just as he wrenched it open. Her sullen expression, the one she bore most often as though she had just stood in dog shit, dropped from her face. Her eyes popped open at the sight of Blaklok bearing down on her, stripped to the waist, tattoos plain to see on his muscular frame, face of thunder, covered in sweat and surrounded by a queer effluvium.

'I was only–' she managed to say, before Thaddeus grasped the newspaper that sat in the crook of her arm.

He held it up before her face and nodded his thanks, his eyes still burning in their deep sockets. She flashed him a bewildered smile as he slammed the door in her face.

Quickly he laid the newspaper out on the bare floorboards. *The Chronicle* was the most popular broadsheet in the Manufactory. In fact it was the only broadsheet in the Manufactory, its stories bearing a particular bias towards the Noble Houses that ran the city and the Sancrarium, the papacy to which they all paid a cursory tribute. In the metropolis that was the Manufactory, journalism was as functional a vocation as street sweeping or lamplighting. There was nothing that passed for freedom of the press, but right now Blaklok didn't give a damn – he only wanted information.

The cover bore several headlines, and Blaklok was quick to rule them out as he scanned the crisp paper. A murder in the Cistern, the betrothal of two unexceptional nobles, a tower in the Spires finally completed. All trivial.

Then he saw it; *Key of Lunos on Display*.

A smile slowly crept across Blaklok's face. That must be it! Though he had never been one for puzzles, this one seemed plain enough. He scanned the rest of the paper just in case. If he was wrong about this he would end up 'procuring' the wrong key, and that could never be good. But there was nothing, no mention of a key anywhere else in *The Chronicle*.

Once he had determined that this was the object of his task, he read further:

Duke Darian Hopplite, fortune hunter and explorer, heir to the House Hopplite fortune and eligible bachelor, has decided to show his recent procurement – The Key of Lunos – at the Manufactory's Repository of Unnatural History. The Key, unearthed by Duke Darian on a recent expedition to the Moon, is an item of great value, and the subject of intense scientific and theological debate. Some say the Key is a vessel for the Almighty, while the scientific community argue the veracity of this, stating that the Key of Lunos is an item of "undeterminable extra terrestrial import".

Duke Darian has declined to become involved in the debate, himself stating that the item: "Looks dashed nice on the old mantle".

The Key of Lunos will be on display for one week, starting Thrivensday.

Thaddeus sat back in the small wooden chair that still leaned against the wall and rubbed his stubbly chin with one calloused hand. This could be difficult. An item owned by a duke of the Noble Houses. Not only would it mean a hanging offence thieving such an item, but now it was to be displayed in the Repository of Unnatural History. Everyone knew security within that monolith to all things weird and weirder was almost as tight as the Chambers of the Sancrarium. The place was full of dangerous flora and fauna, and the near impregnable aegis was there as much to keep the exhibits in as to keep the light-fingered out.

There was nothing else for it, he needed advice. First of all he needed to know exactly what he was dealing with. What was this bloody Key and why was it so important? The rest he would figure out as he went. After all, how hard could it be? The Repository's safeguards might be considered insurmountable by its custodians, but then again they had never tried to stop Thaddeus bleeding Blaklok!

CHAPTER
THREE

CASTOR CAGE WALKED with purpose. He neither rushed nor tarried, but there was a definite sense of resolve to his long stride as he moved down the dank passageway. The High Priest had seemed almost feverish in his eagerness to get the ritual started, and Castor was very keen not to disappoint the High Priest.

With two other acolytes at his shoulders, the three of them cloaked from head to foot in scarlet satin, Castor felt his confidence rising. Soon the ritual would begin, he and his fellows would be gifted with a boon undreamed of, and he felt almost as keen as the High Priest for this to be underway.

At the end of the torch-lit passage stood a heavy steel door and, as he reached it, Castor pulled a rusted iron key from within the confines of his flowing robes. There was a small grille set in the centre of the vast portal and Castor could see nothing but blackness through it. Soft whimpers emanated from within and he felt a sudden pang of pity for the cell's occupant. Castor was by no means cruel, but he understood that he and the other acolytes might sometimes have to perform acts of cruelty to attain their ends. It was a burden he was more than willing to bear.

He slotted the key into the lock and turned it. Despite the age and condition of the rusted metal door, the lock itself was well oiled and the key turned easily, sliding the bolt mechanism inside with a resounding click. Castor pulled the door open and allowed the light from the wall's bracketed torches to bathe the cell, revealing the wretch within.

'Earl Beuphalus,' said Castor with a smile. 'The time is now. Please come with me.'

The Earl cringed in one corner. Dried blood stained his torn clothing and he looked gaunt, two hollow eyes staring from within a pallid face. At first he shook his head and backed away from Castor's brothers as they entered the cell, but there was nowhere for him to go. As the robed figures reached out for him, Beuphalus began to whine and mewl like a puppy being gelded. All the pity Castor might have felt for the man suddenly vanished. This was a Highborn noble of House Westowe. Where was the dignity he had been taught to expect from such aristocrats? Besides that, this man was also a prominent member of Valac's coterie. Where was the fearless edge, the arrogance in the face of the enemy? Castor knew for a fact that were the tables turned he would be sure to give a much more august account of himself.

The acolytes deftly bound the Earl's hands and secured a gag to his mouth. It served to muffle the pitiful grousing somewhat, but Beuphalus still managed to make an annoyingly loud racket. Castor led the way as they dragged their prisoner back along the corridor, through the tunnel of flickering light.

When they reached the end, Castor could hear that the chanting had already started. Butterflies began to beat gossamer wings within his stomach as he mounted the stone stairs to the upper sanctum. Near the summit, the bright yellow light from the corridor's torches mixed with that of a thousand crimson votive candles, throwing an odd titian hue against the walls. As he stepped out into the huge red-lit hall, a hundred hooded heads turned to greet him.

Beuphalus was dragged up behind, and when he saw what awaited him he began to scream behind his gag. The sound was truly awful, and must have caused the Earl great pain, but the congregation gave no response.

The sanctum rose high, a hundred feet, perhaps more, Castor could not really tell. It was bare but for the four-foot altar that rose in its centre and the pit of fire that stood to one side. Lining the walls, standing on racks reaching almost to the ceiling, were thousands of scarlet candles, giving off a baleful light. Even the glow of the fire pit seemed to burn an angry red.

Castor stood, his brothers holding Beuphalus between them, waiting for the High Priest to appear. They did not have to wait long.

From a dark alcove to the north of the hall strode a tall, thin figure. He was adorned in satin, just like the other brothers present, but the robes he wore were black as ebon and his face was not hidden by the shadow of his cowl. A burnished bronze mask adorned his head, at once beautiful and grotesque. Its edges were sharp, splaying outwards like a sunburst and wickedly pointed. There was no mouthpiece but the nostril and eyeholes were like slits; lacerations in a face of evil. From within the sharp eyeholes burned two blue orbs, intense and focused. Castor could see those eyes even from this distance, and it made him shiver.

The High Priest paced slowly to the altar, and with one long arm, beckoned his acolytes to bow. This they did, humming as one as they stooped towards the altar, accompanied by the sighing sound of a hundred satin robes moving as one. Castor took this as his signal, and led his brothers as they dragged Beuphalus towards the altar.

To his credit, the Earl seemed to realise that his end was near, and chose this moment to begin a valiant struggle. Alas, his resistance was for naught – the acolytes chosen to bear him forth were not selected for their weakness of arm. Strong hands held on tight to him, and the squeak of bare feet being dragged on the polished marble floor made Castor smile within the shadow of his hood.

As the Earl was shackled tightly to the stone altar, the High Priest held out one of his arms in silent demand. A hooded acolyte shuffled forward, his head bowed, holding out a worn leather tome, which the High Priest grasped in a claw-like hand and held aloft for all to see.

'Earl Beuphalus of House Westowe,' the High Priest began. His voice was distorted behind his mask, but his words remained clear, echoing throughout the massive hall. 'Heir to vast fortunes. Keeper of slaves. Dweller in towers.' The gathered mass of acolytes tittered at the joke. 'Your plans are known to us. Your intentions clear. As self-professed Guardian of the Codex of Valac you would presume to leech us of power. To use us, our entire order, as a sacrifice to your weak master.'

The congregation muttered disapprovingly. It was as though they sat in judgement of the Earl as he lay trussed to the altar, a jury of a hundred robed acolytes, baying only for blood. Castor doubted there would be any clemency.

'How could you ever presume to overcome us in the service of such an inferior eidolon as President Valac? How could you hope to defeat us, when you are but few, and we are Legion!'

At his words the hooded mass began to chant louder, a buzz of forbidden words, both mundane and demonic. It was all Castor could do not to join in, but his own task was more important. The Earl had to be held steady. Despite the chains that shackled him he was still able to struggle, and the High Priest's aim must be true. With his two brothers, Castor pressed the Earl down on the hard stone.

'This foul tome must be consigned to the flames,' said the High Priest, his voice growing feverish and harsh. With that he flung the heavy book into the fire pit. The flames leapt up, hungry to consume the leather cover and ancient leaves, flickering higher in a frenzy of carmine light.

The High Priest stepped towards the altar, reaching within one gaping sleeve and producing a wickedly curved dagger. At the sight of the blade the Earl's eyes widened and he began to scream anew, but his words were lost behind the gag, now moist with his spittle. His body writhed, straining against the chains that bound him, but it was little use. Castor pressed down, feeling the Earl's thin ribs beneath his taught flesh. Beuphalus had little strength left and his final attempt at resistance subsided into muffled sobs.

Echoing chants resounded around the hall, and it became almost deafening. The acolytes brayed as one, their resounding voices seeming as a single call. But then, that was the point.

With a deft stroke, the High Priest brought the dagger down, its point easily piercing the Earl's sternum. Castor could hear the crack of bone as the High Priest deftly twisted the blade, splitting the flesh and cracking the rib cage apart.

Beuphalus went limp.

Expertly, the High Priest wielded the curved dagger, drawing the flesh apart and prising open the Earl's chest. Long, deft fingers searched keenly within the cavity as the razor sharp blade cut away sinew and cartilage, until finally his hand reappeared, holding the Earl of Westowe's moist, red heart.

Castor could see a stream of blood beginning to flow from the body, now still beneath his hands. It pooled in gutters carved into the stone, its flow guided to small holes that would channel the still warm lifeblood from the altar. His eye followed the trail as it led between his legs, running fast to gather within a pattern carved in the marble floor. As the blood began to pool within the carved sigil it became clearer. The red stood in contrast to the light grey marble, marking out the sign of Legion, his score of limbs spreading wide, his thousand eyes staring, seeing all.

Looking back to his High Priest, Castor saw that the figurehead of the Cult of Legion was standing in triumph, holding aloft his enemy's heart, allowing the blood to run down his arm in streams.

With a flick of his wrist, the High Priest sent the heart spinning into the fire pit. This time the flames grew even higher than when they had consumed the infernal codex. It was like oil had been flung on the flames, giving them an almost lifelike vigour. All at once the chanting stopped and silence fell over the hall.

'Legion!' cried the High Priest. 'We offer the heart of your enemy, and we ask for your boon that we may better effectuate your needs. We await our benefaction that your glory might once more be seen. That you might be liberated from your execrable detention. Bestow your numen upon us!'

Silence.

Castor stood back from the altar, watching the High Priest. The Earl's blood still continued to drip from his body but it was now beginning to congeal, and did not flow down the channels of the altar quite as well as it had.

Seconds passed, and still the assemblage waited. No one dared move, least of all Castor. Everything hinged on this, everything they had worked for and believed in. Should this fail the High Priest would have much to answer for. For the first time in a while, Castor was thankful that he was only a simple acolyte.

A sudden shocked sound came from within the congregation. A group of red robes moved aside, revealing one of their number, bowed in discomfort. Men were murmuring with disquiet as one of the acolytes began to make choking sounds. Before Castor could react, another sound alerted him to more movement in another part of the hall. Then, right next to him, one of his brothers suddenly fell to the ground as though he had been hit by an eight-chamber carbine. The man writhed on the floor, and Castor found himself backing away in disgust and fear.

All the while, the High Priest stood impassively, as more and more acolytes were suddenly afflicted, some screaming, others falling silently in violent spasms.

Some acolytes fled in panic, others backed away from their writhing fellows, knocking over candlesticks and grasping their brethren in fear. As Castor watched, wondering if he would be next, he realised he was standing in the centre of the sign of Legion.

The blood had congealed within the furrows and he could feel it beneath the thin soles of his sandals. He looked down and saw a faint glow, as the outline of the sigil seemed to reverberate with unnatural power. A strange sensation was beginning to consume Castor, a feeling of inculpable elation and blood curdling terror all at once. He looked up, and saw that the High Priest's steely gaze was upon him.

'Accept the gift of Legion,' he said, his voice but a whisper. Despite the noise in the hall, Castor heard the words clearly; they reverberated in his head like the sounding of a bell. And then he felt the pain.

Searing heat, or was it freezing cold, wracked his body in an instant from the tips of his extremities to his very core. Castor wanted to fall, to land on the ground in a heap, curl up into a ball and moan and whine and weep. But he could not. The sigil of Legion on which he stood seemed to hold him in place, filling him with an eldritch light, consuming him and nourishing him, changing him but reaffirming his very being. He felt sinew strengthen and grow, felt his senses heighten. Knowledge forbidden to mortal men flooded into him, and in an instant Castor Cage was one with Legion. He was all of them, and only himself at the same time.

IN THE END there were a mere dozen acolytes who had been granted the boon of Legion. The rest of the congregation stood at the fringes of the sanctum, those who had not fled anyway. The High Priest looked at his chosen few from within a sunburst mask of bronze. He did not need to speak. The Legion knew their task as one mind, and with their boon they could now accomplish it with ease.

This was just a taste of things to come; Castor knew it instinctively. Soon the Legion would be free to spread its power throughout the Manufactory, and beyond.

CHAPTER
FOUR

THADDEUS KNEW THE quickest way to get the information he needed. It might not be the easiest, or indeed the cleanest way, but it was by far the quickest.

The estate of Lord Julius was set a ways from the Spires of the Manufactory, where most of the Highborn dwelt in their sequestered towers. Not the sky-borne grandeur for Lord Julius, oh no. He demanded something even more exclusive.

To an outsider, a visiting dignitary or a travelling merchant-baron, the Manufactory might seem like a huge stinking machine, constantly moving, perpetually churning and writhing within itself. But there were places – secret and cloistered places – that were a world apart from the filthy streets and slime encrusted alleyways of the city. Walled off from the bustle and rancour of the Manufactory were sanctuaries of green, lined with bright blooms and home to fauna other than the usual scurrying vermin.

It was within one of these cloistral retreats that Thaddeus Blaklok would find his answers.

Obviously the grounds had security. Lean hounds patrolled the gardens, snuffling at the foliage, docile until they sighted an intruder. But Thaddeus had always had a way with animals. At first ferocious, the guard hounds had soon been licking his chin and rolling on the ground, whimpering for their bellies to be scratched.

When their play had ended, Thaddeus stole away from his new found canine friends, clinging to the shadows as he approached the great manor. He was all in black, neck to foot. A thigh length greatcoat covered his torso, while the black trousers and boots that he always wore finished his attire. Despite his size, Blaklok moved with the grace of a skulking cat. He had never considered housebreaking as a career, but as he made his way silently towards the well-lit estate, he suddenly considered that he would make a quite excellent second-storey man.

The porch light shone brightly, and Thaddeus moved round to the side where the light was dimmest. There was a door to the cellar, sealed with a simple latch and it took no effort to prise it apart. As he entered the building, Blaklok could only wonder at the naivety of the rich. Did they really think that hounds and reputation alone would keep out a determined intruder? It was true, that for most ordinary footpads, the repercussions of encroaching on the domains of the rich were dire indeed, but Blaklok feared none of that. Let them try and take him if they could. Besides, this Lord Julius was of no named House. He had few friends in high places. His reputation, and consequent deterrent to intruders, was built from what he knew of the dark arts and the occult. For many, that would be reason enough to give him a wide berth, but not for Thaddeus Blaklok. That was the whole reason for him being here.

He crept from the cellar as silent as death, stealing through the house like the reaper himself stalking a centenarian. The floors were carpeted with a lush shag, something Thaddeus was thankful for with his big boots and the heavy feet within them. He had no time to admire the décor; he was here on business. There was little time to stop and marvel at the portraits and stuffed, glassy-eyed animal heads that stared down from the gaudily papered walls. They certainly wouldn't help him find his quarry. But then, that didn't take long in the end.

Lord Julius sat reclining in a paisley patterned armchair. Through the crack in the door Thaddeus could see him, nursing a copy of some doubtlessly tedious book, whilst puffing away on some doubtlessly expensive cigarillo. To his credit, Julius did not seem surprised as Thaddeus walked in, the door creaking as he pushed it open. Most men at least showed a flash of fear as Blaklok loomed over them, but no such indignity from Lord Julius.

'And to what do I owe this unexpected pleasure?' crooned Julius, taking a slow pull of his thin, brown cigar. The air was fusty with thick smoke and Blaklok found his eyes were beginning to well. Nevertheless, he kept Lord Julius locked in his algid stare. Even Julius could not hold it for long.

'Care for a cigarillo?' asked Julius, reaching for a silver cigarette case that sat on a nearby chess table.

'Cut the shit,' said Blaklok. 'You know I don't smoke.'

'Indeed,' Julius replied, a languid smile crossing his face. 'Pure as the driven, Thaddeus. That's you all over. Well, let's get down to business then. And by the way, you really should have knocked.'

'Balls to that. It's better when you don't know I'm coming. The Key of Lunos. What is it? Why is it important?'

Lord Julius snorted, almost dropping the stub of his cigar on his lounge pants. 'This is a joke, yes? You took the trouble of breaking into my house to ask me about some useless extra-terrestrial trinket?'

Blaklok stared hard at Julius, looking deep behind the self-satisfied grin and overconfident air. There was something he was hiding; something in the way he sat, still squirming under Blaklok's gaze.

'You don't believe it's worthless any more than I do.'

'*Au contraire*, my indefatigable friend. It is indeed worthless, despite what Duke Darian and those overzealous curators at the Repository would have you believe. Why the interest anyway?'

'Mind your own fucking business,' said Thaddeus, taking a threatening step forward.

'Now, now! Don't bother with any of the rough stuff; you know it'll only end in tears. Besides, what possible reason would I have to lie to you?'

'Let's find out, shall we.'

Before Blaklok could take another step he heard the creaking of a loose floorboard behind him. He spun in time to see the barrel of a blunderbuss come poking through the door, aimed at his back. His jackbooted foot rose quickly, the powerful leg striking out like a piston to impact against the door. There was a deafening explosion as the blunderbuss went off, spraying the room with iron shot and destroying a four-foot vase that took pride of place in one corner. Before the echo of the blast had subsided, Thaddeus was moving, wrenching the door open to face the gun wielder. He was big, even bigger than Blaklok but that didn't matter, he would still go down; they all did in the end.

Grasping the man's shirt front, Thaddeus struck in with a head butt, feeling the crunch of nose and teeth, the sharp pain in his forehead... good pain. The man stumbled, but it was not enough, he was still on his feet. As the empty blunderbuss slipped from his fingers, Thaddeus pulled him into the room and clocked him with a right. It was a solid blow, straight to the cheek, and the thug fell back heavily into a table, knocking it over and sprawling on his back.

Good on him though, he was still conscious, obviously a tough one. But before Thaddeus could move in to finish him off, something smacked him hard around the back of the head.

Bloody stupid! Of course there were two of them.

Blaklok fell to one knee, the periphery of his vision blurring, like looking through snowfall. He tried to get back up but his legs wouldn't move.

Bloody stupid!

'As I said,' crooned Julius, 'you really should have knocked.'

Through his blizzard vision, Thaddeus could see the second man standing tall, a banded cudgel in his hand. Just lucky it hadn't been another gun.

The one he had sat on his arse stood unsteadily, nothing but ill will drawn across his bloody face.

'I would rather have avoided all this unpleasantness, but you've really left me with no choice, Thaddeus.' Lord Julius was now standing in one corner, away from the hulking brutes. There was no way he would want to get blood on him, after all. 'Make it quick,' he said to his men. 'And painful.'

Blaklok was glad of the chatter; it gave his vision a chance to clear.

The one with the cudgel raised his arm to strike again, but he was slow and ungainly. Thaddeus's piston leg struck out, this time into the cudgel wielder's knee. It snapped back, pointing the wrong way, and the brute screamed like a girl. His bloody-faced accomplice ran in with a vicious kick, but not vicious enough. It hit Blaklok in the face. There would be a bruise later but nothing to cry about, and it didn't stop him rising and snatching the cudgel from the one with the broken knee.

And then he set about them. It wasn't pretty or graceful. In fact it was brutal and fairly ugly, but it got the job done. In the end he was panting like a lion after the hunt and his head was starting to throb, but the two big ones were down, and they weren't moving.

'Now, now, remember who started this,' blurted Julius. He was backed into a corner and suddenly took on a frightened-rabbit demeanour. 'I have a right to defend myself.'

'Shush,' said Thaddeus, dropping the cudgel to the floor; this he wanted to do with his hands. 'No fucking talking until I say so.'

'All right! I'll tell you what you want to know.' Julius's voice had grown shrill, and his arrogance seemed to have fled.

'I know you will,' Thaddeus replied, reaching forward with those big, grasping hands.

'Not the face!' Julius covered his head with his arms. A balled fist hit him right in the guts, punching every ounce of wind from his lungs. Immediately his arms dropped and Blaklok wasted no time, driving a fist into his victim's pinched and imperious features. Blood immediately spread from a bust nose and lip. Another fist to the face and Julius was beginning to redden around the eyes.

'It opens gates,' blurted Julius.

Blaklok paused, his fist still raised. 'Gates to where?'

'Dangerous places. It's forbidden. Just leave it well alone.' Blaklok reached back once more, his knuckles itching to strike. 'The Nine Gates! The Nine Gates!' screeched Julius. 'It can open any of the gates to Hell!'

Blaklok loosed his grip on Julius and took a step back. 'So it would be extremely valuable to anyone wanting to open one of those gates? Someone mad enough to let loose the joys of the Pit?'

'Yes, yes,' said Julius, pulling a handkerchief from his pocket to dab at the blood on his face. 'But for the moment it's quite safe within the Repository. Security on that place is tighter than a fish's fanny. You'd have more chance of robbing the Bank of the Houses than stealing an exhibit from the Repository. And less chance of dying in the attempt. Take my advice, Thaddeus, leave well alone.'

'When I need advice from a stuck up outcast with more money than the sense to hire good bodyguards, I'll be sure to check with you.'

'I'll have you know these men came with perfectly splendid references,' Julius replied, starting to regain some of his former composure. 'So what is it? You want the Key of Lunos for the money? Someone hired you to procure it?'

'I told you once, mind your own fucking business.'

'Well, suit yourself, but you did come to me. I do have a right to know.'

'I came to you because you know everything concerning the Houses, and most things about our 'business'. Not because you're a great conversationalist. And no, you don't have the right to know anything. Speaking of which, this Darian of House Hopplite. Does he know what the Key's for?'

'I very much doubt it. And even if he did, it wouldn't interest him. All Darian is concerned with is his own prestige and how much tipple and tit he can secure for himself.'

Blaklok had heard enough. He left Julius bleeding in his drawing room and exited the manor, this time by the front door.

As he crossed the grounds towards the cloying confines of the Manufactory, he thought of poor unwitting Duke Darian and his unlucky find. It was clear the Duke might be about to get a rather nasty surprise. If Blaklok's 'benefactors' wanted this item, you could be damn sure there would be other interested parties. And if this Key could open the gates of Hell, it was damn sure that things would heat up in the Manufactory in the very near future.

CHAPTER
FIVE

THE REPOSITORY OF Unnatural History, like most prominent edifices of the Manufactory, stood on an innocuous street, in a nondescript part of the city. Gull Road was a quite ordinary byway, and followed the Cutter's River most of the way through the city. It was largely residential, with some parts set aside for warehousing and others strictly commercial. The Repository stood in a busy part of one such commercial section, sandwiched between an exotic meat emporium and a workshop dedicated to the construction of combustion engines. However, the grandeur of the Repository did make it stand out somewhat on this otherwise plain thoroughfare. It was taller than any other building on Gull Road for as far as the eye could see in either direction. It towered upwards, a full eight storeys of blank grey stone, weather worn and blackening from the constant downpour of smog and pigeon shit. The sign bearing its name stared out starkly, leaving little doubt as to the building's purpose. The bold script in which the legend was written seemed the only part of the building that was not a drab and dreary mess, wrought from brass that shone brightly even in the dimness of the Manufactory.

Thaddeus stood at the gap in the wrought iron fence that passed for an entrance. Well worn stone steps led up to an open doorway, and the huge building seemed to be doing a roaring trade, with dozens coming and going at once, squeezing in and out of the wide entryway with expectant smiles and bewildered looks of satisfaction. Two custodians stood flanking the doorway, one with a heavy carbine, the other a thick baton. Their faces were hidden behind helmets and they wore padded leather on shoulders, knees and elbows. It was puissant security, especially for what was, to all intents and purposes, a museum. Thaddeus could not wait to see inside.

Just within the doorway was a rusted turnstile, and after Blaklok deposited the requisite three shills, he was in. Easy enough. Perhaps the Repository wasn't quite the fortress it was reputed to be. Then again, he hadn't tried to get out yet.

He was swept along with the crowd at first as they moved into the wide reception hall. Blaklok could hear the gasps of delight ahead and wondered what could be evoking such a reaction. When he reached the main reception hall he had a hard time stifling a gasp of his own. The first thing to greet the Repository's visitors was a huge metal cage, reaching fifty feet up to the ceiling, with a sign displaying the legend *Lacerta Ferociatus*. Inside was the largest reptile Thaddeus had ever laid eyes on, though it didn't seem particularly ferocious. It sat sullenly in one corner of its cage, eyeing the passers by with disinterest, through black slitted pupils. The creature's leathery bulk was immense, and Blaklok doubted it would have been so cumbersome looking in the wild, where it had to fend for itself and find its own food. A leaner, liberated version of this creature might indeed deserve the title 'ferocious', but not this pitiful creature. 'Languid' was a much better description.

A bunch of schoolboys were leering at the beast, jeering and pulling faces, safe beyond the reinforced cage bars. One, his face covered in a rage of freckles, went so far as to spit a gob of chewed paper through a straw. It spattered on the reptile's long snout, but the monster gave scant reaction, merely turning its head in wan indignation. Thaddeus walked by, feeling a pang of pity, reassuring himself that he would die before allowing himself to be caged like that.

Moving through the Repository was like being assaulted by the mad musings of some crazed naturalist. There were chimeras of all kinds, creatures that should not exist, even in a drug addict's nightmare. There were horses with horns and human hands, winged monkeys with pig's heads and a sulky mermaid sat in a humid pool combing her tangled hair. Spiny tigers and scaly bears. Trees with faces that laughed and cried, and venus flytraps that could consume a man, sat behind reinforced railings. In the huge aviary, hideous harpies sat alongside beaked birdmen, aiming their shit at the paying customers to break the monotony of their day.

Once beyond the madness of the zoological section, the Repository displayed ancient artefacts from bygone cultures and mechanized works of wonderment. It was here that Thaddeus hoped to find the Key of Lunos.

After passing the jewel encrusted skull of a long dead fakir that was said to be cursed, and a seven-foot sword fabled to have been flung to earth by the angel Bath Kol, he finally saw it.

The Key had attracted a modest crowd and seemed inoffensive enough. It stood on a simple plinth, surrounded by a rope barrier. Etched into the plinth was a plain legend that described the artefact:

Discovered in a derelict basilica on the surface of the Moon, the Key of Lunos is an item of unknown origin that has sparked paroxysmal debate amongst theologians and scientists alike. What is known is that the Key, which appears to be an ordinary item crafted of basalt, is impervious to heat and seems all but indestructible. Some have speculated that the object may hold the secret to the heavens, but the truth may never actually be discovered.

Typical, Thaddeus thought, they've even tried to immolate the thing. Ignorant bastards; if only they knew.

He stepped back and began to survey the security. The Key was in plain sight and there seemed to be nothing stopping him reaching out and taking the thing, which was even more suspicious. The item was perched on a dais in the centre of a mezzanine, with two custodians posted at each exit. Each wore a carbine at their hip and carried a studded truncheon. These would be easy enough to overcome, but there had to be more.

Blaklok moved to one side, sticking to the shadows. He was big but he could be discreet when he needed to be. After a few seconds of lurking he saw what he was waiting for. The babbling of high-pitched voices heralded the party of schoolboys he had seen by the great reptile cage. Their preceptor looked flustered, at the end of her tether. The lads were a boisterous bunch, and after seeing the wonders of the Repository's zoological section, rusty old trinkets like the Key of Lunos most likely held little attraction. Blaklok moved forward, searching out his target. The boy with the freckly face, such a good marksman with his sodden missiles, stood closest to the Key. It took little effort to nudge him beyond the boundary; just a little push in the right direction and momentum would do the rest.

As Freckle-Face stumbled towards the Key of Lunos a shrill klaxon blared out from a hidden speaker. Blaklok kept moving, wanting to put himself as far from the exhibit as possible as the full weight of the Repository's safeguards came down. Steel shutters crashed shut behind the custodians, sealing everyone on the mezzanine as they pulled out their repeating carbines. But best of all, a cage of iron telescoped down from the ceiling, encasing the Key and trapping the bewildered schoolboy within.

Immediately the preceptor's voice began to rise above the wailing klaxon as her ward, now trapped within a cage just like the exhibits he had come to gawp and poke fun at, began to make panicked noises.

The custodians rushed in, barracking the boys away from the cage but the preceptor did not seem fazed by their presence. She railed at them, her plump face growing red with anguish as she demanded they release the now wailing boy. To her credit, the custodians took a step back, obviously unused to five-foot-nothing of school ma'am spitting hot red rage in their faces.

It took only minutes for the situation to be brought to order, the barriers to be lifted and the traumatised youth released to the care of his irate preceptor. Blaklok smiled at the state of the freckle-faced teen, no longer so cocksure as he had been when spitting at the wretched reptile earlier.

Thaddeus had seen enough and made his way towards the exit, still pleased with himself until he caught sight of someone that made the smile evanesce from his face.

Tarquin Bates – the weasily little scumbag! What was he doing here?

Blaklok moved in like a shark towards a thrashing fish, the crowd parting like waves before him. But Tarquin seemed to have a sixth sense for pursuers; most vermin did. His ratty eyes locked onto Thaddeus as he moved in, opening wide with surprise as he saw him stalking closer. Then he was off, pushing his way towards the exit, barging the old folk and the young, and slipping past men who were bigger than him, which was most of them.

Thaddeus watched him, moving at his own pace, seeing the crowd squeak and tremor as Bates made his way hastily towards the exit. He let his quarry move out of sight, the guttersnipe was obviously in a panic to leave, and he would never consider that there was a much shorter way to the exit by cutting through the Hall of Automatons. Casually Blaklok moved past the colossal mechanical drudges, it would never do to draw attention to himself.

Moving through the rows of vast metal automatons brought back vivid memories – painful memories, but Thaddeus pushed them to the back of his mind. He had other things to think about right now.

As he came out of the Hall, right beside the exit, Bates was just appearing from within the crowd. He was looking over his shoulder, checking to see if Blaklok was coming up behind, little realising that the hulking shadow on his heels had already beaten him to the pass.

Tarquin Bates squealed as Blaklok grabbed him by the lapels and pulled him into a shadowy corner. He tried to protest, immediately babbling his excuses but a quick, tooth-rattling shake shut him up. Blaklok glanced around. No one in the crowd had noticed and the custodians couldn't see from where they were standing. This was as private as it was going to get.

'Why the interest?' demanded Blaklok, giving that hard stare of his.

'I've always liked museums,' Bates replied, a weak smile revealing his crooked teeth. Blaklok could smell him: mothballs and talcum powder. It wasn't pretty.

'In the Key, you fucking shithead. What's your interest in the Key?'

'What Key? I'm here to see the caged beasties. That mermaid's just lush. Do you think she's re–'

Blaklok released the lapels and took a firm grip on Tarquin's too-small head. He pressed a thick thumb into Tarquin's eye and started to push. Before Bates could scream Blaklok's hand clamped to his throat and stifled the sound.

'Let's try again, shall we? Why the bleeding interest?'

'All right, all right,' rambled Bates, shaking himself free. 'I came to see the Key, but who wouldn't in our line of work? It's like the relic of relics, a direct door to the holy land. Of course I want to see it.'

'And you expect me to believe that?'

'Believe what you want, but look with your own eyes, Blaklok. We're not the only ones come to gawp at the Key. Go on, look!'

Thaddeus frowned, then he raised his gaze to the crowd. He had been so preoccupied with the exhibits, and then the Key itself, that he had failed to notice. But even now, walking amidst the throng he started to see them. Papa

Juno the Hoodoo Man had just strolled in, his long black dreadlocks cascading down his back, rainbow robes flowing to the ground. As he entered he was passed by the Deacon, his head bowed as ever, closely trailed by his initiates of the Art. Blaklok started to move, leaving Bates behind, now forgotten. As he walked, almost in a trance, he saw that they were all around him. He caught sight of a bright green top hat that could only belong to Trey the Rafter, the obese Mother of Mourn walked past within mere inches, not even acknowledging he was there, and a stench assailed his nostrils that could only belong to King Snake, hidden somewhere in the crowd. The further he moved, the more he saw, a dozen within five minutes, all prominent members of the Community, all experts in their craft. Even as he looked, he saw the towering figure of the Slayer of Eight, striding towards him, head and shoulders above the rest of the throng.

Thaddeus turned his back. Of all the 'who's who' of the occult that were here, the Slayer of Eight was the one Blaklok wanted to see the least. It wouldn't do for Thaddeus to be the one who changed the evil giant's name to the Slayer of Nine.

He stared at the exhibit in front of him (something trapped within a reinforced glass cage) and waited for the Slayer to walk by. He could feel the hulking presence behind him, the laboured stomp of great hobnailed boots as they waded past and the stench of animal musk.

When he had gone Thaddeus allowed himself to breathe, then turned his attention to the exhibit he was facing. At first it seemed like an empty glass box, but then he saw something flicker in the corner. The glass cage had the legend: *Elementus Incendium* written on it. Fire elemental. He watched the tiny flame as it flickered from one corner of the glass cage to the next, seeming in a perpetual search for an exit but never finding one. Blaklok could well believe that the tiny entity was going quite mad, cooped up as it was in a six-by-six box.

Suddenly he began to find the Repository of Unnatural History distasteful. The only 'unnatural' thing about this place was the way its exhibits were caged away from the world, put in boxes to be gawped at by ungrateful schoolchildren. Thaddeus could empathise with these miserable beasts much more than he could with the lascivious crowd who merely lapped up the misery.

He couldn't get outside into the smog and noise quick enough.

CHAPTER
SIX

A CROWD HAD gathered outside, embodying a rabid mix of the curious and ghoulish. This sort of thing always happened at the scene of a murder. Some people would be concerned for their safety and that of their loved ones, hoping to glean as much information as they could with which to safeguard themselves against a similar fate. Others merely wanted a glimpse of death; a sniff at a corpse, dismemberment, blood, anything to sate their hunger for the macabre. Over the years, the ghouls had begun to far outweigh the concerned citizens by quite a margin, and today's rabble seemed typical of the morbid bunch that usually congregated for the big reveal when the carcass was finally wheeled out.

Well, they would just have to wait their turn.

Indagator Amelia walked close behind Bounder and Hodge, her fantassins, as they shoved their way through the mob and towards the warehouse. More fantassins of the Judicature stood on guard around the building, watching the gathered spectators. They were dressed in their traditional garb, not an ounce of flesh visible beneath black leather and iron, faces hidden under helmets, even the eyes shaded by a mesh visor.

Amelia ignored them as they saluted her entry; she had little time for the pleasantries of the rank and file. The only fantassins that she was concerned with, or indeed trusted, were her own. Bounder and Hodge might have been dressed up thugs with little moral fibre to speak of, but they were loyal to her and would gladly smash anyone's head in at her slightest suggestion.

Once inside, Amelia could see that there was a bustle of activity in the far corner of the warehouse. Yet more fantassins, surrounded by the grey smocked figures of the morticianeers, flocking around something that lay quite still on the floor. It did not take Amelia's keen investigative powers to deduce that this must be the body.

As she approached, she noted a figure squatting down, examining the wrist of the blood-strewn corpse. The examiner was dressed identically to Amelia, and he looked round with his usual sardonic smile as her shadow fell over him.

'Hello, Indagator. Late again, I see.' The man stood, still smiling his stupid smile, which Amelia did not return.

'Indagator Surrey. So glad you could find the time to attend *my* investigation.'

'Come, come, Amelia. Even you should appreciate the aid of a colleague. We are, after all, the best in the field.'

As he spoke, Surrey glanced intermittently down at her chest, the smile never leaving his face. He seemed to care little whether he was noticed undressing her with his eyes, but some men simply couldn't resist a woman in uniform... even so called 'exemplars' of the Judicature. It wouldn't have been so bad but the plain grey doublet and trousers that made up an Indagator's uniform could hardly be considered prurient.

'Must we persist with this constant duelling,' said Amelia, her tone reflecting her despondency with Surrey's games.

'But Amelia, we play so well together.'

'See fit to show yourself out. I would hate for Bounder or Hodge to accidentally step on you... three or maybe four times.'

Surrey's smile never broke as he strode past the trio. He even had the gall to give Hodge a sly wink on the way.

Amelia turned her attention back to the task at hand. Lying on the concrete floor of the warehouse was a body. The face glared upwards, mouth open in a rictus grin. One of the limbs was stiffened in rigor, telling the Indagator that he had been killed sometime in the past three days. His clothes were in tatters, covered in lacerations, but the cause of death seemed obvious, a huge wound to the chest that still lay open, exposing the whiteness of ribs.

'What do we have?' Amelia demanded of a morticianeer as he hustled by.

The man stopped, adjusting the heavy magnifying lenses that sat on his nose, and turned his attention to the body. 'Well, this happens to be the Earl of Westowe, though I guess he has seen better days.' He opened his mouth in a wide, crooked grin. When Amelia gave no reaction he continued. 'He's obviously male, in his forties. He has minor lacerations to his limbs which occurred *pre-mortem*. His wrists have some abrasions which suggest he was tied down. Cause of death: a blow to the chest with a sharp object and subsequent removal of the heart. I think we can safely rule out suicide.'

The morticianeer began to snort uncontrollably. Amelia could only assume it was his version of a laugh, but then morticianeers were not known for their sense of humour.

'That's very helpful,' said Amelia, pushing the morticianeer along. He went on his way, still sniggering to himself.

Beuphalus of Westowe. Amelia had heard of the Earl, and not in the most salubrious of circles either. The late Earl had certain habits, a penchant for narcotics amongst other things that could only be found in the Cistern. She made a mental note to pay a visit to that subterranean hive later.

Amelia stood for a few moments, taking in the scene, trying her hardest to avoid the dead man's gaze. This was always the worst part of an investigation, examination of the body. It never failed to disconcert her; despite the number of times she had done it.

The lack of blood around the corpse suggested that the Earl had been murdered elsewhere and his body emptied of all fluids. The warehouse itself was abandoned and unregistered, so no leads there. It was most likely a well-chosen spot that the perpetrators must have known was empty.

She knelt down beside the prone carcass to take a closer look at the plethora of wounds, trying her best to disregard that grinning face and dead eyes. No matter how many bodies she saw, Amelia still hated to see the looks on their faces.

The lesions on the Earl's wrists had been made by a thick object. Had it been a rope there would be several telltale marks, but this looked more like it had been done by a handcuff or manacle. As she looked closer, Amelia noticed something further up the Earl's forearm. She reached out, grasping the wrist and pulling the shirtsleeve back to reveal more of the pale flesh. As she touched the body she was suddenly glad of her leather gloves. Even with the scant material covering her hand she could still feel the iciness of the dead tissue beneath her fingertips.

On the Earl's arm was a fading tattoo in the shape of a stylised V. It was surrounded by a thorny vine that wrapped itself around the letter like an eager lover. It more resembled something one might find on the arm of a dockside swabber than an heir to the Noble Houses. She glanced round at her fantassins, showing them the tattoo.

'Do either of you recognise this?' she asked, hoping that the insalutary circles Bounder and Hodge were wont to move in might explain something about the marking. Both men looked at her with bewildered expressions. She made a mental note not to ask for their input in future – they were good at their jobs, but as sources of information they were as much use as a blank notepad.

Then she saw it. On the ground surrounding the body, what at first had appeared to be detritus on the ground was, on closer examination, a collection of man-made impressions. Amelia leaned forward, her head inches from the floor as she tried to decipher the strange devices. They were like nothing she had ever seen, and at first she thought they were part of some exotic language.

'Transmundane script,' said a voice she recognised.

Surrey was still here.

She stood and glanced at him, trying her best to disguise the fact that she had no idea what he was talking about. 'I thought we had established this was *my* investigation.'

'The writings of the occult,' he continued. She wanted to punch him, right in that smug smile of his, but it would be most ungracious at this point. 'I just thought you might not be familiar with it. Not to worry, most people aren't. They find the whole 'preternatural science' thing a little disconcerting.'

Bounder and Hodge took a step towards Surrey, but he did not move, instead widening his smile all the more.

'All right,' said Amelia. At her words the fantassins stopped moving. 'Are you suggesting this was done by a group of raving cultists? Or perhaps even a demon? Did it rip the Earl's heart out and eat it?'

Surrey took a step forward, squeezing himself between Bounder and Hodge to stand beside her. 'There are all kinds of depraved sects within the Manufactory, my dear Amelia. You know as well as I do that in our job we get to see all the best kinds of maniac. However, some say that there are those who can actually commune with the netherplanes. Able to call upon demonic agents to come forth and do their bidding.'

Now it was Amelia's turn to smile. 'There is nothing that occurs in the Manufactory that can't be explained by bioscience and conventional wisdom, Surrey. You know that as well as I.'

'What I know is that the Lexiconium does not just detail murders, rapes and robberies. There is a certain strongroom with journals piled to the rafters full of the weird and wonderful. Arcane mysteries, ancient manuscripts, forbidden dossiers detailing every aspect of this city's secrets. Things that cannot be explained through the precepts of bioscience.'

'You've been spending too much time at the Repository of Unnatural History. Either that or reading too many children's tales.'

'No,' said Surrey, suddenly forceful. The mirth had gone from his face and he seemed deathly serious. 'This is real. The infamous Earl here has quite obviously been partaking of the wrong kind of medicine, and he's come a cropper. You would do well to heed the evidence before you.'

'So you expect me, with the Manufactory full of crazies and footpads, to start my murder investigation by looking for a rampant demon? Surrey, you're more stupid than you look.'

Surrey took a step back, holding up his hands in defeat, the sickly sweet smile back on his pretty face. 'Have it your way, Amelia. But don't say you weren't warned.'

With that he turned and strolled away, but failed to give either of her fantassins a wink this time. She watched him go, right until he walked out of the door, just to make sure he was not coming back.

Amelia smirked. Forbidden dossiers? A strongroom in the Lexiconium? Who was he trying to dupe exactly? Surrey was obviously conspiring to throw her off the scent. He saw that this was a high profile murder; an heir of House Westowe. There would be much prestige granted to the Indagator who could bring the Earl's killers to justice, and Amelia was not about to let Surrey be the one to stand in her way. This was simple murder; the Earl had gotten himself in too deep and paid for it with his heart. It was obvious his murder was a message. Otherwise, why leave the body where it could easily be found? If it was some kind of ritualistic slaughter surely they would have disposed of him in a more discreet fashion than this.

There was only one place to start, and that place was obvious. The Cistern was home to all the refuse of the Manufactory. A breeding ground for the city's unwanted and tainted and fetid. It was also where you could buy anything you desired for the right price, and right now Amelia wanted information.

'I think we've seen enough,' she said, moving away from the body, forcing herself not to glance back in case the Earl's glazed and staring eyes happened to catch hers.

As Amelia left the body behind she began to relax, feeling more comfortable within the confines of her uniform and with her men at her shoulder.

Wrong kind of medicine indeed.

The next time she saw Surrey she would ensure that he would be the one needing the medicine!

CHAPTER
SEVEN

HE HAD LET Tarquin Bates off the hook, but only to see if he could land a bigger fish. There were few who could say they had escaped the clutches of Thaddeus Blaklok with not a mark to show for it, and it was unlikely that Tarquin would be one of those few.

Blaklok kept to the shadows, hugging the filthy brick of street corners, watching from the dark as Tarquin made his way through the arterial highways of the Manufactory. The little shit knew something more than he was telling, and Blaklok was going to find out what it was.

The easy trail that Tarquin left led all the way to the Trader's Precinct, a collection of old storehouses and derelict shop fronts that had been used in bygone years for distribution and barter of goods from the river-barons. Now the river trade was dead and the only thing that pervaded the streets of the Precinct was the stench of the stagnant waterway.

The streets became quieter the further towards the Precinct they got, until they were all but deserted. Tarquin must have had serious business indeed if he risked crossing through this part of the city alone. The Precinct was now home to all manner of waifs and moochers, and Tarquin Bates hardly seemed the type able to defend himself against a determined ruffian. Nevertheless, Bates continued on his merry way, seemingly ignorant of any danger as he wended his way through the filthy streets. As Blaklok followed he realised that there was either a strong fetish watching over the little reprobate or the scum of the Precinct were familiar with Bates and somehow willing to give him a wide berth.

Thaddeus himself cared little for the robbers and footpads of the Trader's Precinct. Usually a threatening look was all that was needed to keep trouble at bay in the Manufactory's dives and ghettos, and here would be no different. It was strange though, that he never once saw sign of any street stalkers or cutthroats. The Precinct was not somewhere he often frequented but still, its reputation preceded it.

Ahead he could see that Bates was headed towards one of the large wooden storehouses that backed onto the river. It was a tall, imposing building that dwarfed all the others in this particular square. Tarquin strolled across the centre of the plaza, now strewn with debris, where once traders would have noisily bartered their wares.

An uneasy feeling suddenly crept into Blaklok's gut as he watched the lithe figure reach the storehouse and knock out a strange beat against the small door. Seconds later it opened a chink, then wider to allow Bates entry.

Blaklok slipped around the outskirts of the square, taking care to stay out of sight of the storehouse. There could be any number of eyes watching from within the rickety building, and he wanted to get the drop on whoever was inside.

When he was within twenty feet he could hear a droning chant emanating from within the wooden confines. It was a dolorous sound, and immediately Blaklok's skin began to bristle in anticipation. A ritual was taking place, and by the sounds of it there were plenty of people present.

He crept round the back of the building, his breathing as shallow as possible lest the stink of the river made him balk. The building was in a terrible state of disrepair, and it was unlikely he would be able to make a stealthy approach due to the creaking wood. Oh well, it would just have to be an *un*stealthy approach then, wouldn't it.

Black boots stomped up onto the porch that surrounded the rickety building. The chanting was growing louder, and Blaklok could only hope that it disguised the sound of his approach.

A door was set in the side of the storehouse and it hung almost off its hinges. It must have once been a sturdy barrier, but now it was merely an annoyance, a troublesome obstacle and heavy with it. Blaklok muscled the door inwards and stepped over the threshold, immediately surrounded by blackness. The droning voices were echoing all around, but Thaddeus could not yet see anyone.

He moved further inside until he saw a weak yellow light emanating from around one corner. As he stole forward he tried his best to be light footed, but, as predicted, the weak floor creaked under his weight. Despite the noise, no hooded acolytes came screaming from out of the dark, nor were there baleful eyes staring at him from the shadows.

As Blaklok reached the corner, he could see the first of the congregation. They wore robes of cloth-of-gold and nodded their heads as they chanted, rocking back and forth.

'*Valac serviam. Valac dominus. Valac patrem. Valac omnipotentum. Valac invicta.*'

And so the chant went on, endless ramblings to a dark god. Blaklok had heard of Valac, a minor President of Hell, but who were this bunch of pretenders? Real demonists didn't wear gold robes and they certainly didn't gather in places like this where anyone could just waltz in.

Blaklok couldn't see Tarquin Bates anywhere in the room, he must have donned one of those ridiculous robes and joined in with the droning. Well, the least Blaklok could do was let them finish their worship before he introduced himself to the flock.

After several minutes it seemed that they were going to carry on forever, and Blaklok began to reconsider his generous offer of allowing them to finish. Just as he was about to introduce himself, one of the robed figures at the front strode forward, taking centre stage. The mantra to Valac suddenly stopped, leaving an annoying ringing in Blaklok's ears.

The one at the front held up his arms, his hood falling back to show his face. A short, well-trimmed beard followed the line of his chin, and Blaklok was sure he had eyeliner on. The man didn't say a word. From a side door appeared two more of the gold robed acolytes, guiding someone between them. From the shadows at the rear of the room, Thaddeus could see it was a small boy, most likely a street urchin from his scruffy garb and filthy face.

In silence, the bearded leader circled the boy three times, then the child's arms were held out by the two figures who had brought him to the stage. There was a murmur of sound from the assembled crowd, they seemed excited, anticipating what was to come, and Blaklok started to get an uneasy feeling in the pit of his gut. Perhaps this bunch was a rabble of pretenders, but they obviously thought they were the real deal. Things were going to get nasty in a minute, and Blaklok was not just going to watch.

Quick as a flash, the head man pulled a knife from within his robes. There wasn't enough time to cross the room, too many people in the way. Thaddeus looked around for something, anything to use as a weapon. Lying next to his foot was a rusted canister, and he swiftly knelt to pick it up. Liquid sloshed around inside it. Good, he thought, it would give the thing some impetus.

As the leader raised his knife high, there was an expectant hush. Blaklok's grunt as he threw the can was heard by almost everyone, and they looked around in time to see the rusted canister fly above their heads; all but the head man, who was still intent on his target. Before he could bring the knife down on his young victim, he took the canister full to the face. The clang of rusty can on nose was drowned out by his yelp of surprise.

One of the robed figures turned as Blaklok stepped out of the dark.

'Defiler,' he shouted, lifting an accusatory finger. Blaklok drove his fist into the man's face, dropping him where he stood, leaving a cloth-of-gold heap on the floor.

As the congregation turned to face him, Blaklok could see that they were all ordinaries, not the lean hungry-eyed fanatics who were usually associated with the worship of demons.

Thaddeus took two more swings, but these were not fighters, and when two more of them hit the ground the rest were instantly cowed. He looked towards the exit and saw a stooped figure trying to slink away.

'Where are you off to, Bates?'

Tarquin Bates froze, then turned, giving his insipid grin.

'What is the meaning of this?' shouted the bearded man, grasping his bloody nose. His gold robe had fallen back and Blaklok could see the expensive attire beneath.

'I'll ask the fucking questions,' replied Thaddeus, strolling forward through the crowd, which quickly backed away. 'No one minds a bit of religious worship and all that, but blood sacrifice? That's a bit strong for a bunch of part-timers like you, isn't it?'

'This?' said the man, pointing at the urchin in front of him who was beginning to look bemused. 'It's not real. We weren't going to go through with it.'

Thaddeus looked from the bearded man in front of him to Bates, who seemed on the verge of turning tail and fleeing the building. 'You expect me to believe that?' By now Blaklok had reached the front of the room, and stood in front of the head man. With a deft snatch he grasped the knife from his hand and hooked one of the bearded man's nostrils on the end of the blade. 'This looks real enough to me. Name?'

'Erm, T-Trajian Arkwright. Of the North Spire Arkwrights,' he replied, not daring to move lest the blade slice him a wider nostril.

The North Spire. An opulent area full of 'old money'. Packed with wannabe families just dying (or killing) to become Noble

Houses. This one was obviously trying to spread his influence in a non-conventional way. Most likely his 'congregation' were made up of other stuck-up arseholes all trying to juice one another for notoriety and prestige. Anyway, this Trajian was obviously scared. It wouldn't hurt to try and milk him for more information.

'So what's all this in aid of then? Trying to commune with Valac are you?'

'N-no,' replied Arkwright, still hanging like a fish on a hook. 'It's more of a w-wake we're having.' Blaklok's brow furrowed. Was this one taking the piss? 'O-our sect leader was murdered recently. Earl W-Westowe. This is just a celebration of his life.'

'Well,' said Thaddeus, lowering the knife. Arkwright gave a sigh of relief. 'It looks like you lot might have upset the wrong bunch. Shows you what happens when amateurs get in over their heads. And as for you, Bates. You should know better.'

Tarquin Bates cringed, the grin on his face wavering. 'I was just here to help them, that's all. Just educating them a bit.'

'And did you educate Earl Westowe? Is that why he ended up dead?'

'That was nothing to do with me, honest. Rumour is he upset someone in the Cistern. Weren't nothing to do with our... worship.'

Thaddeus looked around. They were all scared. Bunch of pretenders playing at demon worship. Where did they think it would get them? He considered giving them a warning; telling them that no good would come of it, no matter what they were promised, but it would do no good. This bunch would never listen.

No one ever did.

'All right then, piss off,' ordered Blaklok, jabbing a thumb towards the door. The gathered crowd needed no further encouragement and began to slink away. 'Not you Bates.'

Tarquin Bates stopped mid-step.

Thaddeus grabbed the weasily figure by his gold cloak and dragged him to one side as the rest filed past.

This was a distraction, and wouldn't help him in his task to secure the Key of Lunos, but Blaklok felt compelled to investigate further. If something was afoot, if there was a war brewing between cults, it would serve him well to know about it.

'So this Earl. Upset someone in the Cistern, did he?'

'Well that's the rumour,' said Bates, showing his array of tombstone teeth. Thaddeus smashed his face against the wall. It hit with a solid thump, knocking the grin, and some of those awful teeth, from Tarquin's face.

'Okay. Okay,' said Bates quickly. 'Rumour is it was a rival cult. But that's just rumour. I wasn't lying about the Cistern. You'll find your answers there.'

'What cult?'

'I don't know all the details, Blaklok. Give a man some credit.'

Thud! More of Tarquin's teeth ended up on the floor.

'Legion! And that's all I know, I swear it.'

'Legion? Never fucking heard of them.'

'Well, you've been out of the game for a while haven't you? No one knows much but apparently someone from the Cult of Legion was asking about the Earl a couple of weeks ago. Where he lives, what he's into and all that.'

'Who was asking?'

'I don't know his name.' Thaddeus readied himself to smash Tarquin's face in again. 'But I know who does!' Bates blurted, holding his hands up in supplication. 'The Ring. They'll give you a name, they know all the goings on down in the Cistern. That's all I know, I swear.'

'You swear? On fucking what, Bates? You've broken every coda there is.' He let go of Tarquin's robe and wiped his hand on his greatcoat.

'Well. It's been pleasant as usual, Blaklok. I'll see you around.'

'One more thing,' said Blaklok. Tarquin stopped again, cringing in expectation of further violence. 'The next time you feel like *educating* a bunch of prigs with more money than sense... fucking don't. Understood?'

'Yes, of course. Whatever you say, old mate.'

'And get yourself a bath. You stink.'

'That was next on my 'to do' list.'

Blaklok watched as Bates scurried away.

By the time he stepped outside, the congregation had dispersed into the labyrinth of the Trader's Precinct. A couple of cloth-of-gold cloaks lay discarded in the square, but otherwise there was no sign of Valac's postulant worshippers.

'Are you gonna pay me, mister?' Thaddeus turned to see the urchin standing behind him, his filthy face looking up expectantly.

'What do you mean?' he asked.

'The one with the beard said I'd get five shill afterwards.'

He obviously didn't realise the danger he had been in. 'On your bike. Count yourself lucky you didn't end up dead and dumped in the river.'

The urchin's face suddenly changed from innocence to rage. 'Well fuck you baldy!' With that he spat a gob of filthy phlegm Blaklok's way and fled.

The spit landed some feet away.

Poor kid, thought Blaklok. Can't even spit straight. What chance has he got in a place like this?

With that, he set off on the long walk to the Cistern.

CHAPTER EIGHT

THERE WERE A thousand ways into the Cistern.

On the murky city streets, steel manholes could be unbolted to reveal tunnels that would lead miles down into the subterranean hive. Certain buildings, disguised as reputable businesses or respectable residences, contained entrances within them that served as conduits to the various underground levels. Then there were the more obvious ways, such as the steam lift that Amelia and her men were now taking.

It was not a comfortable journey, and the noise was hellish, but it was by far the fastest way down. A cage of reinforced steel and wire mesh rattled as though in the grip of a gigantic, angry baby. It plunged ever downwards, screaming as it went and the three occupants were forced to hold on tight to the single railing that ran around the perimeter.

Amelia found the journey quite exhilarating. Though it was not a hundred percent safe, the chances of something going wrong were minimal, and even then very rarely fatal.

Her fantassins, Bounder and Hodge, obviously had contrasting opinions of the journey. Bounder was smiling from ear to ear, his enormous mouth displaying the biggest teeth Amelia had ever seen. Hodge, however, was almost crouched double, obviously fighting the desire to retch, his knees shaking and sweat pouring from his face.

When the cage finally came to rest with a violent hiss and a jetted release of steam, Hodge could not open the mesh gate quick enough. The journey had taken only seconds, but it looked as though Hodge had been at the mercy of a master inquisitor for hours. Bounder on the other hand seemed almost reluctant to leave the cage.

After Hodge had recovered and resumed his usual impassive visage, Amelia led them through the tunnels.

At first it was as though they had arrived in a huge sewer, the tunnel was a wide construction of crumbling brick with water of dubious origin dripping from above and plopping loudly on the moist floor. The stench was tremendous, and Amelia could barely comprehend why anyone, no matter how desperate, would want to live down here. But as they passed through the dingy tunnel, only intermittently illuminated by quivering gaslight, the stagnant atmosphere began to change. Noise began to filter down the passage, growing louder with every squelching step they took. The atmosphere grew less damp and the steam of their breath lessened as warm air began to pervade all around.

At the end of the passage was a huge steel door, open as though they were expected. Within, Amelia could see the real Cistern, and it filled her with disgust.

The three of them entered a scene of debauchery. Thick smoke hung in the air, a mixture of noxious and narcotic fumes blown from a dozen hookah. In the periphery of her vision, Amelia could see bare arses oscillating in frantic copulation, as heavy breaths and cries of ecstasy mixed with vile laughter and hushed conversation. And then there was the music, at once discordant and melodious... or perhaps just odious, banging like a klaxon call: hypnotic and monotonous and deafening.

As soon as she entered she was aware of a score of eyes upon her. Shadowed figures halted their conversations and slipped further into the confines of their booths. Dark faces turned away and slipped into the blackness, or summoned their tipstaffs closer that they might stand in the shadow of their protectors.

Amelia clenched her fists. Did this scum think they could be protected from her? She was the righteous wave that would one day sweep this spume away. There would be a time when the Manufactory would be free of such infection.

But that would have to wait.

For now she had other business.

She walked on, past the addicts and the dealers, the sheep and the wolves, deeper into the labyrinth of the Cistern. Every chamber she passed through was full of the depraved and debauched. The passages seemed endless, leading off into a veritable labyrinth, but Amelia knew her way, she made it her business to know. That was how you stayed ahead of the scum. Knowledge was power in the Cistern, not the strong arm of a hired thug. Knowing the enemy's weakness, finding his lair, where he lurked in repose, unwary, unwitting. And if there was anyone Amelia knew who was unwitting, it was Trol Snapper.

They eventually reached their goal. The lock was a heavy, metal affair, set in a huge, reinforced door. A single shot from Hodge's heavy carbine took care of it better than any key. Bounder was quick to kick the thing in, shoving it wide as he waded in, his huge cudgel swinging this way and that. As Amelia followed close behind she could not help but compare him to a knight of old, wielding his mace in the melee, every swing finding a target. Snapper's men had no chance and those who were on their feet first were soon laid on their backs. A couple even reached for weapons but the barrel of Hodge's carbine forced them to reconsider.

To his credit, Trol Snapper merely sat and watched the spectacle; his long equine face betraying little emotion. When he saw Amelia enter after her fantassins, he visibly relaxed. At least this was not an assault by a rival gang. Snapper knew well that the Judicature were more likely to show mercy than a rival Chamber of the Cistern. As long as it was only his men who were taking the beating, Trol would just relax and watch the show.

Amelia walked forward and sat in a chair opposite Trol's large desk. 'Hello, Trol,' she said conversationally.

'Indagator,' he replied, with a polite nod. One of his men moaned on the floor, and she could see Trol's eyes flicker with doubt, wondering if he was next. 'Is this a social visit... or were you just passing?'

'You know I like to drop in on the Cistern from time to time. When the air of the Manufactory seems too clean I like to fill my lungs with real filth.' Amelia tugged at her leather gloves a finger at a time, removing them to reveal her slender hands. The nails were cut short and practical and the knuckles were well lined, showing a premature age. They were hands that had worked for a long time to lift her to the position she now sustained. And the work had been hard.

She reached forward and ran the middle finger of her right hand along Snapper's desk. All eyes were on her as she silently regarded the end of her finger, rubbing it with her thumb as though smudging the filth she had just swept up.

'Beuphalus? That name mean anything, Trol?'

'Is it what they call that lovely scent you're wearing?' said Trol with a sardonic grin.

Bounder stamped down hard on the leg of one of his felled opponents. The man howled, then was silent. Trol looked unconcerned.

'Earl Beuphalus of House Westowe,' continued Amelia. 'He met with quite a sticky end, Trol. Someone cut his heart out. Sounds like something you might have had a hand in.'

'Please, Indagator. That hurts my feelings. I run a legitimate enterprise.'

'Yes, I'm sure you can show me a full account of dockets and ledgers.'

Trol paused, looking as though someone had just caught him with his hand in the money jar. 'Beuphalus? Let me think. Skinny, glasses, nice threads? I think I may have seen him around.'

Again Bounder stamped down hard and again a moan peeled out through the room.

'All right,' said Trol, holding up his hands. 'I've met your Earl, but I had no idea he was dead until you just mentioned it.'

Amelia stared at Trol for several seconds, and he stared back. She prided herself on being able to sniff out a lie, and for all his blustering attempts at avoidance, Trol looked to be telling the truth. 'Where did you meet him?'

Trol adopted a pained expression, as though thinking of the answer was giving him a headache. 'He would come down into the Cistern on occasion, looking for a good time. When he needed protection, some of my lads would provide it.'

Amelia glanced round the room at the shoddy collection of thugs, some standing helplessly, others lying prone. 'Yes, they seem very good at the protection thing. Who else did he mix with? Anyone from the other Chambers?'

'We looked after him exclusively. It pays to have the favour of the Noble Houses. You should know that better than anyone.'

The aspersion offended Amelia more than she showed. The suggestion that as an Indagator of the Judicature she would curry favour with the Houses was repellent to her. But she knew there were others within her organisation who bent over backwards for the nobles, only too happy to act as little more than lapdogs for the upper classes in return for the few scraps that were thrown from the overflowing tables of the privileged.

'Who did he spend time with? Whores? Dealers? Anyone who would have wished him harm?'

'What can I say, he was a popular man, very generous. Besides, we provided him with all the... friends he needed. What reason would there be to kill him? He'll be sorely missed, won't he, lads?' Trol looked around at his men for their agreement, to which they nodded nervously, still staring at the rock steady barrel of Hodge's carbine.

This was fruitless, and Amelia knew it. She could always take out her frustrations by ransacking Snapper's den, and maybe she would even find something incriminating, but what use would it be? This bog-wallowing turd would only be less inclined to tell her anything the next time she wanted to question him.

Besides, she could wait. They would all get what was coming in the end, when the inevitable tide rose to consume their sins forever.

'Well, it's been a pleasure,' said Amelia, standing up and pulling her gloves back over her fingers. 'We must do this again sometime.'

'The pleasure's been all mine, Indagator,' replied Snapper with a grin.

Amelia tried to avoid looking at him, knowing that locking eyes with his smug face would only encourage her to violence. She turned and walked from the room, as Bounder and Hodge backed out behind her and slammed the door.

Her frustration burned. There were no leads now, other than the ridiculous idea that Beuphalus had been killed in some kind of blood sacrifice. Amelia refused to believe that. Any notion that demonists were at work here would quite obviously have aroused the suspicion of the First Fane of the Sancrarium. Surely their representatives would have liased with the Judicature if there was even a hint of numinous involvement in the killing? Why would she have been left out of such an important loop if that were the case?

The further they retraced their steps through the Cistern, the more it bothered her. The unshakeable feeling that something was going on that she did not know about worsened.

And she hated not knowing.

Amelia found herself suddenly distracted from her self-pity as she passed through another of the Cistern's pleasure rooms.

Pleasure! How could they call this pleasure? It was decadence of the most lascivious kind. Self-delusion; a way to block out the world, to wallow in ravishment and intoxication.

'I assume from the look on your face, this little sojourn was fruitless, Amelia?'

Bounder and Hodge both reached for their weapons as Amelia swung round to face the unexpected voice.

Indagator Surrey was sprawled on a chaise longue, a scantily clad woman with a heavily made-up face was puffing from an elaborate hookah by his side. In his Indagator's uniform he looked oddly out of place amongst this rabble, but there was something about his demeanour that also seemed to fit in so well with the bawdy surroundings.

'Making yourself at home, Indagator Surrey?'

'Ssshhhh,' he replied, with a grin. 'I'm under cover.'

'You're a disgrace,' she said, turning to leave.

'Indeed, Amelia, but I'm further along with your case than you are.'

She stopped in her tracks, turning to regard him, half wanting to leave him to his drugs and doxies, half wanting to set Bounder and Hodge on him.

'Explain.'

'Well, word on the street is there was a break in at one of the Manufactory's more exclusive quarters. Something almost unheard of in this day and age. The residence of a man said to be something of a mover and shaker in the demonist community. Bit of a coincidence isn't it? Two nobles with reputed occult connections, accosted in their own homes?'

'Not this hocus pocus tripe again, Surrey.'

'Well, the last time I looked, Amelia, you had no other leads. I can't imagine the Judicature, or the Noble House of Westowe will be too pleased with your progress so far.'

She could have turned then. Could have left Surrey behind in this cesspit. But what did she have to lose.

'All right, I'll humour you this once. What's his name?'

CHAPTER
NINE

As Blaklok moved through the shadows of the Cistern he felt oddly comfortable in the cloying environment. The cramped tunnels meant that danger could only come from in front or behind and the echoing passages would give plenty of warning if someone was trying to give you the slip… or get the slip on you. Despite its reputation for being a hive of cutthroats and weird beasts, it felt like home to Blaklok.

There was one thing that he could not abide though, and that was the rats. Everywhere you looked they were just scurrying out of sight – that was if they even had the decency to scurry. Other times they would just sit and stare with their pink eyes, nibbling at the shit piled all around or fucking and fighting in plain view. Blaklok hated them, they were too quick by far and they stared at him. He hated being stared at by anything he could not stare out.

Of course, the Cistern was home to rats of a different kind; scavengers and thieves forced from the streets of the Manufactory to the realms of subterranea. The gamins of the streets were one particular unwanted pest, and if caught they would be placed in the labour houses, locked away from the world to slave until they were old enough to be pressed into service elsewhere. But down in the Cistern, the urchins were allowed to run riot… within reason. Sometimes the Chambers would organise a cull if the ragamuffins got out of hand, but that had not happened for years.

Most of these feral children fended for themselves or gathered in tight groups, but there was one gang that was organised, almost well enough to rival the lowliest of the Chambers. The Ring O' Thieves, as it was known, was the eyes and ears of the Cistern. Its members would be quick to fleece the unwary, and even stooped to murder if the price was right, but they were loyal to one another and cared a great deal about the welfare of their fellows. It was this that Blaklok respected, and why he preferred to deal with them and not the Chambers.

He knew the Thieves' burrow well, and had always been made welcome in years past. He only hoped that there was still a member of the Ring who was old enough to remember him.

As he crept up on the entrance to their lair in the dark, he could see the scraggy looking sentry they had posted nearby. The boy was young, nowhere near double figures, and he seemed a bit lax in his duties, more intent on fiddling with what was in his shabby trousers than watching out for danger.

Thaddeus stuck to the shadows, his boots matching the beat of the water that wept from the brick roof of the tunnel. Before the boy realised, a meaty hand was clamped over his mouth. He struggled, his hand flashing from his torn and stained trousers to the blade in his pocket, but Thaddeus quickly clamped his arm in an iron grip.

'Knock, knock,' whispered Blaklok in the boy's ear, and slowly removed his hand.

'I ain't got nuffin mister, honest,' squealed the boy. 'You can check me if you wants.'

'I'm not interested in anything you've got,' Blaklok replied. 'Now, present me to the Chiseller, if he's still top dog around here, that is.'

The boy nodded eagerly as Blaklok released him from his iron grip, and quickly kicked a pile of stinking refuse aside to reveal a small metal grille, about four feet high. Two quick raps with a stick, followed by three slower ones and the grille popped open. The boy dashed in, and Blaklok stooped to follow, hearing the grille crash down with a clang behind him.

The tunnel was cramped and Blaklok had to crouch low as he moved through it. It was hell on his knees but mercifully short, and came out into what first appeared to be a child's playground in the most insalubrious part of town. Scruffy adolescents ran amok in a large room, whooping and screaming at each other like wild harridans. Their faces were filthy, but even the dirt could not mask their delight as they ran free, climbing, fighting and wassailing in a vast feral dance. It made Blaklok want to smile. He hadn't seen so many bright and cheery faces in a long time.

As soon they got to the room, the boy who had led him here disappeared into the throng. The children nearest to Thaddeus suddenly stopped their merry making and simply stared. The reaction spread throughout the room, as the children seemed infected by a wave of stillness that emanated from Blaklok. He and the children regarded each other for several seconds, until a shout of 'Cut!' rang out from the other side of the chamber. Instantly the children were in motion again, running for hidden exits and crawling through tiny rat holes.

From the back of the room strode a rangy youth. He was dressed in a long coat that would once have been expensive, and he wore a battered pork pie hat, skewed at a jaunty angle. The Chiseller marched right up to Thaddeus and stopped, regarding him arrogantly as he chewed the inside of his cheek, as though assessing an intruder on his territory. Then, with a flourish, he grasped the hat from his head and bowed low.

'Always an honour to have the great Thaddeus Blaklok in my house,' he said. 'How long's it been? About five years?'

'Chiseller,' answered Blaklok with a nod. 'Good to see you again.'

The Chiseller beckoned Blaklok to the back of the room where there were chairs and even a makeshift table made from hammered together crates. Blaklok seated himself in one of the chairs and regarded the Chiseller with an appraising stare. The

boy had grown since they had last met, and though he was
barely out of his teens he ran one of the biggest rackets in the
Cistern, all beneath the noses of the Chambers. He deserved
respect, despite his youth.

A young girl suddenly walked from the shadows, bearing a
chipped teapot, and poured two cups of steaming brew. The
Chiseller reached into his inside pocket and pulled out a rusty
hip flask, pouring a generous draft into his own cup. He offered
it but Blaklok raised a hand in refusal.

'Oh, I forgot, you've changed your ways,' said the Chiseller.
'Healthy mind, healthy body and all that shit. Can't see the
point myself. Well,' he raised the mug of tea and tincture, and
blew the steam away, 'what can I do you for?'

'I need a name, is all.'

'Well, names I can do.' The Chiseller slurped at his tea noisily.
'Any name in particular?'

'A man was in the Cistern recently, asking about one of the
nobs from up top, a landed Earl name of Beuphalus. He has
something to do with a cult called Legion. I need to find him.'

Chiseller snapped his fingers and a boy scurried forward.
'Get me Snatcher,' he ordered, and the boy quickly scampered
away into the dark.

The smile never left Chiseller's face as he enjoyed his brew.
Thaddeus merely sat and waited, listening to the sounds of
the underworld as they dripped and squeaked and moaned all
around him. Within seconds, two sets of footsteps approached
from the gloom, and Blaklok could see that the boy was
returning, accompanied by another urchin, this one gaunt as
a cadaver, his hair shaved to the skull but for an inch long tuft
at the front. The boy stopped by Chiseller's side, head bowed.

'Mr Blaklok here, he wants some information,' said the
Chiseller, not even bothering to look at the boy, who Thaddeus
could only assume was Snatcher. 'Remember you told me you
got a crown for telling some bloke about one of the nobs?'
Snatcher nodded vigorously. 'Can you remember who the

bloke was?' Snatcher glanced at Blaklok, then leaned forward and whispered in the Chiseller's ear. A smile crossed his face as he listened to the boy, then, when he had finished, the Chiseller signalled for him to leave. The two scruffy gamins rushed off quickly.

'Geezer's named Castor Cage. Apparently he was asking about this Beuphalus all over the Cistern, and didn't care who knew about it. Snatcher says he's back in the Cistern right now asking more questions. He's interested in the Repository, you know, the one with all the funny fucking animals, and there's a meeting planned with a bloke in Big Betha's.'

Thaddeus nodded. It never ceased to amaze him how much information the Ring could gather, but then people rarely suspected children of being spies; they were often underestimated. It was a mistake Thaddeus promised himself never to make.

'I know it,' he replied. 'What do I owe?'

The Chiseller grinned and held up a placatory hand. Thaddeus could see that one of his canines gleamed gold. 'Let's put it in the bank shall we. Save it for Ron.'

'Later-on it is,' replied Blaklok, standing. He turned to leave, then stopped. The Chiseller was still sitting and smiling. 'I'd stay out of Betha's for a while if I was you,' he said. 'It might get a bit messy.'

'I'll spread the word, Mr Blaklok,' said the Chiseller, after draining his mug dry.

As Thaddeus left the Ring's den he carefully checked his pockets, to ensure he still had everything he had arrived with.

CASTOR CAGE could only be interested in the Repository for one thing – the Key of Lunos – that meant the Legion really were brewing something nasty. It also meant that Tarquin Bates had been a source of valuable information – would wonders never cease.

Blaklok couldn't let this go. He knew his time was running out, that he had to get his hands on the Key as soon as possible, but if there were other interested parties it would behove him well to know about them. If this Castor Cage was meeting someone in regard to the Repository it wouldn't hurt to tag along, would it?

The entrance to Big Betha's was just a simple blue doorway in the side of a tunnel. There was no bouncer or sentry and nothing to give it away as a place of interest within the Cistern. Bouncers were not necessary at Big Betha's; if your name wasn't down you definitely weren't getting in. Luckily, Blaklok was always invited.

As he turned the handle he felt the tingle run through his palm and forearm; a tingle of preternatural recognition. The door gave a sigh as he opened it, the wards placed there allowing him entry. This was a place frequented by the Community, and only they were allowed in. Blaklok had not been amongst their number for some years, and he was relieved he still held some clout, at least in a shady whorehouse.

The inside of Big Betha's contrasted starkly with the tunnel that led to its entrance. Thaddeus could feel the plush carpet underfoot, could smell the fine mix of tobacco smoke and suede upholstery. The room grumbled with the murmur of hushed voices and he immediately felt at ease. Several patrons gave him a flaccid glance, but none seemed concerned at his arrival. It was a welcome change for Blaklok, so used was he to the running and the pleading that so often occured whenever he made an entrance.

Thaddeus walked up to bar and leaned against the polished oak top. It almost felt like old times and he had to catch himself before he threw off his coat and ordered a drink. Luckily, as he saw the ample form of Big Betha approaching, he remembered he was here on business.

'Didn't expect to see you in here again, Mr Blaklok. Word was you'd gone all puritanical.'

'You should know better than to believe everything people tell you, Betha. I just came to relax and take in the ambience.'

'A likely tale,' said Betha, raising one painted-on eyebrow. She leaned against the bar, the tremulous flesh of her upper body moving independently of the tight scarlet bustier she was barely wearing. Had Blaklok not known her from old he would have found the fat bitch quite repulsive. As it was he had grown use to the old whore's look.

'As it happens I'm also looking for an old mucker of mine. Man by the name of Castor Cage. Any chance you've seen him?'

Betha gave a wry smile, seeming to know there was more to this than an innocent reunion. 'As a matter of fact you're in luck. Your old mucker's over there.' She pointed towards a shady booth in one corner. 'He's a regular of mine, though I've not seen so much of him lately. He popped in today for the first time in I don't know how long. Seems a bit out of sorts at the minute. I think he might be poorly.'

Blaklok glanced over, and could just make out a figure sitting in the shadows. Betha continued to prattle on, but he was already striding towards the booth.

The hooded figure never looked up as he slid into the leather seat opposite. There was an uneasy silence for several moments as Blaklok stared at the man, his eyes trying to penetrate the shadowy confines of the hood and see the eyes beneath, but it was no use.

'Castor Cage,' he said finally. 'You know me?'

The hood did not move. This one was tough. Either that or he had no idea who Blaklok was, and of that there was little chance; not down here, not in this kind of place. 'Word is you've been asking questions. What's your business with Beuphalus of Westowe? You the one as cut out his heart are you?'

There was a flicker of movement – the slightest of reactions that an unpractised eye might have missed, but not Blaklok's.

'No? Don't know anything 'bout that one? What about the Repository? What's up with that? Something there you're interested in?'

Still no answer.

'Don't fuck with me, lad,' Blaklok spat, his arm snapping out to grasp the hood. He had meant to grab Cage's ear, to pull him forward over the table, but as his hand made contact he could feel no ear beneath the hood, just a hard leathery skull. Cage's hand shot up, faster than Blaklok could have believed. Before he knew it, he was the one being grabbed, steely fingers biting deep into his wrist, harder than any human's.

And then the table was gone from between them, sent spinning across the room, and Castor Cage was on his feet. The man was huge, standing what must have been close to eight feet tall, and he raised Blaklok high in his one hand, allowing him to dangle like a doll. Thaddeus caught sight of the face beneath the hood for a brief moment, eyes slit like a lizard's, face mottled and rough. It was just the briefest of glimpses before he was sent hurtling across the room.

The oak bar slammed solid into his ribs, knocking the wind out of him, and he fell to the carpet, trying to suck in a breath that just wouldn't come. Blaklok could hear the commotion, the shouts of surprise, Betha yelling across the room, drinks being spilled as people tried to escape the violence.

Still the air wouldn't come and Blaklok tried to rise, tried to face Cage as he came at him again, but when he looked up the giant had gone. He just had time to see the blue door closing before his view was blocked by Betha's gelatinous figure.

Blaklok looked up, able to do nothing more than rise to his knees and gasp in what little air would fit in his deflated lungs.

'You're barred,' chimed Betha, that painted eyebrow rising higher than he had ever seen it before.

Well, that could have gone better, he thought, staggering to his feet. But then, as he felt the sting of his ribs, he reckoned it could have gone a lot bloody worse.

CHAPTER
TEN

GEFFLE LOVED THE snatch at Big Betha's. He spent most of his time there, slurping it up and sticking it in, that was when he could afford it of course. When he couldn't he would just sit in a corner and try to get a sniff, soaking it all up, feeding on it with his senses rather than his wet end. Today had been just such an occasion, a dry spell until he could manage to grift himself some coin. He had been happy to sit and soak it all in, nursing his glass of White-Eye and watching the tit as it sidled past, every girl ignoring him and focusing on the moneyed punters.

However, after several hours of the same-old-same-old, it was turning out to be a bit of a dead loss, and even Geffle was growing bored with the spectacle and preparing to take his leave.

That was until the big man walked in.

It was like a hush descended on the place as soon as he appeared through the door, all big and bald and black-garbed, sidling up to the bar like he owned the place. Geffle knew he was after something, as a Cistern-snitch he made it his business to sniff out the bizarre amongst the innocuous; it was how he earned a crust. There was always someone looking to get some information, and in the Cistern there was always news, and Geffle was usually the man to get it. He had talent, a peeled eye and a pricked ear, and it paid to keep them tuned in at all times because you never knew when something would come your way.

And as the big man sidled in, Geffle got the feeling it was payday.

As Betha pointed him towards a booth in the corner, Geffle followed her gesture, his eyes seeing someone in a dark corner, someone he had not noticed before now. How could that be? Geffle noticed everyone; that was his bloody business. For someone to have entered Betha's under his radar was a cunning feat indeed. Things were growing queerer by the second... and Geffle liked it.

As the big man walked towards the booth, Geffle slipped from his position in the corner and moved closer, keeping to the shadows, never looking directly at his mark. That was the secret you see, if your eyes were not on them they'd never know you were there, they wouldn't get that prickly feeling at the back of their neck warning that someone was following them, and they wouldn't turn around and spot you. It was a clever trick Geffle had learned from a Sandlander who had managed to make his way into the Manufactory. Geffle remembered the lessons the Sandlander had taught him well, right up until he had gutted the wrinkly vagrant. Even now he still wore the Sandlander's hempen belt under his shirt as a reminder of the good times.

When the big bloke had sat down opposite the mystery man in the booth, Geffle took up position right behind them. Now was the listening time; making sure you were stock still, blocking out the ambient noise and focusing on the voices. Well, the voice anyway, because the fellow in the shadows didn't seem to want to say much.

Whenever you couldn't quite hear a conversation it was always the names that stood out the most. Geffle heard two amidst the muffled noise; Castor Cage and Beuphalus of Westowe. Only one of those he had heard of – Earl Beuphalus, one of the nobs from upstairs. Geffle bristled with excitement as soon as he recognised it. This could be valuable indeed if these two were plotting. He knew Trol Snapper looked after the

Earl, and if Geffle had uncovered a plot from a rival Chamber, Trol would pay hearty for the skinny on it.

Trying his best to suppress his excitement, Geffle turned his attention back to his marks. The tingling he was feeling inside was just like the thrill he felt when he was eavesdropping on a courting couple. He loved that the best, listening from the dark when they didn't know he was there, hearing for her gasps of passion to peal through the shadows while Geffle held his cock in his hand, stroking himself stupid. This was much the same – except for the part where he was pulling his old man – and he stretched his hearing as far as it would go to try and learn more. But there was no more to learn.

The heavy table went flying across the room and the sounds of a scuffle replaced the low voice of the big man. He had obviously changed tack: time for talking over, time for fighting started.

Geffle was already underneath the table at his own booth just in case. Well, you never knew did you, it wasn't worth getting a flying glass smashed in your face just for a better view.

He expected the big man to come out fighting, to have the other in a headlock or some such, but that wasn't the case. Like he was being shot from a cannon, the big bald one came flying out of the booth, slamming against the bar and sprawling to the carpet. Geffle smiled; he didn't look so hard now, all in a heap and gasping for air. He quickly tried to get a glimpse of the other figure who had been in the shadows but he was already gone, through the door and away before the dust had even settled. Now there was a wily one, Geffle thought. He would be sure to try and get some lessons from that one if the opportunity ever arose.

He stayed under the table until the commotion was over. Betha, as ever, wasn't too pleased with the disruption in her place, and sent the bald bloke on his way once he could stand.

Geffle tried to look as insouciant as possible as he moved up beside her at the bar. She regarded him with her usual disdain, but Geffle could handle that. As long as he kept spending his coin in her place she was happy to let him patronise her.

'Who was that then?' he asked conversationally.

'You mean you don't know Thaddeus Blaklok?' she said.

Geffle was as surprised as Betha.

Thaddeus fucking Blaklok.

So that was him. Legendary strongarm, dabbler and all round cold bastard. Word was he was out of the game nowadays, but things must have changed. Obviously he had run out of money, that happened to them all eventually. Speaking of which, Geffle would never make any cash standing round in Betha's bordello.

With a curt nod he was out of the door, in time to see the back of Blaklok heading hastily down the tunnel to his right. Geffle made after him, trying to keep as discreet a distance as he could but he quickly reconsidered. If this Blaklok was as good as the legends said it wouldn't be long before he realised he was being tailed. That was the last thing Geffle needed. Besides, the big man was heading towards the Pits, and that was a place Geffle knew he wasn't welcome. He decided it was time to make some money.

The route to Trol Snapper's lair was an easy one, and Geffle almost sprinted all the way there. He was known in the Cistern, particularly around Snapper's Chamber, and he passed without incident. What he expected when he got to Trol's place was certainly not what he got.

Even before he arrived at the door he could hear Snapper's voice raised high, growling and barking like he was wont to do on occasion. Geffle half turned, not wanting to disturb Trol when he was in such a mood, but the promise of coin was just too alluring.

A black powder stain and some twisted metal was all that remained of the door handle. As Geffle gingerly pushed the steel door open, the volume of Trol's tirade grew louder. He was railing at his men, three of whom looked as though they'd just had the shit kicked out of them. His wide wooden desk, which usually looked so pristine and ordered, was in disarray, papers flung every which way as a result of Snapper's ire.

Trol turned, focusing his rage on a man sitting in the corner, a bloody bandage wrapped around his head, his face looking all sullen and lost. 'And you! Fucking useless ape. The next time I tell you–'

He suddenly spotted the miniscule figure framed in the doorway. Everything seemed to stop, even time, as Geffle was caught in Snapper's glare. Immediately he knew he had made a mistake, but he had been so eager to make a report and possibly glean a reward that he had thought the risk worth taking. Now, as Trol bore down on him, he regretted his avarice.

'What the fuck do you want!?' screamed Snapper, turning his attention from his sullen thug to the stranded figure of Geffle, who stared blankly like vermin in the cross hairs of a longrifle.

'I-I was just–'

'Get the fuck out you little shit.'

Geffle turned, eager to escape, grasping the corner of the big steel door to pull it closed behind him.

Then he stopped.

It was like a little voice was speaking at the back of his head. It was a voice that belonged to his greedy, selfish side, the side that wanted to eat something other than fried rat and wanted to suck on those tits at Big Betha's rather than just watch someone else doing it. It was usually less commanding than the self-preserving, pusillanimous side of his nature that had kept him alive for so long down in the Cistern, but on this occasion it was starting to win out.

'I've got news,' said Geffle, before he had even realised it.

Snapper stopped. Despite his fury, Trol knew that when Geffle came with information it was not to be spurned. 'Then what are you fucking waiting for? Come in.'

Geffle gave a half smile and entered the room. It was a mess, with hefty men sitting around looking sheepish, but he did his best to ignore them.

'There's been an altercation at Big Betha's,' he said. 'A fight, two big 'uns, monsters they were. One of them was big and bald but the other, well, I never got to see much of him.'

Trol regarded Geffle with his small blue eyes, and gave an insightful nod. 'So, you've come all this way, and interrupted my meeting, to tell me about a barfight in some fucking spunk-covered hook shop? Are you trying to get fucking killed, Geffle?'

With that Trol picked up the nearest heavy object, which happened to be a hat-stand bereft of the requisite hats, and flung it in Geffle's general direction. Geffle ducked, hearing the clatter of the stand behind him, and looked up in time to see Snapper bearing down, big hands outstretched.

'They were talking about Beuphalus, the Earl of Westowe,' he blurted, eager to finish his tale before Trol could throttle him. 'He's one of your nobs isn't he? I thought you'd want to know.'

Trol Snapper stopped, his meaty hands inches from Geffle's throat. 'What else did they say?' he asked, seeming to suddenly calm.

'All I got was names, then they started fighting, but it was a bit one sided.'

Trol turned and strolled back to the other side of the room, obviously deep in thought. Geffle looked around, unsure of what to do next. He really wanted to ask for cash, but so far Trol wasn't letting on how valuable the information had been.

'They must have had something to do with it,' said Trol, to no one in particular. His men nodded their agreement, and Geffle frowned, unsure of what he was referring to. 'Who were these men?' he said, directing his question back to Geffle.

'One of them was Castor Cage, I've never heard of him, but Betha said the other one was called 'Blaklok'. I followed him a ways down towards the Pits, but I thought I'd best come and tell you before he got any deeper.'

Trol smiled amiably. It always perturbed Geffle, how fast Snapper could change from raving maniac to Mr Nicey in the blink of an eye.

'You did right, Geffle, my little mate,' he said.

'Right enough to earn some recompense?' asked Geffle, quick as a shot.

'Almost,' smiled Trol. He pulled himself up to his full height and regarded his sullen looking crew. 'Right you set of useless cunts.' Snapper's men began to rise gingerly, some distinctly worse for wear. 'Someone's been plotting on our patch, plotting against our good mate the Earl of Westowe, who is now, tragically, deceased. More importantly, we've been put in the fucking frame, and that really pisses me off. So we'll go down the Pits and we'll have a word with this Mr Blaklok.' Trol turned to Geffle with a wide, horse-toothed grin. 'And you're going to fucking show us the way, aren't you Geffle?'

Geffle nodded. Simultaneously his arsehole began to twitch.

Just what he needed – a night in the fucking Pits!

CHAPTER
ELEVEN

AMELIA DIDN'T TRUST Surrey as far as she could kick him in slippers, but there was no other option left open to her. According to the grinning twerp, Lord Julius was an outcast noble, making him far more dangerous than normal members of the aristocracy due to the fact that he had nothing to lose. It was no surprise then that he was apparently deeply preoccupied with the occult; disavowed rich types were always looking for some whimsical avocation. It just remained to be seen whether this Lord knew anything useful.

If Surrey's information was reliable, Julius had recently been attacked in his home. He had attempted to keep the trespass to himself, but apparently neighbours had notified the authorities after hearing the sound of gunfire resonating from his manor. The resultant investigation had discovered that a man had intruded on the house, but been frightened away by the Lord's bodyguards.

This, coupled with Julius's notoriety amongst demonic types, was too much of a coincidence so close to the demise of Beuphalus; another noble who appeared to be embroiled with the occult. Amelia had a feeling there was more to this than a mere housebreaker.

Upon arriving at his estate, Amelia was surprised to see that it covered several acres. Despite being an outcast, Lord Julius had at least managed to retain and sustain his wealth.

As soon as they entered through the elaborately rendered cast iron gate, Amelia realised her error. Three large black hounds were already bounding towards them, tongues lolling hungrily. They didn't bark or howl in their eagerness to attack, and Amelia thought it quite unfair of them to approach in such a clandestine manner.

Before she could stop him, Hodge had produced his heavy carbine and blasted one of the approaching canines into offal. The other two seemed unstirred by the sudden demise of their fellow guardian, and continued their approach unabated. Hodge aimed and fired into the second dog, just as Bounder pulled his cudgel free from the belt at his waist and met the last hound as it leaped forward to attack. There was a dull crunch, and the black dog hit the ground, lifeless.

Amelia felt a sudden pang of regret as she walked past the bodies of the three dead dogs. They had only been doing their master's bidding after all. Nevertheless, dog corpses were much preferable to dog bites, any day of the week.

The crisp blast of the carbine stirred the residents of the manor, and as she approached up the immaculately trimmed paving, the large front door swung inward. Two large figures appeared, initially brimming with menace, but as they saw that it was representatives of the Judicature who had come calling they soon backed down.

On their hard faces, the men bore the bruises of a recent conflict, and one of them was limping heavily. Obviously whoever had broken into the manor of Lord Julius had given these two quite a pasting. She couldn't wait to see what he had done to lord Julius.

'We're here to see the lord of the manor,' said Amelia, not breaking her stride. The two men quickly nodded and led her inside, the one with the limp grimacing in obvious pain.

The inside of the manor was just as impressive as the exterior and Lord Julius quite clearly had impeccable taste... to a degree. Some of the paraphernalia in the hallway – the stuffed animal heads in particular – turned Amelia's stomach, but the rest was assembled in all its antiquarian glory. She spotted at least three originals by Strivengi, an artist much sought after amongst the effete classes. There were also a number of exotic busts and effigies of some unknown origin that looked aesthetically impressive if nothing else. Not a single decoration looked damaged or out of place, and it seemed that whomever had broken into the manor had not done so to pilfer Julius's art collection.

She was led past an ornate staircase to a small door at the rear of the building. The pungent fragrance of roasting meat emanated from a door to her left, and Amelia's stomach began to rumble in response. It plainly wasn't vermin or bush meat Julius would be dining on, if the rich smell from the kitchen was anything to go by. This was truly how the other half lived; surrounded by trinkets and trophies, and fed at their leisure on the best of fare. It was hard to subdue a pang of jealousy at this Lord Julius and his life of privilege. One he had chosen to fritter away in disgrace.

Amelia couldn't wait to make his acquaintance.

He sat in a large chair in what looked to be a cosy study. The pinched face that flowered from his starched collar was yellowing with bruises and one eye was almost swollen shut. Light beamed in through a wide bay window and Amelia was forced to squint as she entered. One of the hulking bodyguards was whispering into Julius's ear as she walked in, and it was obvious the lord of the manor was not pleased with what he had been told. Nevertheless, his scowl turned into a wide and welcoming grin as soon as he spied Indagator Amelia and her men.

'Welcome, welcome,' he said, showing her his palms. It was an unconscious gesture of submission, but it failed to put Amelia at her ease. 'It is always a pleasure to play host to representatives of the Judicature. Please, Milus, bring our friends a drink.' He gestured one of the bodyguards towards a nearby cabinet stocked high with decanters of varying size and shape.

'That won't be necessary. I don't think we'll be here long,' she said.

'As you wish... I'm sorry, my men are remiss in their duties, I'm afraid they failed to ask your name at the door.'

'Indagator Amelia,' she replied warily. She would have much preferred for Julius not to know who she was, but then again whom would he tell? Had he been a prominent member of the Houses it might have mattered, he may have been able to have 'friends in high places' put pressure on her to ignore his indiscretions. But Julius was a fallen man. She could split his head wide and there would be scant consequences, other than perhaps a mess on her tunic.

'And what might I do for you on this splendid day, Indagator?'

Immediately, she knew he was hiding something. His manor had been violated recently, it was common knowledge. The reason for her presence should have been obvious yet Julius was giving nothing away, acting overly friendly as though he was not intimidated by the sudden presence of the Judicature. It was easy to spot and the implication that he could fool her was insulting.

'The break in?' she said, pulling the gloves from her hands one finger at a time. 'Why else would we be here? Do you have a lot of callers *Lord* Julius?' She put a stress on his meaningless title in the hope of baiting him. Showing her contempt for his redundant honorific might goad him into letting something slip.

But it didn't seem to faze him in any way, and he simply smiled wider. 'Indeed not, Indagator. But your colleagues in the Judicature have already been here and taken averments from my employees and myself. I merely wondered why another visit from the Judicature was necessary.'

Amelia gripped her leather gloves tightly, ringing them like a damp cloth. It was a measured answer, and one that could have been true were it spoken from the lips of someone else. But something was amiss here. The more she looked at him, surrounded by his opulence and his bodyguards, the more this stank.

'Have you ever heard of Beuphalus of Westowe?' she asked, hoping once more to catch him off guard.

Julius twitched, an almost imperceptible movement of his mouth, but it was definitely there. Then he widened his grin even further, revealing more of his shiny white teeth. 'Why of course. He was a well respected member of the Houses. Such a pity about his recent... demise.'

Well respected? Was Julius having a lark? Or was he once again trying to hide something? 'So you know nothing about it then?'

Julius twisted his face in mock abashment. 'Why Indagator, what are trying to imply? I'll have you know I have a cast iron alibi for the night in question, several score witnesses to my credit. I don't appreciate being accused in my own home. Particularly not by–'

'Calm down Julius. It was an innocent query. No need to get yourself aroused. Unless of course you have something to hide?'

'Something to hide? Me? Indagator, are you being serious?'

That was it, she had had enough of this vacillating nonsense. The time for diplomacy had gone; it was time to find out what Julius actually knew.

'Am I being serious?' replied Amelia, starting to pull her gloves back over her fingers. 'Bounder, show Lord Julius how serious we are.'

There was no pause, no need for a validation of her implied instructions, as Bounder pulled forth his cudgel and smashed it into the nearest bodyguard's face. It was the man with the limp, and the strength of the blow staggered him. He fell with a howl as his compatriot covered his head with his hands, readying himself for a blow. Bounder placed a firm kick to his exposed privates, and the man went down with a stuck-pig squeal.

Amelia didn't watch as Bounder began to set about them with his cudgel. She merely watched the expression on Julius's face change from smug to uncomfortable to horrified.

When Bounder had finished, neither of the bodyguards were moving.

'A noble, notoriously linked with the occult, is found dead. Soon after, your home is broken into. And you, a famed benefactor of occult organisations. Tell me this is just coincidence, Lord Julius?'

'Well... I... stranger things have happened.'

She glanced over one shoulder to the panting form of Bounder, who took a single menacing step forward.

'All right,' shouted Julius, lifting up his hands. He had obviously been given enough bruises by his prior assailant and was in no mood to receive any more. 'Thaddeus Blaklok's the man you want, he was the one who broke in. And I'll give you odds he's the man who saw to poor Earl Beuphalus.'

'Who?' replied Amelia.

'You're an Indagator of the Judicature and you've not heard of Thaddeus Blaklok? Well, granted, there may not be anything official in the records of the Lexiconium, but Blaklok's reputation precedes him.'

'Let's pretend I know nothing,' she said, her interest piqued.

Julius regarded her slyly. 'Well, I suppose you are a little young. Blaklok was very much before your day but he's made a recent resurgence, unfortunately. He was a well known underground strongarm in his time. Specialising in orphic eradication and cabalistic abrogation—'

Amelia held a hand up to silence Julius. She had heard enough, and wasn't the least interested in his occult fantasising. 'Why did you not tell us before about this Blaklok character?'

'Because the man's a menace. Have you seen my face? My men?' Julius gestured over at the prone forms of his bodyguards lying motionless on the carpet. 'Thaddeus Blaklok is not a man to be trifled with. Had I told you his name he would

know where the information had come from. I don't want to
end up a marked man.'

'So he didn't come here to kill you? Your men didn't fight
him off?

'Of course not,' Julius seemed almost incensed. 'Look at
them, do they look like they could fight anyone off, they're
fucking useless, the cook's more likely give a better account of
herself. If Blaklok had wanted me dead I wouldn't be talking
to you now.'

'It was just a social visit that turned nasty then? Is that it,
Lord Julius?'

'He wanted information. Names and locations of prominent
House members. What they were into, when they took their
respites. When I told him I couldn't help things started to turn
nasty.'

'You couldn't help? Come now Julius, you're a well connected
man.'

'Was! Was a well connected man. Now I keep myself to myself.
When allowed! I'm not a fucking lexicon of the nobility. Not
that Thaddeus Blaklok would believe it. And from the look on
your face neither do you.'

Amelia gave Lord Julius a sideways look. 'Which nobles did
he have an interest in?'

'There were several, I can provide you with a list if you like,
but it'll do you little good.'

'And why is that?'

'Because all roads lead to the same place. Blaklok was
interested in their secret cubbyholes, their places of quiet
reflection and amelioration. Everyone knows where the nobles
crawl to in their hour of need. The Cistern.'

Amelia was starting to get annoyed again. This trail was
leading in bloody circles.

Julius looked scared enough that she had gotten all she was
going to get from him, it was time to look elsewhere.

'Apologies for the dogs,' she said, turning to leave.

Julius glanced over at his fallen men, obviously unsure of her meaning. When he discovered the fate of his guard hounds, perhaps he would show more remorse than he did for his men; though she doubted it.

The scenery as she walked from the grounds didn't seem quite so nice as it had on the way in. There was bitterness in the air now – she had wanted information, but all she had was a name. It was better than nothing, but it still left an acrimonious taste in her mouth.

Thaddeus Blaklok.

Whoever this Blaklok was, he had better look out. The Judicature was on its way, and he was only a man, after all. At least that was what Amelia was hoping.

CHAPTER
TWELVE

IT HURT TO admit it, but the bastard had gotten away.

Blaklok had trailed Castor Cage for almost an hour, at times thinking he was on him, only to find the trail led to a dead end. He would pick up the scent again minutes later, but that too would only lead to nothing.

In the end, Blaklok was forced to admit defeat.

That irked him even more than being slapped around in Big Betha's. He hated giving in; conceding defeat was worse than actually being beaten. At least losing in a fair fight meant you'd been done in by a better bloke. Giving up meant you were a fucking coward, only beaten by yourself.

He had been made to look an idiot in Betha's and now had no way to atone for it. His only consolation was that the bastard Cage would keep. There would be another time for a reckoning; and soon if Thaddeus had anything to do with it.

Anyway, he had let himself become distracted by the circumstantial. All this traipsing around the Cistern was not getting him anywhere but humiliated. He had a job to do: procure the Key of Lunos. No amount of slogging round in the Cistern was going to help him do that.

Thaddeus began to make his way back up through the stinking tunnel towards the surface. Once he was out in the open air with the smog and the pollution he would be able to think better. He might even come up with a plan to break into the Repository, although he couldn't imagine he would come up with anything different to the usual: storm in, break heads, steal goods.

It was thinking of this that distracted Thaddeus from where he was and what he was up to. It was how they managed to get the slip on him. Three of the fuckers, and big lads each, all tooled up to the nines. The first jumped out of the shadows behind him, garrote in hands. Blaklok had been out of the game a while and he had obviously slowed down during his time off, that was how the geezer managed to get so close before he noticed. Nevertheless, he still managed to spot the attack before that garrote was secured around his throat.

Blaklok grabbed the bloke's wrists and twisted, turning them so his attacker's hands were crossed, and then *he* was in the driving seat. He pulled back, thick arms yanking, and the garrote was around its owner's neck in no time. Gritting his teeth, Blaklok tightened his grip, pulling with all his might and trying to strain the life out of the bastard. He was starting to enjoy the wheezing, hacking noises that were coming from his victim when a second garrote flashed over his head. Thaddeus barely had time to reach up with one hand and cover his throat before the wire tightened. It cut into his palm, shearing deep into the flesh, but better his hand than his throat. Blaklok was still holding his own victim, still pulling that wire tight around the bastard's neck, but it was all he could do to fend off his second attacker. The one behind was doing all he could to strangle him, and Thaddeus had his hands full. If he let go of the first attacker to concentrate on the second he could be in even worse bother.

Before he could come up with a plan, attacker number three jumped from the shadows. Thaddeus didn't have time to react as the last one hit him with a thick black sap. The first blow didn't knock him out, and Blaklok was pleased with the surprise on the bloke's face when his attack failed, but it was soon replaced by a stern look of determination as he struck again. This time everything went black.

*   *   *

THE ROOM HE came round in was dim and stank of damp. As his eyes came back into focus, Blaklok could see it was more a vault than a room, metal walls on every side dripping with rust red moisture that gave off a rotting, metallic stink.

He was tied to a chair, the bonds were well tightened and as he tried to move he realised the seat beneath him was secured to the ground. Obviously this little torture chair was built for purpose. There was no gag on his face nor blindfold across his eyes, which instantly told him two things: they wanted him to talk and they didn't care if he saw their faces. It also meant he was probably going to end up dead whether he sang a tune or not.

'He's awake,' said a gruff voice from behind. Thaddeus tried to turn and see who had spoken but he couldn't quite twist his head far enough.

'Right then, let's get started.' The second voice was a deep growl.

Heavy footsteps resounded off the concrete floor and a tall figure walked into view. A black mop of hair sat over a horsey face and a startling set of huge teeth smiled down at Blaklok. This one was an ugly bastard and no mistake, but his suit was well pressed and a fine watch chain glinted on the front of his waistcoat. He took pride in himself despite his ugly mug. Blaklok liked him already.

'Feeling all right?' asked the man, eyes glinting and teeth shining in the gloom.

'Better than you're going to feel if you don't fucking untie me,' answered Blaklok, staring up at that horse's face.

The man laughed, and Thaddeus could hear other voices chortling behind him. They sounded nervous, their laughter false and forced. Lackeys most likely, and this one was obviously their leader.

He leaned forward, still smiling that big-tusked smile, and slapped Blaklok hard across the face. It was a blow meant to shock rather than hurt, but Blaklok didn't shock easily.

'Don't you know who I am? I'm Trol Snapper,' he said, still smiling.

There was a pause, and Blaklok could only assume it was so the name had time to register. It was clear he was supposed to know who this ugly fucker was, and be scared.

'Never fucking heard of you,' Blaklok replied, still staring.

He saw a sudden flash of doubt on those equine features, but it was gone in an instant. This one obviously relied on his reputation speaking for him. Well now he would have to do the talking himself.

'You're as stupid as you look if you don't know me, son,' said Trol. 'But that's neither here nor there. I'm not interested in whether you recognise me or not. Word is you've been asking after a friend of mine. A recently deceased friend of mine, and you're going to tell me why!'

'Like fuck I am,' snapped Blaklok, the words out of his mouth before he could even think about it.

This time Trol's blow was not with an open palm but a clenched fist. It was hard and solid, but not as powerful as Thaddeus would have expected from a man of Trol's size. He couldn't wait to be let loose on this one; he'd show him what a fist in the face was meant to feel like.

'Horatio,' said Trol, glancing up at someone behind Blaklok. 'It's time to do what you do best.' Snapper took a step backwards, flexing his fist as though it pained him.

Another man stepped forward. He was stout, broad featured with greasy hair plastered to his head, wearing plain trousers and a vest. He had seen some action recently, and a plaster was stretched over his flat nose. Blood still caked his mouth and nostrils, and Thaddeus fought the urge to laugh at him.

'Now. Earl Beuphalus. What's your interest in him?' said Trol, slipping his thumbs into the pockets of his waistcoat.

'Who's your dentist?' asked Blaklok, trying to sound as sincere as possible.

Horatio took a step forward and planted his fist into Blaklok's gut.

Now this one could hit.

Blaklok felt the air rush out of him, his insides crying out in pain. He gritted his teeth against the ache and stared at Trol, ignoring his attacker.

'Bet you could eat an apple through a letterbox,' he said, forcing a grin.

Another strike to the gut, this one harder.

Blaklok couldn't help letting loose a whimper of pain. Showing weakness almost bothered him as much as the beating.

'When you kiss your mother you must be able to comb her moustache at the same time.'

Horatio's fist struck his jaw. Stars danced around the periphery of Blaklok's vision but he could still make out the look of anger on Trol's face. Obviously the slights against his mother were a winner.

'You think you're funny?' said Snapper, leaning closer. 'You like to make jokes? We'll see how funny you look with no nose.'

Horatio pulled out a straight razor and, with a flick of his wrist, unleashed the blade. A big hand grasped Blaklok's ear, pulling his head back, and the razor slipped under his nose. He could feel the cold of the metal against his top lip, the razor's edge just brushing the side of one nostril.

'Don't make me ask you again you ugly bastard,' snarled Trol, his big teeth a hair's breadth from Blaklok's ear. 'What do you know about Beuphalus? Were you the one that did for him?'

Blaklok thought hard, trying for another quip about Snapper's mother, but he never had the chance to say it.

There was a deafening crash and the echo of buckling metal. Horatio released Blaklok's head and staggered back, the razor now loose in his grip. Trol stepped back too and the pair of them were gawping like they'd just been slapped.

Another crash, and the sound of heavy metal hitting the ground. It rang like a bell throughout the vault and Blaklok tried his best to turn his head. The carnage was just out of sight; raised and panicked voices were followed by screaming. Horatio ran past Thaddeus and out of sight, quick to join the fray, but Trol remained, backing away as far as he could, his look of bewilderment soon turning to apoplexy.

Blaklok strained at his bonds but it was no good, they would not budge. Behind him all hell was breaking loose and he was unable to do anything about it.

A body fell to the ground beside him, covered in blood and flapping like a landed fish. Then it went still, the eyes staring up, dead and blind. That was enough for Trol, and he took his leave, sprinting off to Blaklok's left. He left a faint nasty whiff behind and Blaklok was sure the buck-toothed bastard had shat himself.

There was a high-pitched scream, and the angry shouts died away. In the end, all Thaddeus could hear was the sound of someone being throttled. It seemed to last an age, that bubbling croak, and when it finally ended Blaklok realised he was next.

Footfalls clicked on the concrete floor, drawing closer with every resonant step. Blaklok clenched his fists, expecting big strangler's hands to reach around his throat at any minute. Instead, the ropes that bound him to the rooted chair suddenly went slack and fell away.

Blaklok stood and spun like a scalded cat, expecting to see some hideous giant, but the figure that had seemingly saved him was the most inoffensive he had ever clapped eyes on.

The man was small, wearing a flat cap and brown raincoat. From beneath the peak of his hat he smiled amiably. 'Hello,' he said. 'I think we should go now.' It was a friendly suggestion, rather than an order, and Blaklok almost laughed. If the room had not been full of bodies he well might have.

'I think that's a good idea,' he replied, and moved quickly towards the large hole in the wall that had previously been blocked by a huge steel door, now so much twisted metal on the ground.

As he moved down the tunnel, away from Snapper's torture room, the amiable figure of his rescuer trotted alongside, his small legs too short to keep up with Blaklok's stride.

There were a lot of questions that needed answering here. But he guessed they could bloody well wait, at least until they were away from the heaped corpses.

CHAPTER
THIRTEEN

IT WASN'T LONG before Blaklok had to stop and confront his newfound 'companion'. He looked down at the man, who was a good head-and-a-half shorter than he was, staring his stare into those amiable little eyes.

'All right, what the fuck's going on?'

The man smiled slyly. 'All will be revealed, Mr Blaklok. Please, let's continue. Although Snapper's men were easily dealt with, there will be more. And I was forced to carry out your rescue somewhat indiscreetly. Who knows what kind of ruffians might be after us.'

With that, he doffed his cap and led the way towards the surface.

Blaklok could do nothing else but follow.

They walked for what seemed like hours. It was a circuitous route through the winding tunnels of the Cistern, and one that Blaklok didn't recognise, but he wasn't about to complain. He was happy to put as much space between himself and the bowels of the Cistern as he could, especially now he knew there were several Chamber members out to do him mischief. Besides, something about this little fellow in his brown coat and flat cap was most agreeable. He felt compelled to follow, like it was his purpose to do so.

When eventually they made it to the surface, Blaklok shivered at the sudden chill of the wind. It reminded him that he had lost his greatcoat when he had been in Snapper's ample clutches, and only served to anger him further. Now there were two new enemies who needed to be settled with: Cage and Snapper. They would get theirs, sooner or later.

The little man led them through the darkening streets, eastward towards the Fell Marches. Though not the most ignominious part of the Manufactory, neither was the Marches the most salubrious of districts. Like many of the city's slumlands, this place was bereft of Judicature interference. The rule of law was kept, in the most part, by its citizens, and the Marches were lucky in that respect. A union of workers held sway here, mostly honest men who just wanted to keep the peace for the good of their families. Extortion and coercion were rare in the Fell Marches, but that was not to say they never happened. Honest working men were just as likely to use brawn over diplomacy, and it was not unheard of for violence to spill out onto these usually peaceable streets.

As the gaslights were being lit along the grimy street, Blaklok was led into a dark doorway. No door hung from the rusted hinges, but by now he didn't care. He just wanted somewhere to sit and think a while.

The stairs were rotten and old, and made a deathly racket as the pair of them ascended. Blaklok couldn't help but notice his tiny benefactor's footfalls hardly made a sound, despite the decrepitude of the stairway.

After walking along a dank passageway flanked with seeping walls, they came to a plain door. The man smiled as he pulled a tiny key from inside his coat and unlocked it.

It was pitch black inside, and a cool draft wafted in from somewhere to his left. It smelt of mothballs and incense; a welcome change from the damp stench of the corridor.

With a hiss, the little man had lit a taper, and ignited a small gaslamp. It bathed the room in yellow light that danced off the walls, and Blaklok was surprised to see how comfortable the room looked. A cosy looking armchair sat in one corner, and immediately Blaklok headed for it, not waiting to be invited.

The little man did not complain as Blaklok made himself at home, even smiling as he waddled across the room to close the door. The pain in Blaklok's gut still ached and his jaw hurt, but at least his palm had stopped bleeding. He had also bruised his shoulder when Castor Cage had flung him across Big Betha's but he was never going to let any of that show. Thaddeus merely sat and watched the little man as he turned and walked towards a small stove that sat in one corner of the room.

'Tea?' he asked.

Fucking tea! thought Thaddeus. That seemed to be the answer to everything these days. *Leg fallen off? Have a cuppa. Dog dead? Have a cuppa. Soul been stolen by the Demon Prince of the fifth tier? Never mind, have a cuppa.*

'Yes,' Thaddeus answered. *Well, if you couldn't beat them…*

'My name is Quickstep, in case you were wondering,' said the little man as he lit the stove. Thaddeus remained silent, although he had been wondering. 'I know it's an odd one,' he said, turning and grinning from beneath the shadow of his flat cap, 'but that's because it's not my real name.'

'No shit,' said Thaddeus. At any other time he would have beaten the crap out of the little fucker to find out the truth, but right now he just wanted to sit and drink his tea. Besides, most of the people he knew went by some alias or another. It didn't really matter. And this Quickstep had just saved his life – or his nose at least.

Quickstep busied himself at the stove for a few moments until the screaming howl of the kettle signified it had boiled. Within seconds he turned, bearing two very different cups. One was a battered enamelled mug, white but for all the chips and scuffs on it. The other was a porcelain cup and saucer that looked as though they had been stolen from the tea set of some aristocratic antique dealer. Blaklok was presented with the battered mug.

'I suppose you'll be wanting to know what all this is about?' asked Quickstep, sitting himself on the sofa opposite Blaklok's armchair.

'I suppose I will,' he replied, taking a long sip of tea. The brew was still too hot and it burned his lips, but he didn't let on.

'Well, needless to say, the mission you're on is an important one, but you knew that already.'

'What do you know of it? Were you sent by–' Thaddeus stopped himself before he said any more.

'I represent parties who are interested in the Key of Lunos. As do you. Whether those parties are one and the same is not for me to say.'

'Because you don't know?'

Quickstep smiled and lifted his teacup from its saucer. He took a sip, lifting his pinky finger in a dainty manner. After a long draft he placed the cup back on the saucer with a resounding clink. 'I think what we don't know about all this far outweighs what we do. Nevertheless, I'm willing to tell what I know if you are.' He raised an eyebrow suggestively.

'Go on,' said Blaklok, eager to hear what Quickstep had to say. Whether he would feel like reciprocating afterwards remained to be seen.

'Very well. I represent the Fane of Zaphiel. We're not quite as popular as the other Fanes, but we are still a loyal part of the Sancrarium.'

'I've heard of you. But how have you heard of me?'

'Oh, we might be small but our eyes and ears are large. Despite appearances the Fane of Zaphiel packs quite a bit of clout.' Blaklok could not argue with that, particularly after seeing the mess Quickstep had made of Trol Snapper's vault. 'We have been watching your... progress. Needless to say, I was sent to put you back on track.'

'What does the Fane of Zaphiel want with the Key of Lunos?'

'Nothing,' replied Quickstep. 'But we realise that there are other parties – nasty, loathsome parties – who want the Key badly, and who would use its power for ill. We also know that you're not one of those parties, so we are willing to help you.'

Richard Ford

'Exactly what 'parties' are we talking about?'

'Well, you've already had an unfortunate run in with one of their representatives. Hopefully the next time you encounter the Legion you won't take them so lightly.'

'So it's the usual is it? This Cult of Legion want the Key so they can open one of the gates and summon their demonic master? Wankers!'

'If only it were that simple,' replied Quickstep, with a frown. 'The Legion won't stop at summoning one demon. They are named well. If they are not stopped the Manufactory will have more than its usual infestation of rats and almsmen to worry about.'

Blaklok gripped the mug, rubbing his thumb over the rough scuffmarks as he thought about the implications of what he had been told. The Legion wished to release their horde into the Manufactory. Conceited fools. What did they hope to gain? What did any demonist hope to gain other than immortality and power. They would learn their lesson the hard way, like all their kind inevitably did. Getting bummed by your demonic master was never pleasant.

'Any suggestions for getting my hands on the Key?' he asked.

'The Repository is well guarded,' Quickstep replied with a grin. 'But I'm sure a man of your–'

He stopped suddenly, his head flicking toward the open window, the fragile cup and saucer falling from his fingers. Blaklok watched them fall, tumbling towards the stained carpet and releasing a limp splash of brown brew.

Then the window imploded.

Both men were showered with glass and shards of the wooden frame, and instantly Blaklok was on his feet. Quickstep had leapt up in time to meet a hulking robed figure as it shot through the empty window frame and loped forward on powerful limbs. Blaklok barely had time to register what the creature looked like – lean and muscular with ridges on its leathery flesh and spines on its back that

105

protruded through its blood red robe – before Quickstep had smashed the thing in the face with a balled fist. The beast was knocked backward with a howl, curling up and grasping its wounded snout, as a second robed creature crept into the room. This one's advance was more measured, and it seemed to be focused on Blaklok. He recognised the baleful eyes that stared at him with a hateful glow.

It was Castor Cage.

Thaddeus took a step forward, intent on settling the score with this weird hybrid of man and monster, but more robed creatures were already creeping in behind, grasping the broken window pane and pulling themselves into the tiny room.

'I suggest you make yourself scarce, Mr Blaklok,' said Quickstep, moving in between Thaddeus and the advancing beasts. 'Your task is more important than brawling with these foul monstrosities.'

Blaklok stared at Castor as he skulked forward, fighting the longing within to launch himself forward and settle the score. But he knew Quickstep was right; he had to concentrate on retrieving the Key of Lunos. The Cult of Legion would have to wait until later.

He turned and ran for the door. As he moved he heard an enraged growl, as the creatures bounded forward. Once again, Quickstep let loose his own brand of fury, and Blaklok could hear the uproarious racket as a battle royale ensued. He didn't look back as he ran down the corridor and away from the fray. Heads began to pop out of darkened doorways, lured by the sounds of violence, but not one of them would leave to investigate. The inhabitants of the Manufactory knew better than to stick their noses in where they weren't needed.

Back on the gaslit streets, the chill night air made Thaddeus long for his greatcoat, and he couldn't get back to Mrs Fotheringay's boarding house quick enough. Quiet as death he opened the front door and padded down the hall towards his room. It wouldn't do to wake the old trout at this hour; the last thing he needed was her whining about him keeping odd hours, especially when he had a robbery to plan.

As he reached his door, Mrs Fotheringay suddenly appeared at the end of the hallway like a ghostly apparition, her hair in curlers and her face covered in some enriching balm. It made her look even more gruesome than usual.

'Ah, Mr Blaklok. Out late this evening, I see.'

Thaddeus nodded curtly, fumbling his key in the door, desperate to open it and be free of the carping harridan.

'It's just that I expected you earlier,' she continued.

Thaddeus nodded again, then felt cold relief wash over him as the key clicked into place and released the door's deadbolt.

'Only you had visitors earlier.'

He opened the door, then froze.

'Visitors?' he asked, deigning to turn and look at the wrinkled prune, standing there in her hideous paisley nightgown.

'Yes, a trio from the Judicature, said they needed to ask you some questions. Led by quite a charming young lady, actually. I let them in your room, hope you don't mind.'

Thaddeus heard the heavy *clack-click* of a carbine being cocked.

Its wielder was standing in his room, the weapon pointed right at his face.

A woman stood to the gunman's right wearing the crisp grey uniform of an Indagator. Her expression was reminiscent of a cat that had just clawed its very first mouse.

'Thaddeus Blaklok, I presume?' asked the Indagator.

But it was quite plain that she already knew the answer.

CHAPTER
FOURTEEN

FROM THE OUTSIDE, the Ministry of the Judicature was as grey and stern as its walking, talking representatives. Bare, weathered stone walls surrounded a building covered in interlocking walkways that linked sharpened spires and crenellated turrets. It was a grim edifice of rock and iron, whose exterior matched the austere corridors within.

The building teemed with stiff doubleted Indagators, armoured fantassins and sullen administrants, but none paid Blaklok any heed as he was led through the panelled corridors and down staircases embossed with intricate engravings, his hands chained behind him. The place was spotless and there was a stench of polish and disinfectant more overpowering than any infirmary Blaklok had ever had the misfortune to enter.

Within the bowels of the Ministry, it was an entirely different scenario. The further they sank into its depths, the more the buzz of hushed conversation was replaced with an eerie quiet, occasionally interspersed with a distant cry of pain, until the only sound was the soft clicking of Indagator heels. The disinfectant smell was traded for the stench of piss and shit and damp, but after the Cistern it was almost welcome.

All the while Blaklok was looking for his out, his need becoming ever more desperate the further into the depths of the structure they went. But these three were seasoned, they knew exactly what they were about. At every step there was a heavy carbine pointed at his head, his hands were bound and his chaperones kept a generous distance from him in case he happened to attack. Every time Blaklok thought he had an edge, or could see an opportunity for escape presenting itself, it was gone as quickly as it arrived.

That pissed him off no end.

By the time he got to the interrogation cell he had run out of chances.

Blaklok was manacled to a high-backed metal chair, and his situation was suddenly becoming all too reminiscent of Trol Snapper's vault. Torture and an endless line of monotonous questions were imminent, Blaklok could tell. When would these people learn they couldn't get anything from him? Pain was irrelevant, an abstract concept and meaningless to a man who didn't feel it. When you were not motivated by hope, when you knew your future was even more bleak than one wracked by constant pain, you were never going to break.

'Thaddeus Blaklok,' said the woman, standing in front of him. There were no other chairs in the room, that way the interrogators were always standing above you, looking down, keeping you small. 'I'm curious as to why I can't find any trace of you in the Judicature's archives?'

'Beats the shit out of me,' replied Blaklok, trying to retain an air of nonchalance. It was difficult though; this woman had a keen look to her, despite her youth. Something about her was getting under his skin. The two tipstaffs that stood to either side of her looked intimidating enough but they were inconsequential, there was nothing behind their eyes but violence. But she was something else.

'I'm hoping that beating the shit out of you won't be necessary,' she said. 'Although from what I've heard it's not an attitude you share.'

'Just get to the point, love. I haven't got all day.'

'Have you somewhere else to be?

'What the fuck's it got to do with–'

He was cut off by a steel banded cudgel playing a drumbeat on his thighs. Blaklok clenched his teeth against the pain, never taking his eyes off her.

So much for the violence not being necessary.

'Why did you kill Earl Beuphalus?' she asked conversationally.

'So you're trying to pin that one on me are you? Typical fuck–'

The cudgel hit him in the ribs. It wasn't hard enough to crack one but it still cut him off mid-sentence. And Thaddeus hated to be interrupted.

'Let's say I have a strong hunch,' she continued. 'If not you then who?'

'How the bloody hell–'

He was stopped by a punch to the jaw.

'Shit! You fuck–'

Followed by another.

'You cunt, I'm go–'

And another.

Blaklok fell silent.

His mouth and nose were bleeding, and this bitch didn't seem to care what answers he was going to give until he told her what she wanted to hear. For now it was time to retreat.

Her questioning went on for almost an hour, the same old sounds interspersed with a cudgel blow or a fist on flesh, but Blaklok took it all silently. He was deep inside now, listening from within a cavernous hole, watching and waiting.

When it was finished they dragged him to a cell. By then he was too weak to overcome them, even when they un-manacled his wrists.

He lay on the floor of the cell for untold minutes. It was time wasted but Blaklok needed it to bring himself out of his torpor. Besides, it was a well deserved break from the incessant beatings he had been taking for the past two days.

When he eventually managed to sit up, peeling his bloody face off the cold stone floor, he saw that there was only one way out of his current situation. The cell door was thick and solid, the lock only accessible from the outside. Four walls surrounded him and no windows.

It was time to call in the cavalry.

As he thought about it, a smile crossed his face. Those fuckers would get such a surprise when they opened up the cell to find him gone.

There was no salt or chalk handy. No chipped stone to make a mark on the floor and not enough dust and grime to mould into the shape of the sigils he needed.

It would have to be blood.

Blaklok only hoped he had enough left to spare; his face and chest were covered in the stuff.

After working his jaw to get the blood-ridden saliva flowing, he let a line of scarlet drool spew from his mouth. It wasn't much but it was a start. This he carried on for several minutes, shaping a basic summoning circle on the floor. Then, holding his nostril taught, he snorted out some more cruor-riddled sputa within the circle, licked his finger and wrote the requisite sigils required for the ritual. By the time he was on the last symbol his drool was running out. It would have added insult to injury if he'd had to open a vein to finish the cryptograph. He just managed to complete the last part as his mouth went dry.

There was no summoner's pentacle, he would have to perform this conjuration dry. Well, he was in enough shit already, how much worse could it be if he opened a portal to the Pit with no protection?

Falling to his knees, Blaklok began the incantation. As the black words spilled from his lips, the parched feeling in his throat and mouth was replaced with the taste of hot bile. It was as though his body was rejecting the abhorrent language he was uttering, as though every fibre of his being recoiled in the face of such degrading blasphemy. Blaklok fought for control, struggled to stay in charge of his will and his faculties. Hot winds blew into his face and he felt his bladder suddenly fill. His fingernails dug into his palms and the stench of rotting eggs flared within his nostrils, but still he kept his eyes closed. It wasn't as if he had never looked into the abyss before, but the sheer memory of the sight was enough to keep his lids firmly clamped.

All the while he continued his foul litany until the words themselves seemed to take over, and he no longer had to concentrate on the pronunciation and inflection. All he had to worry about was not shitting himself.

Then came the noise. It was like ice and fire, high pitched and booming all at once, a raging torrent in his face. He could only imagine this must be the closest he would come to feeling the exhilaration and the shit-storming terror of falling to his death, without actually having to fling himself from the tallest tower in the Spires. At least he hoped he would never experience it.

And then all at once it was gone. The wind, the heat, the fear, all but the stench; that sulphurous linger, now mixed with a damp animal stink.

'We were not expecting to see you again so soon.'

Rankpuddle's voice was like slime running over Blaklok's skin. The spinning had also started in his head and he knew it would only get worse if he opened his eyes.

'I've run into a bit of a problem,' he said, feeling a little foolish to be having a conversation with his eyes shut.

'We cannot say we are not a little disappointed. Thaddeus Blaklok came highly recommended. We are finding nothing to justify such a recommendation.'

'Well boo fucking hoo. Right now I'm all you've got. Or is there someone else you can turn to?' Blaklok paused, waiting for a reply, but none was forthcoming. 'Yeah, I thought not. So I suppose we'll both just have to make the best of a bad do. Can you get me out of here or not?'

Rankpuddle began to make a throaty noise, like he was

choking on his own vomit. Blaklok could only assume it was what passed for the creature's laugh.

'Thaddeus Blaklok asks if we can get him out of here. That is jocular.'

'I don't see what's so funny you stinky little shit. And if you don't stop laughing–' He opened his eyes and instantly regretted it. Rankpuddle was standing before him, but the room was reeling, causing the hideous creature to flicker from right to left in his field of vision, then snap back to its starting point like a broken record. Nevertheless, Blaklok kept his eyes open, fighting the dizziness, willing it away.

'Of course we can get you out of here, Thaddeus Blaklok. As long as you can pay the price?'

Typical demon; always on the bastard want. It couldn't be much, a low class imp like Rankpuddle wouldn't dare ask for a bestowal of umbra, not for such a simple petition of aid.

'All right, what are you after? Is it blood? I don't know how much of that I've got left to give. It cost me enough to get you here.'

'For this, Thaddeus Blaklok, the price is bone and flesh. Can you pay?'

Blaklok's fists clenched. Anywhere else, with time to prepare and the resources available, it would have been a simple and easy request. A rat, a chicken, sometimes even insects were acceptable depending on who was asking, but stuck in here there were few options.

'I don't suppose I can have this one on the cuff?'

'For this, Thaddeus Blaklok, the price is bone and flesh. Can you pay?' repeated the demon.

'Guess not,' said Thaddeus quietly.

A toe would have probably been much preferable to one of his fingers but he didn't have a blade handy and he had never been flexible enough to bite his toenails. Thaddeus looked down at his hands. He splayed his fingers, counting them for the last time, then stuck the little finger of his left hand into his mouth. As he bit down he stared at Rankpuddle. The little stinky shit – there would be a reckoning for this as well as the rest he owed.

The pain coursed up his hand as teeth split flesh. Every fibre of his being was screaming for him to stop, but Thaddeus had long ago learned to ignore the expostulation of his body. In a second he was down to the bone, his teeth grinding against it as he twisted his jaws, and all the while he stared at the cursed imp, fighting the urge to scream in rage lest it be mistaken for pain, or worse – fear. He could hear the crack of cartilage as the proximal separated from the metacarpal, and with one final wrench of his jaws he pulled his hand away.

With his right hand he plucked the severed digit from his mouth and flung it towards the squatting creature.

'We thank you,' said Rankpuddle with a smile. His yellow dog's teeth were bared and Blaklok could see the black gums attached. Then everything began to swim. Not just his field of vision but his hearing too, even the rank smell of sulphur seemed to undulate on his palate, mixing with the acrid stench of burning.

He fell hard.

His back hit a metal surface and pain jarred through him, right down to the tip of his missing finger. Blaklok barely had time to reach out and grip the siderail before he was flung from the roof of the monotrain. Black smoke billowed in his face as the steam engine powered itself along a single elevated track, far above the twisting streets below.

Silently Blaklok cursed the shit-eating demon back to hell. Was this his idea of a joke? Transporting him straight onto the roof of a moving monotrain might have seemed like a laugh, but how was he going to get the Key if he fell to the ground below? He was already a finger down, he doubted he would be in any fit state to finish the job if he was bounced off a pavement from a great height.

The train pulled into the station with a clatter of sleepers and squealing of breaks. Thaddeus was only too happy to jump from the roof, still clutching his bleeding hand.

So many scores to settle and so little time. But they would all have to wait, for now it was back to business.

Enough of the pratting around, there were heads to break and a Key to steal at the Repository. Blaklok's blood was up and he was ready to do what was asked of him.

Just let somone try and stop him!

CHAPTER
FIFTEEN

HE KEPT TO the back streets, striding past the whores and cutthroats, through the slick filth and steaming vents. Even in his fury he knew better than to walk the main thoroughfares and attract attention. In the back alleys no one would pay him much mind. The anger raging in his eyes and the clothes covered in blood would not attract much notice here amongst the pimps and soaks.

Despite his ire, Blaklok's mind was still churning – rumbling with lucid thoughts, all the whys and wherefores. He had been set up, his name put in the frame for Beuphalus's death. That could have been done by any one of the three parties he had pissed off in the recent past. Lord Julius perhaps, but Thaddeus thought him too caitiff. Trol Snapper maybe, but why would a criminal of the Cistern have the Judicature do his dirty work for him? Most likely it was the followers of the demon Valac. It was more like the actions of the nobs to get the Indagators to do their shitwork, and Blaklok had pissed them off royally by interrupting their boy-murdering party.

Whoever was responsible, it would have to wait. There were bigger arses to kick right now. The Cult of Legion was abroad and in obvious union with their patrons, from the demonic look about them. The bestial creatures that had broken into Quickstep's tenement had been human once; you could see that in their eyes. Part of Blaklok pitied them. Most of him just wanted to beat them silly. If Quickstep was right they were

117

after the Key of Lunos, and if they were as clever as they seemed they would know that other parties – Blaklok and Quickstep included – knew about their aims. In turn, that would mean they were probably even now planning their break-in of the Repository, if they weren't in there already, stealing the Key from under the noses of the Repository's curators.

This angered Thaddeus to the quick. Didn't they know the Key was *his* to steal? It wasn't for a bunch of soul-selling, demon-loving pricks who wanted to unleash hell on the Manufactory!

He was close now, almost at the Repository. Part of him was ready to storm up the stairs to the entrance and start smashing skulls, but he stopped himself. He remembered the custodians in their armour, carbines cocked and ready. It might be easy to take two or three down and maybe he would make it inside the building but he would never get to the Key by taking the direct route.

Thaddeus looked around the grimy street he was on. In one corner he noticed a shifty looking figure in a doorway; pimp or pickpocket, he didn't know which, and didn't really care. In all honesty it could have been the most devout and bounteous bloke in the Manufactory, Blaklok would still have picked him.

Without a word he walked towards him. The shady figure saw Blaklok coming and started to look round, panicking as the huge bald frame bore down. He barely had time to scream as he was dragged into the shadows and given a mild pasting.

Blaklok used the bloke's shirt to wipe down his bloody face. The coat he wore was too small but it still covered Blaklok's grimy vest. The hat covered most of his bruised and yellowing face, and by the time he walked from the shadows of the doorway he looked almost presentable.

As he reached the Repository's entrance and strode up the stairs he kept a wary eye on the two custodians who stood guard at the door. Hopefully they wouldn't question him, but if he was stopped he would simply have to improvise.

One of them glanced in his direction, Thaddeus could see him leering from the corner of one eye, but he carried on regardless, trying to appear as innocent as he could – a hard enough task in itself. Just as the custodian made to move in his direction there was a sudden squeal from the street behind. The custodian stopped, his attention momentarily diverted by the noise, and in that brief second Thaddeus was gone, straight through the door and away. He glanced back before the huge oaken door closed behind him and saw a group of teenage schoolgirls giggling and squealing as they passed. On any other day Blaklok would have found them an annoyance... but not today.

He moved through the museum, gliding past the other patrons and barely noticing the cornucopia of strange and sad creatures. His focus was on the Key, only the Key, and nothing would distract him from it. Several times his shoulders bounced heavily off someone in the crowd but Blaklok never noticed as he mounted the stairs to the mezzanine above.

Something was wrong here; he could feel it. Despite the seeming façade of normality something was up – or at least it was about to be. It was the almost imperceptible rumbling from up ahead that first gave it away. A barely existent murmur amongst the crowd that made him stop in his tracks.

Then he heard the screams, and he was off like the clappers; like a baited hare rushing from its hole. While most of the museum's other patrons began to head away from the cries of alarm Blaklok headed straight for them, barging his way through the retreating crowd, and as he got within eyeshot of the Key of Lunos he saw the telltale red robes of the cultists of Legion.

The bastards had beaten him to it!

Above, the mezzanine was in chaos, with men, women and children running in all directions in their haste to escape from the fiendish thieves. The creatures were running rampant, clawing and rending at civilian and custodian alike.

Blaklok couldn't see the Key, it had been removed from its plinth, the sturdy cage that safeguarded the exhibit having already fallen, but there was no one trapped inside.

Two deafening blasts rang out as a custodian let rip with his carbine, but the cultists seemed unstoppable. As Blaklok closed in, one of the red-robed beasts leapt upon the firer, rending and tearing with tooth and claw. Blaklok could hear the strangled screams but he was no longer looking, his eyes busy scanning the rampaging monsters to see which one held the Key of Lunos.

Then he saw it, it was held in an animal's grip but Thaddeus recognised those keen eyes, those familiar features recognisable as once human. Castor Cage was bounding right towards him, the Key clutched in one black taloned hand.

Blaklok raced forward, determined to bring Cage down before he could escape but at the last minute the cultist changed direction, leaping over the banister of the mezzanine to the ground twenty feet below. Blaklok silently cursed, begrudgingly admiring Cage for his superhuman abilities, and then leaped after him.

He hit the ground hard, falling on his side, his shoulder slamming into the marble floor. After scrambling unsteadily to his feet he caught sight of Cage bounding towards the exit. Thaddeus set off running, mixing with the fleeing crowd and quickly realising he would never make it to the door in time to stop the escaping cultist. All around was confusion, and the custodians of the Repository were starting to fire randomly into the crowd in the hope of bringing down the robed beasts that ran amok.

Blaklok moved forward, stalking one of the custodians who was firing wildly. His elbow smashed into the helmeted face, shattering the visor and dropping the custodian to the ground. Before the man fell, Blaklok snatched the carbine from his limp fingers.

He took three swift steps forward, enough to give him a decent view of his target, then swiftly aimed and fired. Three deafening reports blared out, answered by three metallic explosions as the carbine rounds impacted against the lock of a metal cage. The huge lizard inside suddenly stirred from its slumber, seeing the door to its prison slide open just a crack.

Quickly it took its chance and moved, something Blaklok had been counting on. As the beast burst from the open pen, Castor Cage was just bounding past. The lizard roared its triumph, blocking the cultist's path, and Blaklok could see the look of horror on Castor's face. He wasted no time – as the two creatures faced off against one another, Blaklok ran, his focus once again locked on the Key.

Castor Cage made to move around the creature but it shifted its huge bulk to block his escape route. With a feral roar, Castor leapt to attack, clutching the Key protectively to his chest. The lizard growled in reply, sweeping a huge claw at the mass of scales and red robes as they shot towards it. Cage was hit squarely, a vicious blow that would have finished any normal man. He was flung backwards, his arms spreading wide and his fingers loosening on the Key. It spilled on the shiny marble floor, bouncing away from the cultist's grip, and came to rest right at Blaklok's feet.

In less than a second Cage had recovered, spinning to his feet, but the Key was already in Blaklok's tight fist. Rage crossed Cage's feral features as he recognised his foe, and he made to charge, but Blaklok had already raised the carbine. With a sly wink he pulled the trigger, sending a blast right into the charging cultist's chest. Cage was flung back towards the rampaging lizard, sliding along the smooth marble and leaving a trail of crimson ichor.

Madness still raged all around as the custodians tried desperately to stem the tide of beastly cultists. Blaklok was not about to wait and assess their progress, and moved quickly towards the exit. Luckily the huge lizard had the same idea and made its last bid for freedom.

As the beast headed for the door, Thaddeus was happy to run after it, easily moving through the carnage it left in its wake. The custodians rained shot after shot at the beast but it kept on moving, heedless of the wounds being inflicted on its scaly hide. With a triumphant roar the lizard bowled through the phalanx of custodians and smashed its way out of the door. Blaklok could see daylight streaming through the wide-open portal left by the creature.

He was nearly out.

Gunfire suddenly blazed all around him, and Thaddeus realised the custodians had spotted him, the Key held firmly in his grip. Some shouted for him to halt, while others were content to rain shots in his direction. Blaklok ducked, trying to find cover against the onslaught, and moved behind a wide pillar. Shards of marble were blown from the massive colonnade, trimming its width as Blaklok cowered behind. He looked around for a means of escape, seeing the door, blasted wide and beckoning to him, but if he tried to make a break for it he would be cut to shreds. To top it all, the bloody figure of Castor Cage was slowly rising from where Blaklok had gunned him down.

Did nothing stop this fucker?

He glanced around desperately looking for an out. Then he spotted it, glowing like a beacon of hope amongst the chaos. The fire elemental winked and flittered within its glass case, perpetually searching for freedom, bouncing from each of the walls in its transparent prison.

Blaklok's first shot cracked the reinforced glass, his second sent shards flying across the room. The flickering creature was free. For a second it paused, as though not quite able to believe it had a way out. Then it shot forth, zooming across the hallway like a meteorite, expanding with each passing second until it was a torrent of shooting flame. There was a howl as the inferno began to engulf all in its path, igniting exhibits and custodians alike. Carbines were emptied into the creature but they only seemed to fuel it as it rampaged around. Blaklok was not about to wait and see what happened next.

Taking huge strides he was out from behind the pillar and headed for the street. One of the custodians still had the presence of mind to try and stop him, firing a shot that fell well wide of its mark as Blaklok dived through the door into daylight. He crashed down the stairs and came to rest on the hard pavement of Gull Street. The bedlam inside the Repository could still be heard as screams, howls, growls and fiery light streamed from within the smashed doorway.

Blaklok stood and opened his palm, looking at the Key in his hand. He allowed himself a smile. His mission was almost complete.

'Going somewhere with that, Mr Blaklok?'

It was a woman's voice, and one Blaklok recognised.

The Indagator stood with her hungry looking tipstaffs at her shoulders. One had a carbine raised and aimed; the other held a banded club at his side. They both had white knuckles and eager stares, desperate to be given the order to let rip.

Blaklok glanced down at the heavy carbine in his hand, seeing into the empty chambers that no longer held any ammunition.

'Bollocks,' he whispered.

CHAPTER
SIXTEEN

'THERE'S NOWHERE TO run to, Mr Blaklok,' she said with a wry smile. 'Even for a man of your astonishing powers of escape.'

Blaklok rarely hit women, and only then when expressly necessary, but this bloody Indagator was starting to get right on his wick. Let him meet her without the armed henchmen and see how smug she was then.

'Isn't that the Key of Lunos?' she continued. 'What would a man like you want with such an important artefact?'

'I don't think we've been formally introduced,' replied Thaddeus conversationally. He was looking directly at her but all the while scanning the periphery of his vision for some way out, some distraction he could take advantage of. If they took him back to the Ministry of the Judicature he didn't fancy having to bite off another digit. That was if he was given the opportunity. Considering the miraculous nature of his last escape he might find himself trussed up under twenty-four hour watch, and that would make escaping *really* difficult.

'How remiss of me, Mr Blaklok,' she said, feigning embarrassment. 'I am Indagator Amelia, First Class of the Judicature. And these are–'

She never got a chance to finish the sentence.

Screaming like a thunderbolt from the doorway of the Repository came a searing, blinding streak of fire. One of her henchmen turned and fired his carbine at the conflagration, while the other ducked, covering his head.

Blaklok didn't need any further encouragement. He dropped his own carbine and set off running. It was only then he noticed what a mess had been made of the street. Whether it was the fleeing museum patrons or the rampaging lizard he could not tell, but detritus was strewn all over Gull Street. Discarded footwear, an overturned newsstand and even a smashed-in steamtram were strewn across the thoroughfare. Blaklok was only glad he wasn't the one who had to clean it all up.

As Thaddeus sprinted down the street, a glance over his shoulder revealed that this Amelia woman was not about to give up the chase so easily. Even as the fire elemental danced in swirls, celebrating its new found liberation, she and her men began their pursuit. A carbine blast ricocheted off the railing to one side of Blaklok's head, and he realised that if he continued down Gull Street he would be an easy target.

He bounded to his right, through a gap in the cast iron fence and towards the door ahead of him. It was only when he had burst through the doorway he realised he was inside the exotic meat emporium that stood next door to the Repository.

Immediately he was assailed by an almighty stench.

Considering the fact people paid good money to eat what was prepared here, there seemed to be little diligence paid to cleanliness. Carcasses hung from hooks, meaty thighs ending in cloven hooves next to unidentifiable fowl, stripped of feather and clipped of beak. The walls and floor were daubed in gore, and Thaddeus almost slipped on the goo underfoot.

Two of the emporium's workers glanced up as Blaklok burst in. Both were attired in bloodied aprons over stained smocks that might once have been white. One wore a mask and chainmail gloves, and wielded a gigantic cleaver. The other seemed old and greasy, a half-chewed, half-smoked rollup dangling from the corner of his mouth.

Blaklok wasn't about to hang around for introductions. He piled on through the emporium, dodging the hanging meat, ignoring the stench and the squelching noises his feet made on the tiled floor. The butchers shouted something at him as he raced by but he wasn't interested – it was hardly likely they were offering him a deal on cutlets.

The back of the emporium was cordoned off by a segmented plastic sheet that hung from ceiling to floor, and Blaklok burst through the slimy curtain, making a mental note to bathe vigorously when he next got the chance. The back of the emporium stank worse than the front, and he almost gagged as he moved deeper into the building. Here, more butchers went about their work, cleaving, slicing and sawing at what looked like the most dubious cuts of meat Blaklok had ever seen. He had never considered becoming a vegetarian, he liked the taste of dead flesh far too much, but he would rather have eaten his own head than sample the goods from this particular outlet.

Behind him he could hear the door to the emporium burst open and angry voices shouting out curt demands. The Indagator and her lackeys were not far behind.

Blaklok was suddenly instilled with a greater sense of urgency. Gripping the Key ever more tightly he bowled past the slabs covered in animal parts and the crates that sat beside them. Try as he might not to glance in them he couldn't help himself, catching sight of what lay within and instantly regretting it. He was sure he caught sight of an eye staring out from some creature's head. It had seemed almost human.

Dismissing it, Blaklok spotted a back door to the place.

As he burst into the backyard he sucked in a huge gulp of fresh air. It was still tainted with the stench of raw and decaying flesh but it was a relief from the cloying rot inside the emporium.

He hurtled through the gate and sprinted down an alleyway. The place was awash with rats and pigeons, fighting over scraps left by the meat emporium. As Blaklok's footfalls splashed through the creatures in their brawling melee they paid no heed, so intent were they on their battle for carrion.

Behind he could just make out the sound of raised voices as his pursuers continued after him. Dropping a shoulder Blaklok barged through a side gate and down another alleyway. The sight of a rusted fire escape filled him with hope. If he could make it to the rooftops he was sure he would be able to lose the hunters. The back streets and rooftops were his domain, and he was as surefooted as any when it came to treading the gables and gambrels overhead. He could only hope that this Indagator and her men were not so well practised.

Without stopping Blaklok launched himself towards the ladder, quickly scaling it to the first balcony. From his elevated position he could just make out his trio of pursuers, the two tipstaffs lumbering along, closely followed by the Indagator Amelia. As he scaled the second tier they spotted him.

The thug with the carbine let rip another blast but it fell well wide, as Blaklok continued to climb. He heard the woman say something, most of it inaudible against the clanging of his boots on the rusted ladder, but one word did stand out against the rest:

Alive!

She wanted him alive, which meant they weren't going to gun him down when his back was turned.

Well that was the best news he'd had in ages.

Even so, he at least needed to make a good show of escaping, it wouldn't do to be caught twice by the same mob in less than a day.

His pursuers began their climb after him, just as he reached the top. The roof was flat, interspersed with blackened chimneys and skylights. A loft of pigeons were startled into flight as he began to traverse the blackened asphalt, never slowing, always looking out for the next place to tread high up above the streets. The rooftops flashed by as he ran, looking for the higher ground, always taking a step upwards, higher and higher above the clangour below. Who could tell whether his pursuers were afraid of heights? It might help him the higher he got. A scared enemy was a careless enemy, but these three had shown him that the last thing they were was careless. Any advantage he could get might give him the edge he needed, and he was sorely in need of an edge.

Blaklok leapt a gap between the flat roof he was on to a sloping one and stopped, allowing himself a glance back.

Those bastards were gaining!

The one with the gun was no more than twenty yards behind, and he was taking aim. In an instant Thaddeus was away again, hearing the blaring report of the carbine, quickly followed by the clap of the shot blasting apart slate not three feet from him. This fellow was definitely shooting to miss. Either that or he was the worst shot in the Manufactory.

The further he ran, the more random and sprawling the rooftops became, seeming more like a maze, but Blaklok simply didn't seem able to shake this lot. He knew it would eventually come to a fight, but he had to find ground to his advantage before he got himself cornered. The roof he was running up steepled at the top, then sloped downwards. Thaddeus half skidded, half ran down the other side, leapt across to another flat roof and waited.

As he watched, the one with the carbine soon appeared and stopped in his tracks, aiming his weapon and waiting for his fellow tipstaff. While the one with the gun kept it raised and aimed, the other one slid down the roof and made to leap across.

That was when Blaklok moved.

The gunman couldn't take his shot for fear of it being a fatal one, and by the time he could aim to wound, Blaklok was using his mate as a barrier. The tipstaff was in the air, leaping into space, gripping that cudgel he liked to use so much. Blaklok's leg came up, aimed at his midriff. Moving through the air there was little the tipstaff could do to avoid the blow and it hit him hard, unbalancing him as he fell. Before he could sprawl to the black tar of the flat roof, Blaklok had him in his grip. The cudgel went spinning, and now they were on level terms, Blaklok's strangler's hands gripping tight to the fucker's throat.

He was a big one and no doubt, thickly muscled about the neck and shoulders, but obviously unpractised in unarmed combat. A man should never rely too much on one weapon – without it you were helpless.

In an instant, Blaklok was using him as a shield, backing away as quick as he could, throttling his prisoner all the while. The gunman followed but when he came to the edge of the roof he had to stop.

Blaklok glanced back; the roof's lip was only feet away, and there was nowhere to go from here. This looked like it would end in a stalemate, and no mistake.

Panting for breath, Amelia crested the top of the roof and stumbled down the other side. She said nothing as she saw her man in Blaklok's clutches. She either didn't care, or she was trying to make it appear so.

If she was acting she was making a bloody good job of it.

Without a word she snatched the carbine from her tipstaff's hand and jumped the gap in the roof, calmly closing the space between her and Blaklok. Thaddeus closed his grip on her man's throat, causing him to gag. His face reddened as he was slowly asphyxiated, but she gave no reaction, smoothly cocking the carbine and taking aim. Again, Thaddeus could only wonder whether she was play acting or whether she really didn't give a shit about her man.

He winced at the sudden, deafening report – he didn't mean to, he just hadn't been expecting it.

Suddenly the tipstaff in his grip went slack, dead weight, and he couldn't hold him up any longer. The man screamed, clutching his leg where he had been shot. Well, that answered whether she was acting or not!

'I hate to have to repeat myself, but there's nowhere to run to, Mr Blaklok,' she said, lowering the carbine. Her man moaned on the ground, trying to staunch the blood flowing from his wound. 'Shall we dispense with all this futile nonsense and return to the Ministry?'

Blaklok considered her words, while his fingers absently traced the edge of the Key that was now secured in his trouser pocket.

There was a sudden buzzing in his ears, an annoying dull noise like an engine. Blaklok had never suffered with migraines but he guessed this was what one would be like.

Surrender was not an option. But this bitch was serious – serious enough to shoot one of her own men. She obviously hated losing just as much as he did. Maybe his theory about her wanting him alive was a bit premature. Maybe she would kill him after all if he kept on running.

As he thought this, the buzzing grew louder, and Blaklok began to wonder if it was just in his own head. The expression on Amelia's face gave him the answer.

She quickly raised the carbine again as the sound became deafening. Her shot screamed straight past him, but Thaddeus was already moving, sprinting for the lip of the rooftop, ready to make his leap of faith.

As his legs powered him out into oblivion he saw it, rising like a great, beautiful monolith, all round and smooth. The airship rose up fast, steam pumping from its churning engines as it ascended. Blaklok reached out, those big hands wide, hoping more than anything that they would find a hold.

He started to fall, gravity sucking him towards the hard ground hundreds of feet below.

Quickly he realised he was going to die.

One hand squeezed tight against the lip of the open hatch, and his flicker of despair was instantly replaced with the heart thumping burn of relief. Looking over his shoulder he saw Amelia fumbling with the carbine, her man still squirming at her feet. She was shouting but he couldn't hear a word over the airship's engines.

Allowing himself a smile of triumph, Blaklok pulled himself aboard, still staring, resisting the temptation to give the Indagator a jaunty wave as he sailed away.

'Ah, Mr Blaklok.'

The voice was raised above the din of the engine, but it was strangely familiar. 'I didn't think we'd be seeing you again so soon. I believe you have something that belongs to us…'

CHAPTER
SEVENTEEN

BLAKLOK TURNED SLOWLY, but even before he saw the telltale cloth-of-gold robes he remembered where he had heard the voice before.

Trajian Arkwright, the beardy little shit.

He was standing, smiling smugly, surrounded by the other delusionals. They were lined up next to one another, Arkwright at their centre, grinning at him like a bunch of halfwits.

'The Key,' said Trajian. 'Hand it over.'

'You must have a fucking death wish,' said Thaddeus, taking a step forward.

'Ah, ah.' Arkwright raised a tiny revolver.

Blaklok stared at it, thinking hard about his next option.

Could he cover the distance in time? Could he take a bullet from that little peashooter and still make his escape? Could he make it out of the open door behind him before Arkwright could fire? A quick glance over his shoulder ruled out the last option as he realised that the airship had ascended high over the streets of the Manufactory. There was no way even *he* could survive that fall.

'Let's not have any further unpleasantness,' Arkwright crooned. 'Now. The Key, if you please.'

'What fucking Key?'

It was a poor attempt at subterfuge but the best he could do at such short notice.

'The one that's bulging in your pocket, Mr Blaklok. Or are you just pleased to see me?'

Bollocks.

Blaklok reached into his pocket and pulled out the Key of Lunos.

'Just toss it over here.'

Thaddeus could see the eagerness in Arkwright's eyes, matched by that of his followers. Something wasn't right. How could they know anything about its power? A bunch of wannabe, demonist losers could not possibly have the arcane knowledge to come after the Key.

Nevertheless, fact was they wanted it, and Blaklok was in no mood to simply hand it over.

'What's to stop me tossing it out of the door?' he said, suddenly moving his arm and dangling the Key between thumb and forefinger precariously over the void.

'It would be nothing more than an inconvenience for us, Mr Blaklok. It would just take a little longer to find. For you, I can promise, the inconvenience would be much worse.' Arkwright brandished the revolver with menace. 'Now, just pass it to me.'

Trajian was getting annoyed, Thaddeus could tell. As much as he enjoyed winding up arseholes like this, he kind of got the feeling it wasn't long before he would get shot. With a flick of his wrist he sent the Key spinning towards Arkwright. In a flash, one of his cloth-of-gold sycophants moved to intercept and snatched it out of the air.

'President Valac appreciates your compliance,' said Arkwright, with a leer.

'Fuck him,' Blaklok replied.

Arkwright merely smiled. He had a plaster on his nose where Blaklok had hit him with the rusty canister, and Thaddeus only regretted not finding something heavier to throw back at the riverside.

'Put those on,' said Arkwright, signalling to one of his acolytes who brandished a set of shiny manacles. Blaklok stood impassively as the man approached gingerly, holding the manacles at arm's length as though they were covered in pig shit.

Now was Blaklok's chance – taking a hostage would be the quickest way out of this mess; use a human shield, disarm Arkwright, take back the Key and be home in time for tea and biscuits.

Before he was within striking distance, the man threw the manacles at Blaklok's feet.

Not a bad move, all things considered. Though there was fear in his eyes, the bloke wasn't quite as stupid as he looked – had he got any closer, Blaklok would have had him.

Once he put the manacles on he would put himself in an even more vulnerable position, but there was little choice. This was why he never planned anything; because once your plans went to shit your arse was left hanging in the wind. Since there had been no plan, and Blaklok had pretty much made everything up off the cuff, he could take a little solace in knowing he hadn't fucked up. Not really. And whatever happened next was purely fate.

It made him feel a little bit better about being at the mercy of a bunch of stuck up nobs.

Reaching down he picked up the manacles, casting his eye over them to try and discern any imperfection he might be able to exploit later. Unfortunately they seemed very well made; the best money could buy.

He really hated rich people.

When he had snapped the manacles over his wrists Blaklok noted that some of Valac's followers visibly relaxed, some sighing openly in relief.

Who were they trying to kid? They obviously didn't realise who they were dealing with. He could do just as much damage to these arseholes with manacled hands as he could without. Given half a chance he would bloody well show them.

'Please feel free to sit, Mr Blaklok.' Arkwright sounded jovial, almost friendly. As he was speaking he never took his eyes off the Key of Lunos, turning it in one hand, whilst keeping the revolver trained on Thaddeus with the other. 'It will only be a short trip to our destination but you look rather fatigued. The events that have befallen you since our last meeting have obviously not been pleasant.'

'Where are we going?' replied Blaklok, remaining on his feet.

'All will be revealed. In good time.'

This was getting worse. Blaklok had a sneaking suspicion his earlier assumptions about this bunch being ignorant in the Arts, or in the least the assumptions he had made about Arkwright, might have been wrong. Then again, he had only made those assumptions because they had been in the company of a certain back street bilker.

'Where the fuck is Tarquin Bates? Is all this down to him?'

Arkwright diverted his attention from the Key and stared Blaklok right in the eye. Then a wide grin crossed his face.

'I can assure you, Mr Blaklok, Bates has nothing to do with this. He was merely the hired help. Though he may have thought he was using *us*, I can assure you it was quite the opposite. You see, certain obsequies have to be adhered to for our plans to work properly. Despite Bates' lowly nature, he does have the requisite knowledge, which we would have found it difficult to procure elsewhere, particularly after the murder of our patron, Earl Beuphalus.'

'Requisite knowledge for what?' asked Blaklok, but part of him already knew the answer.

'Why, to raise the President, of course.'

At that, the rest of the gold-clad acolytes began to chant in unison: '*Valac serviam. Valac dominus. Valac patrem. Valac omnipotentum.*'

Blaklok suddenly felt cold, and it wasn't just the cutting breeze blowing in through the hatch of the airship. 'Tell me you're not thinking of using that thing, are you?'

'Why of course we are, Mr Blaklok. Why else would we have gone to all this trouble? We were going to bide our time in the beginning. After all, there's no rush, the President's not going anywhere. But word on the grapevine was that an attempt was going to be made on the Repository, so we decided it would behove us well to be waiting. And there you were. And here we are.'

'You've got no idea what you're fucking doing,' snapped Blaklok, taking a step forward.

Arkwright raised the revolver once more.

Thaddeus could see in his eyes he would use it if he had to. There was a look of complete commitment, his dedication to a cause. Blaklok had seen that look in others many times, and he was sure plenty of others had seen the look in him.

'On the contrary, I can assure you we know exactly what we're doing. The Earl of Westowe had planned to procure the Key of Lunos legally from its current owner, but with him dead we had to make alternate plans. Not only that, but we also lost our codex. That's why we needed to solicit the aid of Tarquin Bates. He was most helpful too, teaching the relevant rituals and summonation rites. So now we have the power and the knowledge, Valac will soon walk among us once more. His time is almost here. And with no small thanks to you. And Mr Bates of course.'

'Fucking Bates,' said Thaddeus quietly.

'Oh don't blame him. He was as much a pawn as you are. Only he won't be taking as much of an active role as you will, Mr Blaklok. A front row seat has been reserved for you. I just know you'll enjoy the show.'

The droning chant of Valac's followers continued, rising above the din of the airship's engine and grating on Blaklok's nerves. He pulled the manacles tight until they bit into his wrists, but it was no use. He considered striking forward, maybe he would be shot, but maybe he would still be moving, still able to finish Arkwright before he was finished himself. But then who would stop the rest of these fanatics?

There was no one else.

Bide your time, he told himself, breathing deep and trying to keep control. There was no need to unleash the beast yet. The opportunity would present itself in good time, and when it did, these fuckers were going to get just what they deserved.

The airship droned onwards, just like the voices of the acolytes, and Blaklok soon found himself having to turn his back on them.

Through the open door the view truly was breathtaking. Blaklok seldom took the time to appreciate the Manufactory, but then again, he rarely got the opportunity to view it from this angle. From up here you could not see the grime and filth of the streets, the wan and woebegone faces. All you could see from here were the rooftops and towers, the lights and the lanes and the riverbed as it meandered through the city's centre like a great dead serpent. From here, you could also see the sky clearly, and not through the usual obscuring pall of smog that blanketed everything. He hadn't seen the sky this clearly since he had been outside the Manufactory, only a year ago. Things had been simpler then, but he knew well how nothing stayed the same. Nothing ever stayed simple... not for Thaddeus Blaklok.

You reap what you sow, someone had once told him. Of course, Blaklok had beaten the shit out of that fucker, but it still didn't make the adage any less true. The sentiment was clear – Blaklok was cursed – and current events were only reinforcing that sentiment. Well, he would fight this curse, just like he fought everything else. And like everything else he came up against, he would win or he would die.

Just let them try and stop him.

Blaklok suddenly noticed that the airship was slowing down, the steam engines that powered it growling less intensely as it slowly turned, aiming itself towards one of the grasping towers that clawed up towards the heavens.

The acolytes had ceased their chanting, much to Blaklok's relief, and he turned to face them, seeing that Arkwright still had his revolver aimed and ready.

'Well, Mr Blaklok. We appear to have arrived.' Arkwright smiled.

Blaklok didn't think he had ever wanted to break someone's teeth more.

The airship cruised low over the tower, and slowly came to rest. Blaklok could see more cloth-of-gold clad acolytes securing mooring ropes on the ground. With a screech of rusty wheels, a set of metal steps were pushed toward the side of the airship and clanged against the gaping hull.

Arkwright wafted his revolver at Blaklok.

'Shall we?' he said.

Thaddeus had little choice but to obey.

CHAPTER
EIGHTEEN

THE GRINDING ENGINES of the airship powered down, dying out like the last breath of some wheezing, cankerous monster. As they silenced, Blaklok could hear more chanting, the droning litany of President Valac being repeated, ad nauseum.

When he reached the bottom of the metal stairs he was immediately surrounded by a dozen acolytes, their golden robes glinting in the bright sun. Some held carbines while others brandished hand weapons: knives, clubs, one even bearing a knuckleduster. While the acolytes' weapons looked effective enough, their faces told a different tale. They were nervous, bearing little conviction behind the eyes, and Blaklok doubted they would bring themselves to use their weapons in anger. Unfortunately, he couldn't guarantee that they wouldn't use them out of desperation, and a shot fired in fright would kill him just as dead as one fired in anger.

'Take Mr Blaklok to the chapel,' ordered Arkwright, closely following him down the stairs from the airship. Blaklok glanced back, noting the revolver still trained on him.

He was ushered away from the great grumbling vessel, and across the wide flat rooftop, high above the Manufactory. The sun was warm against his face and a fresh wind blew gently against his skin. Even in this moment of endangerment, Blaklok still appreciated the fact that he was, for once, high above the cloying streets, up in the relatively clean air and bathed in sunlight.

'Magnificent, isn't it?' said Arkwright. Blaklok resisted the temptation to reply. 'This is one of the towers of House Westowe. Pledged to us by its former owner. Truly magnificent what money can buy these days, wouldn't you agree?'

Blaklok's fists clenched tighter. Money didn't give them the right to this. Fresh air and the beauty of a cloudless sky should be the right of every citizen in the Manufactory, not the exclusive privilege of the rich.

'Soon it will all be His. *Valac dominatus*. You should be proud that you will bear witness, Mr Blaklok. It is the dawning of a new era. A golden age, ruled over by a god. And we will be his lieutenants.'

'You'll be his fucking entrées, you ignorant prick,' replied Blaklok.

Some of the acolytes stared at him, shock written on their faces, but Trajian Arkwright merely laughed.

'You are the ignorant one, Mr Blaklok. We have been promised a seat at his right hand. It has been foretold. Valac is beneficent with his rewards, and we will bathe in the shadow of his reign.'

Now it was Blaklok's turn to laugh, which seemed to compound the nervousness of those gold-clad acolytes that crowded around him. 'You lot really have no idea, do you? You're just pawns... less than pawns, you're not even on the fucking chessboard!'

'No!' screamed Arkwright, suddenly enraged. Blaklok felt the tiny cold barrel of the revolver pressing into the back of his head. It appeared he had finally managed to hit the spot. 'Valac loves us. He cherishes his followers, and we will be rewarded. We will stand by his side for eternity. *Valac serviam!*'

His last words were repeated by the surrounding acolytes, and Blaklok realised he was wasting his breath. There would be no reasoning with these fanatics. He could only hope there would be a way to stop them before it was too late.

He was led to a staircase that swept down to the floor below. Here Blaklok could immediately see that the followers of President Valac had already busied themselves with their preparations. The wide, circular chapel was surrounded on all sides by huge glass windows set in carved frames, depicting their demonic master. He seemed almost benevolent; a striding figure with the requisite horns and forked tail, but his face was serene. On every facet Valac was depicted performing some kind of gracious act – anointing his followers, blessing the land, sitting atop a gilded throne watching over his kingdom.

Blaklok almost guffawed at the naivety.

In the centre of the room had been carved a summoning circle. It was set into the marble floor, the pentacle carved in relief, the chthonic symbols gilded in silver leaf. Blaklok had never seen such ostentation in honour of a demon before. Communion was usually made in dank and dirty cellars, with charcoal sigils streaked across blood-spattered floors. This place really was fit for a king.

Then he realised, with rising panic, that there were no safeties in place. No guards against a hostile summonation, no salt, no lead, no standby sacrifice. When Blaklok had been forced to make a dry conjuration it had been out of pure desperation, but this… this was simple madness.

One of the acolytes secured Blaklok's manacles to a stone pillar, as Arkwright sidled up beside him. 'I hope you will enjoy the show, Mr Blaklok. I'll see if I can put in a special word for you when the President arrives. Perhaps he will allow you to be his pet.'

Blaklok stared, and for the first time he spotted the glint of insanity behind Trajian Arkwright's twinkling eyes. 'You're all going to die,' he said.

'Not us,' Arkwright replied with complete conviction. 'We are about to begin our lives anew. Lives that will last an eternity at the right hand of our master.'

Arkwright turned, stowing his revolver inside his golden robes, and raised his arms high. Blaklok could see the Key of Lunos clutched tightly in one raised hand.

'We are moments away from apotheosis, my friends. *Valac patrem!*'

'*Valac patrem,*' cried the acolytes in a single voice. Even now they were assuming their positions, faces twisted in glee, smoothing their robes and preening their hair as though they were keenly awaiting a secret lover.

Arkwright strode to the centre of the summoning circle and was surrounded by his acolytes, each of them joining hands with their neighbour and beginning the droning chant.

'We have been gifted,' said Arkwright spinning on his heel and showing the Key to the assembled circle, as though blessing them all with the sight of it. 'We have the means. We have the will. Nothing can stop us.'

Blaklok began to strain against his manacles. They were padlocked to a bracket that was secured to a stone pillar. Though the manacles themselves were of good quality, there was a chance he could pull the bracket free of the pillar if he worked quickly enough. His muscles strained as he pulled with all his might. The grip of his left hand was not as strong as he'd have liked due to a recently lost finger, but he put that to the back of his mind. The manacles cut into his wrists but still he wrenched at them, staring at the bracket and willing it to move. There may have been the most minute of movements but it was no use, he was still tightly secured.

In the meantime, the chanting had grown louder. '*Valac dominus. Valac patrem. Valac omnipotentum. Valac invicta. Valac serviam.*' The chant was almost joyous as it was sung through bewildered smiles, gleaming from the hooded golden robes of the acolytes. And in the midst of them was Arkwright, his eyes locked with steely intent on the Key of Lunos.

Blaklok silently scolded himself again. He should have taken the fucker out when he had the chance. Should have snapped that neck like a twig before he could do any harm. Well that would teach him to show mercy when it wasn't warranted, but it was too late to castigate himself now. He had to do something. But that wasn't going to happen with him trussed up like a sacrificial goat.

He pulled again at the bracket and it began to move. A little dust at first, just a tiny spray dislodged from the pillar as the bolts that held the bracket began to loosen. Blaklok took some heart in this, trying to block out the droning chant, trying not to panic. With another tug, the bracket began to wobble, but the manacle about his wrist was cutting deep. The flesh was parting and blood was starting to run in rivulets down his arm.

He had to ignore it; there were more important things at stake.

By now, Arkwright had joined in the chanting along with his followers. His voice was raised higher than the rest, shrill and loud, as though he wanted the limelight all to himself.

It was starting to get hotter, and that was never good. A warm wind was blowing straight through the chapel, but there was nowhere it could be coming from.

Nowhere on this earth, anyhow.

Blaklok turned his attention back to the manacles. The pain was getting more intense, even for him. His wrists felt like they were ready to split right off, and that wouldn't have been an altogether bad thing. He reckoned that even handless he could have taken down these wet bastards.

'Come, Valac!' Arkwright's voice peeled out above the din, momentarily diverting Blaklok's attention from his painful task. 'President of Hell. Lord of the Eighth Gate. Master of Serpents. Keeper of Hidden Secrets. We are ready to receive you. We have toiled long and hard for the means to offer a guiding light to the teeming masses of this foul city.'

Blaklok was annoyed at that last comment. Especially since he was the one who had done all the toiling to retrieve the Key of Lunos, but he had little chance to complain. A blinding light suddenly glared from the Key. It looked like it was burning white hot, but Arkwright appeared to feel no pain. This was it, the demon was coming.

Thaddeus strained once more, desperately pulling at the bracket, feeling it give a little more with each agonising tug, but it simply would not come all the way.

'Yes!' screeched Arkwright. 'He is here!' With that he placed the Key of Lunos down in the centre of the pentagram and stepped back from it, retreating all the way to the edge where he joined the rest of the chanters. He joined in with their endless litany and they all looked on eagerly as the light emanating from the Key intensified.

Blaklok had to close his eyes as he kept tugging. The blood now covered his arms, but he knew he had loosed the bolts that secured the bracket to the wall. He was almost free, another few seconds and he would be able to stop this before it was too late.

Then he realised that a disturbing hush had descended on the room.

Slowly he opened his eyes and felt the cold, unnatural chill that told him he was in the presence of the unearthly. The gold-cloaked acolytes were now standing in silence. Some gawped, open-mouthed and astonished. Others smiled dumbly, a pall of orgasmic glee having fallen across their faces. The rest could only weep, but whether from fear, happiness or some twisted sense of accomplishment, Blaklok couldn't tell. Arkwright himself merely looked victorious, his eyes burning with intense madness.

And in their midst, rising from a crouching position, a sulphurous miasma emanating from its bare flesh, was President Valac.

The demon was twice the size of a man, maybe more, naked and matted with thick, wiry fur. A huge hairy cock dangled flaccidly between its legs, denoting it as male, but Blaklok knew demons bore nothing that could be described as gender.

This thing was an *it* from the tip of those wicked horns to the bottom of its massive cloven feet.

It embodied every stereotype and myth ever written about demons – the horns, the snout, the hooves, the skin. But its face was not ferocious. Indeed, it seemed almost limpid, and imparted an aura of calm throughout the chapel. Part of Blaklok wanted to stop struggling against his bonds and merely stare in awe, but he knew better. He knew the odious, deceptive nature of the unworldly creatures that resided in the Pit, and before things could go tits up he resumed his straining against the bracket.

From the corner of his eye he saw one of the acolytes lurch forward, dropping to his knees before Valac. 'Master. We beseech your blessing,' he pleaded, tears straining from the corners of his eyes.

President Valac reached down with its huge, hairy hand, a faint smile playing across its fat red lips. It gently rested the hand on the acolyte's head, as though anointing him, and the man closed his eyes, tears of joy running across his wide smile.

With a final wrench, Blaklok dragged the bracket from the wall, six-inch bolts lurching from their housing within the stone pillar. He almost cried in triumph, but the pain in his wrists cancelled out any sense of accomplishment he might have felt.

Thaddeus turned to the gathered acolytes, their demonic master standing in their midst.

The President's face regarded its congregation with an ambivalent stare. Then it looked down to the one at its knees. Valac's blank stare suddenly took on a ferocious sheen. Its teeth bared in a half-grin, half-leer as it reached down with talons that had a second before seemed so innocuous, grasping like a vice, piercing gold robes and flesh. The man screamed in pain as he was lifted, just for a second, before his head was crammed into the demon's maw and snapped off by powerful jaws.

A scream rose to the ceiling of the chapel as panic ensued.

Well, thought Blaklok, *you can't say I didn't fucking warn you.*

CHAPTER
NINETEEN

GOLDEN ROBES FLUTTERED in panic as Valac's acolytes began to flee in terror. Blaklok's eyes were on the Key of Lunos, now lying at the centre of the summoning circle, but the huge demon still stood astride it. It reached out another hand, grasping a fleeing figure by the hem of his robe and lifting him high, examining the struggling man like a child might observe a dangling worm. As the victim began to peal out a high pitched scream, Valac lowered him towards its jaws, taking a deep bite of the man's torso, crunching through ribs and flesh and into organs, allowing the rich red juices to run in rivulets down its chin.

The man didn't scream for long.

Blaklok looked around for Trajian Arkwright, determined that he should not escape the hellish justice of his master, but he was lost in the confusion as bodies ran every which way in terror.

Trajian would have to keep, for now Blaklok had to retrieve the Key and stop a ravenous demon from slaughtering scores of innocents. Obviously these acolytes were an exception – Valac could have as many of these injudicious bastards as he could stuff in his huge maw.

The demon finished rending the flesh from its now flaccid victim and dropped the body to the ground, as though discarding a stripped spare rib. It glared around at the confusion, its former acolytes now fleeing in terror, and it roared. The sound filled the chapel and made Blaklok cringe. He felt the fear wash over him and struggled to fight against it. This was not real terror, not the primal kind you got from being scared for your life. This was a horror only the demonic could imbue – a fear for your very soul that even death could not liberate you from.

And as the noise of the hellbeast's roar subsided, Thaddeus saw that its eyes were solidly fixed on him. Two burning embers lodged deep within a face of solidified magma.

Blaklok fought against the terror but it was no good, the eyes had him transfixed. His knees were trembling and his bowels were about to loosen. He knew his very soul was in jeopardy.

With a deafening crash one of the ornate windows burst inwards, showering the chapel and the few remaining acolytes with multicoloured glass. Valac turned in time to see hideous red robed figures bound into the sanctity of the wide room. As they did so, more scarlet cultists came storming through the door, pushing past those in gold, as eager to enter the room as Valac's followers were to exit.

Blaklok recognised the feral, bounding forms of the Cult of Legion, and even noted the wild-eyed features of Castor Cage, but he soon realised they were not here for him.

'Seize the Key!' cried the cultist to their fore. To all intents this one was human, not bearing the vile demonic taint of some of the other red-robed monsters, but his face was hidden behind a large mask, shaped like a bronze sunburst. 'We must have the Key!'

Valac roared once more, this time at the defilers encroaching on his sanctum, but these intruders did not seem to be afraid. Three snarling beasts leapt at the demon, rending him with their talons, and Valac gave a wail of pain. As it was distracted, more red-robed figures scurried forward, reaching desperately for the Key of Lunos where it lay discarded on the ground.

Blaklok was suddenly enraged, his fear of President Valac dissipating as he saw the creature now combating several smaller demons. As he took a pace forward, Valac grasped one of the creatures that had clamped jaws around its broad shoulder and flung it aside – right at Thaddeus.

It was like being hit with a block of stone, and he fell back, cracking his head against the marble floor. The beast of Legion quickly scrambled to its feet and leapt back into the fray, but Blaklok was stunned, and not for the first time in recent days. He stood in time to see one of the red-robed men grasping the Key, thrusting it towards the masked leader. 'I have it,' he cried gleefully, just as Valac swept its wickedly clawed hand around to decapitate him. The body fell forward, spilling the Key to the ground, and Blaklok did his best to lurch towards it. But before he could reach it, the masked figure had stretched out a long arm and clutched his prize.

'We have it,' he said, his voice distorted behind his mask. 'Let us leave this foul place!'

With that, he and his robed followers made for the door, leaving three of their beastly fellows, including Castor Cage, still engaged in a vicious battle with the demonic President.

As much as Blaklok wanted to stay and watch these monsters tearing into each other, he had to get the Key back. His legs trembled as he moved towards the exit, narrowly avoiding the flailing, snarling beasts that were fighting for their lives in the centre of the chapel.

Once he made it through the archway, Blaklok staggered through a twisting corridor that led to a wide landing.

By the time he got there he was too late, a huge winch was grinding and squeaking as the tower's lift descended towards the ground. To the side was a staircase that twisted hundreds of feet down, and Blaklok could see several golden robed figures falling over themselves in their eagerness to clatter down the stairs.

He needed a quicker way.

Pulling off his shirt he tore it in two and wrapped it around his bloody hands. Then, gulping a deep breath of air he leapt for the pulley cable that was quickly descending. The pain in his palms was instantaneous as he gripped the cable and felt the friction burn his flesh. The stub of his missing finger seemed to scream out in protest as he tightened his grip, desperately trying to alleviate his fall.

Blaklok slipped for several feet, feeling the rush of air sweep past as he fell, until finally he managed to slow himself.

His palms were on fire but still Thaddeus clung to the cable for dear life. The lift car was almost fifty feet below him, and to fall now would make an awful mess of its roof.

Above he could hear the roar of angry demons, and he looked up, in time to see a huge bestial face glaring down at him.

Valac!

The demon reached out, its bulk filling the lift shaft as it began to descend. Blaklok duly shimmied down the cable as fast as he could, away from the approaching monster, but with its superior size and strength it was easily gaining.

Seeing that the cable was aiding Blaklok's escape, Valac reached out for it, trying to stop its descent, but the thick steel simply ran through the beast's grip. It roared in frustration, clambering faster, and Blaklok had to fight to resist the temptation to let go, and drop away from the ravenous demon.

He was almost at the elevator, shimmying down the cable for dear life, when the cabin suddenly hit the ground with a grinding of breaks. Thaddeus dropped, landing on the roof and wrenching open the access panel as Valac let go of either side of the shaft and dropped after him.

Blaklok fell into the lift, seeing the red robes of the Cult of Legion running for the tower's exit. Desperately he scrabbled out to safety as Valac landed on the lift with a smash of metal and wood, crushing its roof and sending metal panels flying.

As the demon fought to free itself from the lift shaft, Blaklok rose unsteadily and made after the Cult of Legion and the Key.

They were sprinting, their red robes billowing behind them, but Blaklok was faster. As they made their way out onto the street, Thaddeus was on them, crunching his fist into the side of one red hood to his right, smashing his booted foot into the knee of one to his left. The men went down screaming, and the rest turned. Their leader, eyes glaring from within the bronze mask, simply stared, grasping the Key of Lunos to his chest.

'That belongs to me,' said Blaklok, mustering as much menace as he could. 'Do yourself a favour and–'

With an unearthly roar, President Valac burst onto the street. Passers by began to scream in terror as the demon appeared, its hungry eyes regarding them with evil intent.

Blaklok was torn – the Key was right in front of him, he could almost taste it. It would be nothing to reach out and take it from the masked man, but Valac was loose, and the innocents on the street had the look of an all night buffet about them.

As the red-robed cultists backed away, Thaddeus turned to face the beast. The fear was still in him, the soul rending terror that threatened to spill out into his underclothes, but he couldn't allow this creature its liberty. It did not belong here on this plane.

This was Thaddeus Blaklok's domain, and while he was here there was no room for fucking demons.

Valac began to stride towards the crowded street and Blaklok ran forward, yelling at the top of his lungs. The demon turned, recognition sparking in its eyes. Blaklok could see its body was rent and torn by claw and tooth marks – the beasts of Legion had made a valiant attempt at bringing the demon down. He could only hope he would do half as well.

With a hideous grin, the demon took a step towards him, flexing its razor talons that were now covered in gore. Blaklok desperately scanned the area for a weapon, anything would do, but there was nothing to hand. People were scattering all around, and every instinct inside him told him to do the same but he knew he could not.

With a beastly grunt, President Valac swung a huge claw. Blaklok ducked, feeling the air part inches from his head, and he rolled to the side. He was on the demon's flank, with time to spare, and he leapt up, stepping off the monster's bent thigh and stretching up for the head. Before Valac could stop him, Blaklok had grasped one of its horns and wrenched it back with all his might.

The demon roared in pain as the horn crunched and twisted within its head. Blaklok knew that had the demon been manifest for more than a couple of hours it would have felt no pain, but newly summoned it was vulnerable.

It reached up, grasping with its talons, but Blaklok had already leapt clear, hitting the ground hard and rolling to his feet. Valac snarled, staring with hatred at the annoyance in front of it, the audacious mortal that had dared to do it harm. With a sound like the sucking vent of an airship, the demon drew in a deep gulp of air.

Blaklok knew what was coming, could sense it almost preternaturally. He also felt the long intricate tattoos that stretched down from his shoulder blades reacting instinctively. His flesh began to burn as the sigils that had been needled into his skin reacted to the hellfire that was brewing in Valac's gullet.

As the demon spewed forth a gout of flame, Blaklok closed his eyes. His mouth opened on reflex, spurred by the reaction of the ritual that had been enacted on his body so many years before, the tattoo itself taking control, using his mortal flesh as a conduit of occult power.

The burning liquid, hotter than any earthly furnace, shot towards Blaklok in a cone of fire, straight into his waiting mouth. Tears streaked down his eyes and he could see the blinding light of the fire beyond his closed lids, but there was no pain. His flesh did not blacken, his nostrils did not clam up, and when it was done, all that remained was a thin line of steam exuding from his lips.

He opened his eyes. Valac looked drained – calling up the hellfire had obviously taken a toll on its fledgling form, but it was still more than a physical match for Blaklok. It reached for him again with those grasping claws and, this time, Blaklok's reaction was slower. Even imbued with the power of the divine, the consumption of so much hell-spawned fire had its side effects. The claw came ever closer, and Thaddeus stumbled back, desperate to avoid the demon's grip, but he would never be quick enough.

This was it!

The blaring report of a dozen carbines peeled out from somewhere behind, as Blaklok slipped and fell on his backside. Valac roared to the heavens as its body erupted in a dozen places, black ichor spurting from its arms and chest.

As he began to stagger to his feet, Blaklok saw the Judicature approaching, heavy carbines unleashing a deluge of shot against the demon. He had never been so pleased to see the masked fantassins of the Judicature in all his life.

Valac turned, bounding off as fast as it could, as the gunmen kept firing, corralling the demon away from the crowds that stood transfixed.

Blaklok knew he had to make his own exit before he was captured and questioned, but the hellfire he had consumed still bubbled and roiled within him, making him groggy and sluggish.

He stumbled away from the Judicature, slipping on the cobbles, and glanced back, hoping against hope that he had not been noticed in the excitement. Then he saw her, her tipstaff by her side – well, the one she hadn't shot anyway. How did she keep doing this, where did she keep cropping up from?

Thaddeus began to move with greater urgency, but he knew Indagator Amelia had seen him. He stumbled away down the street but she would be on him in no time.

With a squeal of breaks, and pumping of steam, a huge metal wagon screeched to a halt beside him. It stank of rotting cabbage and sewage, and it took several moments for Blaklok to realise it was one of the lumbering refuse carriers that intermittently trundled down the streets of the Manufactory, cleaning up in those districts that could afford such things as garbage collection.

Desperately he grasped for the door to the cab, if he could get inside hopefully he could coerce the driver into getting him out of here, but the door was already opening. Strong hands reached out, grabbing the manacles that still bound his hands, dragging him inside and dumping him on the floor of the cabin.

Once he was within, the engine of the carrier sputtered and growled into life, causing the whole cab to lurch as it sped off down the street.

His wrists were screaming for release, but Blaklok was far too grateful for his rescue to be annoyed about the pain. He glanced around the cabin. It was large; big enough to seat half a dozen refuse workers, and all the seats were taken. Big, burly men, dressed in suits with polished shoes.

These were the best dressed refuse workers Thaddeus had ever seen, their allotted district must have been prosperous indeed.

'So, we meet again,' said a familiar voice.

Thaddeus looked up to see the enormous horsey teeth beaming down at him.

'You do remember me, don't you?' asked Trol Snapper. 'I'll be offended if you don't.'

Before Blaklok could answer, something hard hit him on the back of the head.

CHAPTER
TWENTY

THIS WAS GETTING to be an annoyingly familiar situation – bound up tight and staring at bare muggy walls.

As Thaddeus opened his eyes he could taste blood and feel the sting of the manacles at his wrists. The aching in his limbs had only intensified and the friction burns on his palms stung like mad. A lesser man would have cried out at the pain – would have given in to the helplessness – but not Thaddeus Blaklok.

His grin grew wide.

Here he was again, stuck in a hopeless situation, surrounded by enemies, with death at hand.

Death.

His constant companion.

The monkey on his shoulder.

How much longer would their friendship last? How much longer before the reaper grew bored of their perpetual waltz and decided it was time for the dance to end?

Not long, with any fucking luck.

There was movement to his right, someone shuffling, realising he was awake and reacting in a panic. Hushed voices briefly conversed and Blaklok heard a door open somewhere behind him, allowing a little more light to encroach on the room as it swung wide.

Blaklok felt sick. Not due to his dire situation – this was far from the first time he had been bound and threatened – but an unnatural malady squirmed and roiled within his gut. He had consumed hellfire, taken it into himself, and there was no way it was going to stay in there for long. A belch worked its way up from his abdomen, and he could feel it burning his insides all the way. When it finally came it was only the daintiest of belches but it still stung his throat and mouth, bringing tears to his eyes. The stench of it hung in the air; rotten eggs and putrid meat and burned corpses.

He knew this was only the beginning. Sooner or later all hell was, quite literally, going to break loose.

Behind him he heard the click of expensive shoes against the hard floor and could guess at who had arrived.

Trol Snapper was dressed in his best again, smiling that big donkey smile.

'So, we have you again,' he said. 'I was led to believe you were a resourceful man, Mr Blaklok. It appears you're not resourceful enough to avoid *me*, are you?'

'Look,' said Blaklok, feeling sicker with every passing second. 'No pissing about – you have to let me go.'

As much as he wanted Snapper and his goons to suffer, even Blaklok wasn't vindictive enough to unleash a belly full of hellfire at living, breathing mortals.

Snapper laughed, and it was aped by other laughs from behind Blaklok's back.

'Well, whether you're resourceful or not is questionable, but bright you definitely ain't.'

Other figures stepped forward. They were big and hulking; more thugs come to join in the fun. Snapper at least had plenty of men at his beck and call if nothing else. 'I hope you're not expecting your little friend to come and help you again. This time we won't be disturbed. This time it's just you and us.'

One of the brutes stepped in and laid one on Blaklok's jaw. Another put one in his gut. That did nothing for the boiling and roiling within his stomach and he belched again. The thugs reeled at the stench, taking a step back, and Snapper's face contorted in disgust.

'What the fuck is that?' he said, lifting a handkerchief to his face. 'You want to lay off the spicy stuff. It obviously doesn't agree with you.'

With that, the thugs recovered, laying in with more blows. They went at it with gusto, and within a few moments Blaklok was bleeding and winded, trying his best to fight down the sickness that was churning and writhing inside.

'I don't know, boss.' It was a light voice, coming from somewhere to Blaklok's left. In the shadows he could see a diminutive figure watching from a safe distance. 'He doesn't look well. He's gone all green like.'

'Keep out of this, Geffle. In fact, why the fuck are you still here?'

The figure in the shadows went silent.

More blows rained in, just like the last time he had been at Snapper's mercy, only on this occasion no one seemed interested in asking any questions. This time they just wanted him hurting... or worse.

And with each blow Blaklok felt the hellfire boil more intensely, bubbling up in anticipation of an almighty eruption.

'Look, I'm not fucking kidding,' he managed to say through a gap in the beating. 'Do yourselves a favour and–'

He was cut off by a fist to the face.

'All right, I'm bored with this,' said Snapper eventually. 'String him up, and let's get the knives out.'

There was a hum of approval as rough hands grasped him, untying him from the chair and hauling him up.

Blood had started to run into his eyes, and one side of his face was swelling, making it difficult to see. But this was the least of Blaklok's concerns, because it was coming, and nothing he could do would keep it in.

Not that he owed these bastards any favours.

A foul whistling began to escape from his throat, like an engine venting steam. One of the thugs took a step back, his eyes suddenly widening, but the rest kept a grip on him.

Well, more fool them.

He belched again and this time red-hot bile ran up over his lips and dripped onto the floor. It steamed and sizzled, making a seared mess of the hard granite. That was enough to ensure the rest of them let go, stepping back in horror and watching as Blaklok retched and gurgled. He could feel the unnatural heat burning in the pit of his stomach. It ran up into his nostrils, creeping up his spine and into the back of his head and infecting his brain.

It had to be now or it would begin to consume him – the foul, unnatural pestilence spreading into him like a canker, and taking him over completely.

Blaklok opened his mouth wide and vomited.

The hellfire roared as he spewed it forth, searing his lips and cracking the skin. He was protected in the most part by the fell incantations that had been said over the sigils on his body, but it still hurt like hell. As his flesh had been tarred and burned so many years ago, so his soul had been made resistant to certain aspects of the Pit. Fortunately for him, this was one of them.

Unfortunately for Snapper's men, they did not share his supernatural resilience.

The hellfire spattered against the chest of one unfortunate, and his clothes and the flesh beneath immediately took, engulfed in a liquid flame that melted everything in its path. The poor bleeder didn't even have a chance to scream.

More of the evil torrent splashed against another thug's leg, melting his thigh to the bone. This man did have an opportunity to scream as his leg was slowly corroded away by the molten deluge. He fell to the floor, grasping his slimy stump and raising a racket to the rooftop of the small room.

Thaddeus reeled backwards, flecks of the molten liquid still falling from his lips, hissing as it hit the granite floor. Snapper's eyes were wide as they peered from over the handkerchief he still had positioned over his face. The little man, Geffle, streaked from his hiding place in the corner and headed for the door, moving so fast he had to hold his flat cap to his head lest it fall off in flight.

The other thugs standing in the room were all staring at Blaklok, unable to comprehend what had just happened. He retched again, as the hellfire threatened to spew forth once more, and they all made a break for it, falling over one another as they squeezed through the exit.

On the floor, the legless thug was still screaming his lungs out and Blaklok turned to regard him… just as he belched another deluge. It covered the hapless victim, silencing his screams and melting him into the floor.

Blaklok fell to his knees, gasping for air, hoping against hope that he had now expunged the hellfire completely. He looked up and saw Snapper still staring down. As much as he wanted to get up and smash Trol's face to a pulp, he simply didn't have the energy.

'You're– you–' was all Snapper could say before he too thought it expedient to flee from Blaklok's presence.

And then he was alone in the room with two bubbling corpses. He was still manacled, still had the burns on his palms and torn and bloodied clothes. Still had the bruises on his face and the blood on his cheeks, only now he at least had an escape route.

All was silent as he struggled to stand, and followed the rest of the fleeing crowd out through the open door.

From the look of the corridors he wasn't in the Cistern, which was a surprise. He would at least have expected Trol and his men to take him back to their hideout, but they obviously didn't want to be interrupted again.

Not like last time.

As he walked through a seemingly endless maze of whitewashed passages it began to grow harder to breathe. Even walking was difficult. It seemed holding the hellfire had taken more out of him than he had anticipated.

The periphery of his vision was growing hazy and he knew he had to get himself some help, and soon. But who in the Manufactory would he run to? Where in this whole warren of the venal and the wicked that they called the City of Bastards could Blaklok find a friend? Enemies aplenty, that was taken as read, but a friendly face was taking the piss.

Finally he made it out into the open air. Looking back he saw he had exited a large building, something like a stately home but with bars on the windows. A single word was emblazoned on the front in chipped paint: Sanatorium.

Nice, he thought. It would have been quite apt had he ended his days in there.

As Blaklok made his way through the overgrown grounds of the abandoned madhouse he thought again about where he could go. Where could he flee to in the Manufactory? Who would take him in?

Only one name sprang to mind... the Apothecary.

He was neutral, and consequently his place was neutral ground. The Apothecary never took sides, never played one off against the other, never double-crossed. He valued one thing, and one thing only – hard, cold coin.

That did bring up a problem in itself, by virtue of the fact that Thaddeus didn't have any coin, but he would have to cross that rickety bridge when he came to it. It was well known that the Apothecary took no credit, but maybe he could be persuaded to make an exception.

Not bloody likely, but what choice did Blaklok have?

He stumbled on, fighting against fatigue and unconsciousness, eventually running on memory and instinct as he hit the streets.

With a little luck he would be able to make it to the Apothecary's before he passed out. With a little more luck, the Apothecary would be at home.

Whether he would let Blaklok in or not was another matter...

CHAPTER
TWENTY-ONE

A DEMON. IN the Manufactory.

A real life, sulphur-stinking, fire-breathing, people-rending demon.

Here. In the Manufactory.

The halls of the Judicature were in turmoil, bodies moving swiftly and with purpose hither and thither like it was the last day on earth and they all had to finish their paperwork before the cataclysm began. Lectors barked orders, fantassins blurted requests, tipstaffs garbled reports and in the midst of it all administrants shuffled their papers from desk to desk, trying their hardest to keep on top of the clamour.

In the confusion, Amelia walked with a calm air, seeming to move in slow motion amidst the mass of rushing figures. No one would notice her amongst all this upheaval. She was merely one more agent of the Judicature carrying out her duty. No one would care if she entered the Lexiconium without the requisite authorisations. Not an eyelid would be batted if she helped herself to the confidential information held within.

It was not in Amelia's nature to behave in a clandestine or underhand manner. She had always been an exemplary pupil, and a by-the-book operative of the Judicature. But recent events had spurred her into action that was out of character. Almighty's sake, she had shot her own man. If that wasn't an act unbecoming of her position, she didn't know what was.

But things had become insane over the past few days, and she just knew it was all to do with this man Blaklok. He was the key to everything – even this infernal beast that had decided to make an appearance in the city.

She just knew it.

And if she could find out who he was and where he had come from she was sure everything else would eventually resolve itself.

The Lexiconium was the Judicature's Hall of Records, a repository full of tomes, ledgers, essays, periodicals and every other form of script that had been set to paper. Every word ever written within the walls of the Manufactory – and even some beyond – was documented in the Lexiconium.

Amelia had always been something of a bookworm, and she knew if she was allowed long enough within the stuffy confines of the record rooms she would eventually get to the bottom of this.

She strolled in through the double doors, flashing a knowing nod at the librarian behind his high desk, piled almost to the rafters with used tomes ready to be slotted back into their places within the rows of bookshelves. Everything was ordered in the Lexiconium, it was a sanctuary amidst the chaos of the outside world. Amelia didn't spend nearly enough time in here, but without the necessary authorisations she simply couldn't get access. Now, with all this mass hysteria regarding creatures of the Pit allegedly being unleashed on the world, that didn't seem to matter.

Librarians and administrants moved with purpose through the rows of shelves, carrying piles of papers or pushing trolleys rammed full of journals and codices. No one gave Amelia a second glance as she made her way towards the far end of the massive hall, her heels clicking rhythmically on the polished floor.

The criminal archives were towards the far end of the Lexiconium, hidden away in a shadowed room. A single gaslight burned in the corner, supplemented by a few candles spewing molten wax down their sides, and Amelia began to wonder how she would find anything in the dimness. But within minutes her eyes had adjusted to the gloom and she was meticulously poring over old records and scanning through ledgers covered in dust. It reminded her of her childhood days in her father's study, watching the old man work until late into the night, scribing his manuscripts by the light of a single flame.

For the next five hours she worked, researching frantically, uncovering all kinds of skullduggery and misdemeanours, but of Thaddeus Blaklok she found not a trace. There was no mention of his name; no tattooed bulldog of a man involved in the occult had ever been brought to the attention of the Judicature in the last ten years. Either he had never been caught, or any trace of evidence against him had been purloined – whisked away by unseen hands, considered not for the eyes of a lowly Indagator.

Just as she was about to give up, just as the crick in her neck from bending low to stare into faintly scripted tomes almost made her scream, she suddenly found something.

It was a simple report of murder scribed by an Indagator Rush, who Amelia knew had retired from the Judicature a few years ago to end his days out in the Dolmen Precinct. His report contained details of the killing: a woman and her children, cut to pieces and partly consumed by a most vicious perpetrator. The murder had taken place beyond the city's walls just less than a year previously, out in a small settlement to the north, which was curious in itself – Indagators rarely troubled themselves with crimes perpetrated beyond the limits of the Manufactory. Nevertheless, Rush's investigations had led him across the length and breadth of the Manufactory in pursuit of his quarry until he finally had him cornered in the Cistern. Rush's description detailed a large man with eyes like a shark's, huge strangler's hands and a body covered in mysterious sigils.

Whether this was the man she had been pursuing was unclear, but Amelia felt her insides start to knot as she read on. Rush had the man cornered, he and his tipstaffs had him

Kultus

bang to rights, but just before they could apprehend him he disappeared into the dark. Rush reported the loss of three men in the pursuit, all of them killed in a variety of gruesome ways, and their suspect was a man of exceeding guile and strength.

The similarity was too much to ignore. Surely this was him? Amelia flicked through the ledger looking for more details but was surprised to discover there were none. The murderer escaped, never to be heard from again.

This had to be her man, Blaklok. Perhaps he had lain low since murdering a woman and her children and for some unknown reason had decided to resurface.

The ledger contained no other details, and Amelia was frustrated by the dead end. Then she stopped, flicking back through the report. Perhaps the dead woman and her children would offer a clue to Blaklok's past. Perhaps he had some link to them other than being the harbinger of their doom.

Frantically she thumbed through the pages, from the beginning of Rush's report to the end, but there were no other details of the woman and her brood. This seemed odd to Amelia. Standard practice was to include as much detail in a report as possible, and for a man such as Rush to omit such information was curious indeed. With no further leads, Indagator Rush would have been the next logical line of investigation, but it turned out that the man had died of heart failure six months previously.

She had hit another dead end.

After placing the ledgers and reports back in their proper place, Amelia left the archives room and walked back through the Lexiconium. It was as she walked, noticing the eyes of two administrants fall upon her, that Amelia suddenly began to feel naked and vulnerable. It took some moments for her to realise that it was the fact that Bounder and Hodge were not at her side that elicited the feeling of exposure.

Bounder was still in the infirmary and, knowing that she would come to no danger within the walls of the Judicature, she had allowed Hodge to stay with him. At first she had felt a deep pang of guilt for having wounded her tipstaff – Bounder was a faithful underling and had proved himself invaluable over the past months. But his reaction to being shot in the line of duty had been most disappointing. He had looked at her with accusing eyes, as though it were her fault! Did he not realise that such things were bound to happen in the line of duty? It was all part of the job, after all. If she had been the one on the receiving end she would have considered it her obligation to take a round in the leg with a stiff upper lip.

Not so Bounder.

He mewled and cried, staring at her like a puppy that had been kicked by his master. It cut her to the quick to see him react in such a manner, and consequently she had been forced to leave him to his self pity. Hopefully, by the time she returned, he would see that there had been no other choice. Apprehending the criminal Blaklok was the only priority, no matter the cost.

'Indulging in a little extra-curricular study are we, Indagator?'

The words hit when she wasn't expecting them and a wave of nausea suddenly flooded over her.

Not here. Not now, when she was already feeling low.

Surrey was lurking just outside the Lexiconium, leaning against a marble pillar, his hands tucked casually inside his trouser pockets, that slanted smile creasing his smug face. She suddenly began to regret Bounder's condition and the fact she had allowed Hodge to stay with him. This was just the kind of situation two burly thugs were designed to guard against; alone with Indagator Surrey, it didn't bare thinking about. She suddenly wished she still had Hodge's carbine to hand.

'Don't worry,' he said. 'I won't tell anyone.'

'What do you mean you won't tell anyone? I have the proper authorisations.' Her feigned indignation was perfectly acted, but Surrey only smiled wider. He was a good judge if nothing else.

'Yes, of course you do. And I have been promoted to Grand Overseer.'

She tried to ignore him and turned away, heading off down the corridor towards the freedom of the Judicature proper but, like a bad penny, Surrey popped up again from around another pillar.

'Still hunting our troublesome friend, are we?'

'What do you mean?' she said, stopping dead and turning to face that laconic smile. She had not once discussed Thaddeus Blaklok with Surrey, and how he knew about him was a mystery to her.

'I simply meant the object of your investigation. Mr Blaklok, isn't it?'

'What do you know of him, Surrey?' She took a threatening step forward and Surrey raised his hands in mock surrender. 'If you've been sending me on wild goose chases with this occult nonsense so help me I'll–'

'Please, Amelia, calm down. I was merely making an innocent enquiry.'

'I mean it, Surrey. What do you know? There are no records, no evidence. No one seems to want to talk about him and now he's disappeared. Who is he?'

'All I can say is you won't find anything documented. You were lucky to track him down once. Now he knows you're on to him you won't find him again.'

'What in the Pits are you hiding, Surrey? Tell me what you know.'

'Perhaps I've said too much already.' Surrey looked suddenly serious, something Amelia had never noticed in him before. He glanced around, checking that there were no eavesdroppers, then he leaned in close. Amelia could smell a faint whiff of alcohol and mint on his breath, and some unknown cologne wafting up from within his doublet that she didn't find altogether unpleasant. At any other time she would not have let him get so close but now she was intrigued. 'All I can say is that Blaklok is watched over by higher powers than the Judicature. Maybe higher than the Sancrarium itself.'

Richard Ford

Amelia was suddenly sceptical. No mere street thug could afford such protection. She backed away from Surrey, thinking this a ruse just to get close to her.

'You must think I'm one of your street-side doxies, Surrey. Blaklok's a yob. A quite exceptional one, but a yob nonetheless.'

'No!' said Surrey, reaching out and grasping her arm. His grip was tight and his expression deathly serious. 'He's so much more than that. I don't know much but I know this. It's no coincidence he has re-emerged when there's a demon on the loose. And my guess is that's not the only Pit-borne menace the Manufactory's got to look forward to before this whole mess is resolved. Take my advice, Amelia, stay out of it until the whole thing's blown over.'

She pulled herself away, still able to feel the pressure of his fingers on her arm. 'You're mad, Surrey. Get some help. And leave the real investigation to those of us who are dedicated to the job.'

Surrey was smiling again. She couldn't tell whether he had been acting concerned or if it was merely another ruse. 'Well, if you're determined to pursue this, I can't stop you. If you really want Blaklok, there's only one piece of advice I can give you.'

'And what pearl of wisdom is that?'

'Simply follow the carnage.'

With that he turned and set off down the corridor, whistling a tuneless dirge as he went, as though he had not a care in the world.

Amelia watched him go, at once tempted to follow him and hoping never to see him again. She settled on letting him go.

Had he been genuinely concerned? Was his advice genuine? One thing was for sure: following the carnage was just about the only thing she had to go on right now, so she guessed it was advice she had no choice but to follow.

CHAPTER
TWENTY-TWO

THE STREET WAS quiet as he waited outside the ramshackle building. From the shadows, Blaklok could see the comings and goings as the night drew on. Twilight beckoned and the well-to-do and the women and children steadily filtered away. Once the gaslights were lit and shadows began to bruise the streets the carrion hunters started to appear.

Shady figures peeled themselves from the dark, accompanied by painted women and brutish peons. They did a kind of slow dance around one another, stopping to converse before moving on. It was as though they were trying to leech from one another, looking for some weakness or advantage, and when they realised there was none they would move on. It was the way of the Manufactory's night stalkers. In every district the moonlight would bring them out to do their seamy deeds in the dark.

This was all in Blaklok's periphery. What he was really concerned with was the lofty apartment, elevated some way above the streets. A rickety staircase led up to a single doorway, well lit and open.

But no street whores or peddlers used this entrance for their trade.

They all knew this belonged to the Apothecary.

It wasn't the Apothecary himself they were afraid of offending. It was his patrons. As Blaklok watched he saw half a dozen members of the Community come and go. Even the Deacon appeared, without his usual entourage, walking up the stairs without a sound to rap on the Apothecary's door. Blaklok could see that the illumination around the entrance seemed to dim as the Deacon arrived, as though the light was afraid of him.

From his hiding place he watched it all. The bleeding and the aching had stopped a while back as he rested, but he knew that if he was going to complete his mission he would still need help.

That was where the Apothecary came in.

One thing he couldn't do was take the stairs like the normal patrons – though normal might not quite be the word for them. If he was seen by the Judicature or a passer-by that would be the end of it, and Blaklok still had work to do.

As the moon began to reach its zenith, barely visible through the curtain of reeling smog, Blaklok heaved himself from his hiding place and made his way towards the apartment. It would usually have taken him little effort to scale a drainpipe, but in his current condition he felt like a geriatric negotiating a particularly tricky flight of stairs. From the rooftop, he saw the skylight to the Apothecary's rooms, and stealthily made his way towards them. Silent as a tomcat, he crouched down, peering over the rim of the window to make sure he would not be disturbed once inside. He couldn't see anyone amidst the clutter of the brightly lit room. The entire place was a mess; distillers bubbled on a long bench next to tables cluttered with vials and strange looking instruments. Books were packed onto shelves that lined the wall, fighting for space against the cobwebs that surrounded them, and Thaddeus was sure he could see things scuttling along the floor amidst the pattern of the dusty carpet.

He gently lifted the skylight and shifted himself in. It was a short drop to the ground, and Blaklok managed it without making a sound.

He could hear music emanating from within an adjoining room, and after padding quietly across the threadbare carpet Blaklok peered inside.

The Apothecary had his back turned, hunched over a bench, instruments working frantically at some contraption or other. In one corner a gramophone played a lilting tune – cellos and violins by the sound of it, but Blaklok had never been much into music.

Masked by the sound, he crept forward. Perhaps he could find some kind of healing salve and be gone before the Apothecary even knew he was there.

No such luck.

'Good evening, Thaddeus,' said the Apothecary, without turning around.

Blaklok let out a sigh of defeat, suddenly feeling more fatigued than ever. He looked around until he espied a wooden chair covered in a pile of books. Sweeping them to the floor he sat himself down.

The Apothecary turned, smiling a wide brown-toothed smile from within a mass of hair.

Blaklok had nothing against beards, but the Apothecary just abused the privilege – he was the most hirsute human being Blaklok had ever seen. Matted hair covered his head from the top of a high brow to cascade down his back. His curly brown beard started just below his cheekbones and covered him to his chest. But for that, he was a skinny wretch, and it was most likely that his hair and beard weighed more than the rest of him put together.

'Well, you've certainly seen better days,' said the Apothecary. Thaddeus nodded, lacking the energy to come up with anything witty to say. 'Guess you'll be wanting my help, then?'

Thaddeus nodded again and the Apothecary stopped what he was doing and walked to one of the shelves. As he fumbled among the jumble he motioned towards what resembled a dentist's chair in one corner. 'Make yourself comfortable, Thaddeus. It looks like you could do with the rest.'

Blaklok was not in the mood to argue, and he gingerly made his way towards the chair, reclining within its leather confines. It smelt of mould, but the leather was the most comfortable thing he had sat on in almost two days, and to him it felt like rapture.

Within seconds the Apothecary was at his side bearing salve, bandages and a needle and thread.

'How did you know I was behind you?' Blaklok asked as the Apothecary went to work.

'The Deacon mentioned you were waiting in the shadows. You can't hide anything from that one.'

'And you still left your skylight unlocked?'

'How else were you supposed to get in? I know you never use the front door like normal people.' He smiled at Blaklok, his brown teeth just visible beneath the curly hair of his beard. 'Unlike the rest of the guttersnipes in this foul city, I'm not afraid of you, Thaddeus Blaklok.'

Thaddeus almost returned the smile. It was a novelty to hear someone say that. It made such a change from the usual begging and screaming he had to endure.

'So, rumour has it there's a real life demon on the loose. That wouldn't have anything to do with you, would it?'

'No,' Blaklok replied. 'That's down to a bunch of part-timers who got in over their heads. But I suppose I'm the one who'll have to sort out the shit.'

'As always, Thaddeus, as always. I take it the demon's responsible for most of this?' The Apothecary waved his hand over Blaklok's battered body.

'Some of it. The rest is just general wear and tear.'

'Quite. I've not seen you look this bad since the Clockwork Rebellion.'

'This is nothing compared to that. This is–' He suddenly winced as the Apothecary dabbed at his burned palms with a piece of moist gauze. 'Before you do any more, you should know: I can't afford to pay.'

'Well, that would normally be a problem,' said the Apothecary, not pausing in his labours. 'But your account has already been settled.'

'By who?' asked Blaklok, but then he remembered his benefactors had their hands in all sorts of pies. 'Never mind. I think I know who you're talking about.'

'Well, if you'd care to enlighten me I'd much appreciate it. Shadowy figures giving me coin just in case you show up isn't the way I would normally expect business to be conducted. But the settlement of account was most generous, so I guess I shouldn't complain.'

The Apothecary moved to Blaklok's face, pausing, as though he didn't really know where to start. After placing a slab of cold meat on one of Blaklok's black eyes, he began to poke at the burns around his lips.

'Hellfire residue. You *have* been in the wars,' he said, picking at the ripe scabs with a pair of tweezers. 'And here I was thinking you'd left all this behind you.'

'I had,' said Thaddeus. 'But circumstances change.'

'Indeed they do. But don't you ever wish you'd stayed gone? You had an out and you took it. Not many would come back to this dump.'

'As I said, circumstances change.' Blaklok didn't try to mask his annoyance, and the Apothecary duly halted his inquisition.

The pair continued in silence, with Blaklok reclining further into the leather seat to allow the Apothecary to administer his healing touch. Perhaps it was the smell of the healing salves or the comfort of knowing he was on neutral ground, but soon the pull of being stitched and the ache of having bandages applied to his cuts and scrapes faded, and Blaklok gave himself over to the solace of sleep.

BLAKLOK DIDN'T OFTEN dream.

When he did so he found himself plagued by night terrors – never more ferocious than those he faced in the waking hours – but terrors nonetheless. For this reason he had mostly managed to filter dreams from his sleep altogether, but on this occasion he dreamed an old and long forgotten dream.

He was happy.

The sky was not filled with smog and the stench of garbage. There was no cacophony assailing his ears. The clamour of unwashed, ungrateful souls did not surround him. There was no forest of concrete and pathways of stone pressing in on him from all sides.

He was free.

Birds twittered. Green grass caressed his toes. The sun was on his face.

Of course, he knew this was a dream, but that knowledge did not impair its lucidity.

They were there, just beyond his vision. The three of them, standing where he could only just see them, tantalisingly out of reach.

He tried to walk to them but could not move. He reached out a hand but they did not see.

Then he began to focus, his vision fighting through the blur. In seconds the haze was gone, their faces clarified and he saw them standing there – red and ruined.

He screamed.

BLAKLOK'S EYES WERE open but the room was in darkness. A cool sweat had set itself around his neck and down his spine, and it made a soft peeling sound as he lifted himself from the reclining leather chair.

It took his eyes some seconds to adjust to the gloom. He moved through the dark, searching for any sight or sound, but there was nothing but a dim glow coming from the adjoining chamber.

Inside, a potbelly stove still shed some light and warmth as the last of its embers burned down, and beside it was the Apothecary, asleep in a battered armchair.

Thaddeus was unsure whether he should just slip away in the night. The old man had been paid, after all. But then he had done his work so well. Blaklok felt invigorated, his wounds stitched and bound, his bruises having lost their swell. Maybe he would stay and give his thanks when the Apothecary awoke.

Then he noticed something from the corner of his eye – an adjoining room he hadn't noticed before. Closer inspection revealed it was a hidden door left half open.

He crept up silently and pulled the door back gently, relieved that the hinges did not creak. When he had made enough of a gap he stepped inside. A dim gaslight burned in one corner and there was a sound of something bubbling, like a boiling kettle, emanating from a recess.

Blaklok moved further inside, straining to see in the darkness. At the far end of the room was a metal tank, and Blaklok could tell this was where the sound was coming from. He moved closer, stooping to peer in the tank and suddenly stopped. Inside was a human arm, floating in some form of bubbling liquid.

Weird indeed, thought Thaddeus, but perhaps not the weirdest thing in the Apothecary's rooms, if he chose to investigate further.

As he turned to leave he was sure he saw the fingers of the arm suddenly twitch. It made him stop dead, but before he could look again, the Apothecary's voice filled the room.

'Inquisitive as ever, Thaddeus.' Blaklok could only nod. 'I suppose you want to know–'

'I know not to stick my beak in where it's not wanted,' he replied, walking from the room and past the Apothecary. It didn't do to pry unless the job called for it, and this was neutral ground, everyone knew it. 'I'll be off now. Got appointments to keep, you know how it is.'

'Indeed I do, young Thaddeus.'

Blaklok made for the door, but stopped on the way. His eyes were drawn to two small objects on a shelf. He recognised them from times past – times when objects like that had been in common use. Going by recent events, they might come in handy again.

'Mind if I take these?' Thaddeus said, motioning to the shelf.

The Apothecary gave a shrug. 'Feel free. Your account more than covers it.'

Blaklok nodded his thanks, and carefully placed the items in his pockets. He would have to find a safer way of carrying them later, but for now, just having them to hand was safeguard enough.

'Not leaving by the skylight?' the Apothecary asked, as Thaddeus began to unbolt the front door.

'Don't think that's necessary now,' said Blaklok.

He opened the door and strolled off into the night.

A ROMANTIC
INTERLUDE

IT HAD NEVER felt such pain before.

When last it had trodden this plane of men they had not borne such weapons. The sting of their fire belchers still tore at its flesh, leaving welts that were slow to heal. These creatures were meant to be its chattel, not to stand against it with such venom and fury.

Valac knew that it was weak, and would remain so until it had consumed of the flesh enough to build its strength, but that did not stop the rage inside.

These men had grown bold in its absence. They dared to attack it, instead of prostrating themselves at its feet and begging to be consumed so that it could thrive.

The demon moved silently through the maze of underground tunnels. It didn't know where it was or what its next move would be but, for now, rest was the only priority. When it could walk no more it sank to its haunches in the muck and filth.

It was cold here, and dark.

Valac hated the dark; it shed no light on its magnificence.

It had been dark in the Pit, and the demon had hated that, and it pained it to have to hide in the shadows now that it was free. It yearned to be out, basking in the light, feeling the radiance of the chattel as they worshipped it.

Valac yearned to be exalted.

After millennia in the Pit it was all it desired. But for now it would have to hide down here in the shadows until its strength returned.

It lifted a hand to its head in the dark and felt the horn at its brow. It was tender to touch. The man-brute had hurt Valac – a mere man had the audacity to cause it pain. There would be a reckoning for this, and soon, but for now there had to be healing.

In the dark, alone and in agony, the great demon began to weep tears of mercury from eyes of burning coal. They splashed down and sizzled in the muddy water that submerged its hoofed feet, then ran away across the surface in silvery rivulets.

For hours the beast healed and wept in the dark, planning its vengeance and growing stronger. Soon it would need sustenance, and then the men of this place would know true terror, and Valac would feast and the men would worship at its feet.

There was a sudden sound.

It grew closer, and Valac pressed itself into the recesses of the tunnel hoping to catch the interlopers unawares. As the intruders drew nearer, Valac realised there was more than one of them. Its jaws began to drip in anticipation of the feast, and it could only hope to be quick enough to catch them all before they fled in terror.

Something glinted up ahead, a glimmer of gold in the dark.

As Valac watched, robed figures appeared, their faces wan and pale, frightened but determined as they moved through the tunnel.

It recognised them – these were the idolaters who had summoned it here. They were the real reason for its current suffering.

Valac stood, filling the tunnel, ready to leap among them and sunder them apart, but despite the terrified looks on their faces, the robed chattel did not flee. Instead, one of them walked forward, dropping to his knees in the filth at Valac's feet.

'We beseech thee, our President. Please, what have we done to anger you so?'

It was quite admirable that the weak fleshed chattel had the resources and guile to track it down. They must be cleverer than Valac thought. Perhaps it had been rash to begin feasting on them so soon, at least without allowing them to prostrate themselves at its feet first.

'I am Trajian Arkwright,' the chattel continued. 'Humblest and most loyal of your servants.'

'No, that is I, almighty President,' said another of the weak-fleshed, dropping to his knees beside the first. 'Please, give us your divine guidance that we may serve your aims.'

Soon they had all prostrated themselves, and Valac began to feel a little better. Maybe these were worthwhile peons after all.

Then again, Valac *was* ravenous.

It reached down, grasping the one that called itself Trajian in both its huge clawed hands, lifting his head into its mouth. The chattel screamed as jaws bit down, instantly falling silent as the head was bitten off and swallowed whole.

The rest were thrown into a panic, fighting each other to escape. Valac was in half a mind to pursue them, but in truth it was done with these worthless minions.

Besides, it had larger game to hunt.

The headless corpse it held in its hands bore the stench of another of the weak-flesh. It smelled faintly of the man-brute that had evaded Valac; the hulking chunk of pink skin that had wrenched at Valac's horn and consumed his breath in an instant. This was the one Valac would have, and soon, if there were any justice on this plane.

Eagerly, Valac consumed the rest of the body, gold robes and all, and licked its sodden lips in satisfaction.

As it prepared to leave it saw another of its worthless minions cowering on the ground. Suddenly, Valac felt the dangling flesh between its legs stirring. It had been millennia since it had indulged in carnal delights with the weak-fleshed. Despite its eagerness to hunt and feed further, Valac decided it would sate its other urges first.

The chattel squealed and struggled as Valac picked it up, but the resistance only served to arouse it further, pumping molten ichor through its veins until the phallus between its legs had grown vast. The squealing grew more urgent as it pressed itself into the writhing creature again and again. Within seconds Valac had spent its lust and spewed its demon seed, and the subject of its advances was still and limp. The President threw the spent flesh to the ground and smiled.

How it would enjoy indulging itself on the man-brute. That one would feel him for hours, again and again as it satisfied itself; spurting its seed a dozen times before it was finished.

There would be a reckoning, all right. The man-brute had better prepare himself for that!

CHAPTER
TWENTY-THREE

As EVER, THE Apothecary had done exemplary work. Thaddeus flexed the fingers and one stump of his left hand, happy that it no longer throbbed. He could still feel the tip of his little finger, even though it was absent, but the fact that the wound was neatly stitched, covered in a pain-numbing balm and didn't stink anymore was almost as good.

Now all he had to worry about was retrieving the Key of Lunos from a bunch of skin-changing demon worshippers whilst avoiding the attentions of the Judicature and a Chamber of the Cistern. He also had to find President Valac and banish it back to the Pit before it could reap any more harm among the innocents of the Manufactory – though actually finding innocents in the Manufactory might well have been a harder task.

Blaklok was sure there had been a time when he'd faced a tougher task, but it didn't spring readily to mind.

Fact was he had no lead. No one seemed to know anything about the Legion or where their coterie might be based. He had scanned a copy of *The Chronicle* that morning, and despite several articles on demons and their followers, which were obviously influenced by the score of sightings of a rampant demon President in the city, there was nothing that would lead him to the whereabouts of the Legion.

Though he hated to do it, Thaddeus was going to have to retrace his steps and return to Lord Julius. He was the only one who seemed to have any idea at all what was going on. If he didn't know anything about the Legion he may at least be able to reveal more about the Key, such as where it might best be used for the most potent effect. It was tenuous, but any lead was better than none.

After managing to purloin some clean clothes, Blaklok had made his way across the city, using the usual less trodden byways. With news of a demon on the loose, the streets were quieter than most days, and it did not take him long to reach the affluent district in which Lord Julius resided.

This time as he trod across the gardens of Julius's estate there were no hounds to come bounding across the lush grass. Blaklok found it curious that the manor's resident safeguards were not as vigilant as they should be, and rather than accept the absence of guard dogs as simple good luck it made Thaddeus even more cautious. He stole into the house more carefully than he had done before. Once inside there were no sounds or smells, no chatting servants, nothing cooking in the pot.

The place appeared all but deserted.

In the drawing room where Blaklok had been forced to give Julius's bodyguard a pasting, all was quiet. The same pictures lined the walls, the paisley armchair sat empty and a clean ashtray sat by its side on a small table. There would normally have been nothing untoward about this whole situation, but something was niggling at Blaklok – something was wrong.

Even if Julius was simply out and about there should at least still be someone at the estate looking after the holding. Then again, Julius was an ostracized member of the aristocracy... where would he go? He couldn't exactly make house calls on old friends when he had been excised from every social circle in the Manufactory.

Had he been kidnapped perhaps? Maybe the same set of goons who had sliced open Earl Beuphalus had come for Julius. Or maybe the Judicature had decided to clamp down on dabblers in the occult since a rampant demon popped up and started eating people off the street.

Either way, his pursuit of the Key was at a dead end.

This wasn't good. Not only had he found himself defeated – a fact that galled him more than anything – but the parties he was working for would not look kindly on failure. Even Blaklok might find it a struggle to get out of this one with all four limbs still in working order.

There was a creaking – a creaking Blaklok recognised. It was the floorboard that had saved his life the last time he had paid Julius a visit.

Spinning on his heel, Thaddeus stretched out one meaty leg and booted the door shut. He flushed with satisfaction as it hit something solid. Lurching forward he grasped the handle and pulled the door wide, reaching out with his shovel-like hands, ready to start tearing and beating, and shouting and threatening.

But what he saw made him stop dead.

The old man must have been about ninety, he leaned against the wall, stunned by the door that had just hit him in the face. Blaklok instantly felt a pang of guilt. He was more than happy to give any of Lord Julius's underlings a pasting to get what he wanted, but not some old codger. That wasn't what Blaklok was about.

'Don't hurt me,' begged the old man, raising a hand to his bloody nose.

That didn't make Blaklok feel any better about himself.

Grasping the old geezer firmly by the arm, Thaddeus guided him into the drawing room and sat him down in the paisley chair.

'I can't sit here,' said the old man. 'This is for Master Julius only.'

'Don't worry mate,' said Blaklok, trying his best to sound friendly. 'He won't mind. Trust me on that.'

The old man pulled out a handkerchief and dabbed at his nosebleed. 'What are you doing here anyway? This is private property you know.'

'I'm an old friend,' Blaklok lied. It didn't help his guilty conscience to be spinning a yarn to the old timer, but it was better than the truth. 'Thought I'd pay my old mate Julius a visit.'

'Well, young Julius doesn't get many visitors these days. I can't say I've ever seen you before.'

'I've been out of town until recently. I'm just here to catch up.'

'Oh, that's nice,' said the old man, reclining in the paisley chair as though he had forgotten all about having a door kicked in his face.

'And who are you, old fella?' asked Blaklok. He surprised himself at his interest in the man, but he quickly put it down to an uncharacteristic attack of the guilts.

'Me? I'm old Ned, the gardener. Been in the service of Master Julius, oh, since before he was born. Took up in the service of Julius senior about fifty years ago. Been here ever since. It's a noble calling, is gardening. These hands have pruned more bushes and watered more flowers than I care to remember. Of course the soil's not what it used to be, what with the smog and all, but my fingers are still green enough to keep this garden blooming.'

Blaklok nodded, suddenly regretting he'd even asked.

He stood and looked around the room, wondering if Julius had left some sort of clue. 'Do you know where Julius is now?'

'Sorry, can't help you there. I'm as in the dark as you. I was going to ask if he wanted geraniums or crocuses on the beds out front but he's not here is he?'

'No he's not,' said Blaklok, walking towards the bureau at one end of the room.

'So, you say you're a friend of his,' said the old man. 'That's nice. Julius never had many friends when he was young. And those friends he made growing up were a bad influence if you ask me. You seem like a nice sort.'

Blaklok looked up. Old Ned must have been well into senility if he thought the hulking brute who just kicked a door in his face was a 'nice sort'. It also didn't say much for Julius's previous friends.

'Yes, I always thought he should have more friends,' continued Ned. 'He spent far too much time on his own, looking through those dusty old books.'

As Ned prattled on, Blaklok continued searching through the room. Ned didn't seem to notice or care, so locked was he in his bout of nostalgia.

The bureau drawers contained little of interest, nor any indication that Julius was involved with the occultists of the Manufactory. By the contents of his bureau Julius could have been just another rich aristocrat fallen from grace. That was, until Blaklok came to the bottom drawer. He slid it open, at first barely noticing something towards the back, hidden beneath a pile of yellowing parchment. Then his attention was grabbed by a flash of bronze.

He stopped dead.

Ned's words seemed to drift off in a haze as Blaklok reached inside and took out the object, holding it in his hands as though it were an ancient and legendary artefact.

A carved bronze face stared back from the mask he held in his grip. Its edges were sharp, splaying out in a sunburst, the features were pointed and evil looking. Julius was the high priest of the fucking Cult of Legion!

'Oh, you've found Julius's mask have you,' said Ned chirpily. 'He likes to wear that round the house now and again. Obviously when he thinks no one's looking. It's all to do with the Legion. I think that's a benevolent fund he patronises. That's the only fun he gets nowadays.' Blaklok had stopped staring at the mask and was instead staring at the old man in disbelief. 'He's always prattling on to himself about it – Legion this, and Legion that. I think he's getting a bit obsessed, but you know young people these days. Well, of course you do, you're one of them. Of course I don't say much about it myself, it wouldn't do to upset him.' The old man chuckled to himself.

'And do you know where this benevolent fund is based?' Blaklok asked, trying to stay calm. He was really chancing his arm here, the old man probably knew nothing more, but it was about time he was afforded a break.

Ned frowned, staring up at the ceiling as though the answer might be written there. 'Yes,' he said finally. 'I do.'

There was a pause.

'And could you tell me?' said Blaklok, straining to hide his impatience.

'I can do better than that,' replied Ned. 'I can show you.'

He struggled from the depths of the armchair, and Blaklok was about to follow him from the room when the old man turned and walked towards the wall behind him. This was great. Most likely the old git had made all this up as part of some demented fantasy.

'It's here,' he said, pointing to one of the pictures that hung on the wall. 'I've seen Julius whispering to it, sometimes late at night. Don't tell him I told you that though, he might get annoyed if he thought I was spying on him.'

Blaklok moved to Ned's side and stared at the picture. It was a rendering of a tower; Blaklok recognised it as being somewhere in the Spires. Though it wouldn't have stood out as being spectacular amongst some of the other structures in that area, Blaklok was sure he would recognise it if he saw it again.

'Thanks, Ned,' he said, throwing the mask back onto the bureau, and making his way to the door.

'Think nothing of it,' Ned replied. 'Oh, and if you catch up with Julius be sure to ask whether he wants crocuses or geraniums, will you?'

Blaklok didn't answer.

When he finally did catch up with Julius, flowers would be the least of his worries.

CHAPTER
TWENTY-FOUR

THERE WAS FORBIDDEN ground in the Cistern onto which not even the most brutal of the Chambers dared encroach. It lay at the apex of the mass of sprawling subterranean pathways, easily accessible to those who knew how to gain entry, but known to only a privileged few. Seldom would any of the gang leaders of the Manufactory's underworld even contemplate entering to seek an audience with those who dwelled within this aegis unless the reason was of the direst import.

Trol Snapper was hoping that his reasons would be considered just so dire.

He wasn't sure who he was more afraid of: the man who he was traversing sanctified ground to see, or the fire-spewing madman who was responsible for the hideous deaths of his crew.

Either way, he knew he had to do this, had to tread these hallowed walkways to the inner sanctum of the Cistern to see the man who controlled the Chambers, the man who was shown fealty by even the most brutal and insane criminals of the Manufactory.

Trol had very little left in the way of a crew now. Three men flanked him, relatively green newcomers to his gang who, after their recent experiences, looked ready to flee at any moment. And of course there was Geffle, who had decided to tag along for... well, Trol didn't actually know why, but he allowed the little shit to accompany him, because even a coward like Geffle was better back-up than nothing at all. Anyways, if things turned tough when he was presented to the Montserrat, perhaps he could divert all blame onto the thieving little bastard.

It was always worth having a back up plan.

As the four men moved further into the bowels of the forbidden tunnels they were met by two of the biggest, nastiest looking men Trol Snapper had ever seen. Neither spoke, even when Trol gave his best and most winning smile. They simply opened the huge metal door that barred the way and joined Trol and his three men as they tramped through the dripping passage. With one of the hulks at the front and one at the back, the narrow tunnel darkened somewhat as they moved through it. Though Trol could see little, he could feel the intermittent drip of water as it splashed against his tailored suit. From the smell he could tell this water was far from clean, but it would have been foolish to complain – it wasn't like either of these titans was suddenly going to provide him with an umbrella.

The tunnel wound on, until they came to a massive reception room. More troglodytic guards stood vigilantly at the room's edge, brandishing carbines and all manner of vicious looking hand weapons. Behind him, Trol could tell his remaining crew were beginning to get nervous. His three bodyguards were glancing around skittishly, and Geffle was dancing from foot to foot, his eyes darting around, looking for the nearest escape route in case things started to turn nasty. But there was no escape route down here; this place was more secure than the Church of the Sancrarium itself. If things went badly there would be no escape.

One of their brutish guides walked forward and smashed his meaty fist against another massive metal portal. The sound echoed around the reception room like the tolling of a death knell. Trol could feel his insides turning cartwheels. He was about to meet the Montserrat, and his excuse for the intrusion better be a good one or he wouldn't be leaving here with the same number of appendages he had arrived with.

The door swung wide, and Trol could see a massive bull-like head peering through. There was a terse conversation, and bullhead nodded, his face grim, his eyes looking up to fix on Snapper and his crew. He beckoned them forward, and Snapper fought to retain control of his legs, pressing them forward despite their reluctance to move.

When he walked through the door he saw that the bull-faced guard was even bigger than the two brutes who had brought him here. How that was possible he did not know. There were certain drugs one could obtain in the Cistern, and some speculated they were used by the Militia of the Manufactory to increase the size and aggression of its fantassins, but Trol had never seen a man this big before. If this meeting went well, he would be sure to ask the Montserrat what he was feeding his men and use it on his own crew. They might have better luck in the future when they had a lone, bald thug tied to a chair. Instead of being beaten by short flat cap wearing intruders and melted by corrosive vomit they might actually be able to give a good account of themselves.

Trol took several steps into the room, following the guard, until the man stopped and stood aside. Shifting his bulk from Trol's view, he revealed a large, lavishly decorated room covered in drapes and hangings. Burners stood in every corner exuding a sweet spicy scent and the carpet beneath him was thick and lush.

'Wipe your feet,' said the bull-headed thug.

At first Trol didn't realise he was being addressed, until he looked down and saw the filth that he had accumulated on his shoes during the walk. Quickly, he, Geffle and the three gangers started to vigorously wipe their feet on a large mat in the doorway. When they had finished, the guard beckoned them further into the room. 'Through there,' he rumbled.

Gingerly, Trol made his way through the drapes and hazy mist given off by the burners, and moved into the depths of the room. As he penetrated further he could just make out a massive wooden desk that almost ran the entire width of the room. To each side of it was another guard, each one looking identical to bull face. And at the centre of the desk, sitting within the confines of a massive leather chair, sat the Montserrat.

He was tiny, his black hair slicked back from a high forehead, his shirt collar high and crisp, his jowls sagging over the top of it. The tiniest wisp of a moustache was drawn across his top lip, and from above his plump cheeks two beady eyes stared at Trol as he approached.

'Ah, Snapper,' said the Montserrat, a toothy grin crossing his face as he recognised Trol. 'To what do I owe this pleasure?'

Trol felt relief wash over him. The Montserrat was in a good mood. This might go a long way to making his admission of incompetence and the loss of his crew not seem half as bad.

'Well, boss, there's been a bit of a problem on our manor,' said Trol, sliding into a low wooden chair opposite the Montserrat. It made it a little more difficult to see the little man perched at the other side of the huge desk, but Trol's feet were killing him.

'Oh, yes?' replied the Montserrat. 'What's the problem?'

'Well, first we got shaken down by the Judicature. But that wasn't our fault. We were set up, put in the frame by some roustabout. Isn't that right Geffle?' Geffle nodded so hard Trol thought his head might pop off. 'So, like you'd expect, we went off to find the fucker – and we did – gave him a good pasting too. Ain't that right?' This time, Geffle and the three members of Trol's crew nodded in unison as though their lives depended on it. 'But then we got ambushed. This bloke must have had friends in high places. We were attacked from all sides. There must have been twenty of them, all tooled up they were.' He glanced back at the four men behind him. They still nodded at the lie, but this time it was with somewhat less conviction. 'So anyway, he got away, and some of the boys ended up buried. But that didn't stop me, boss, oh no. We found him again.'

This time it was the Montserrat's turn to nod, showing he was keeping up with the tale.

Spurred on by such encouragement, Trol continued. 'And we had him again. But this time it was a demon. Like the one in the papers. Spewing gluey death all around. Me and the boys barely made it away with our lives, we did. That's the gospel, just ask the lads.'

Trol turned to face the 'lads' and saw that each was staring wide-eyed. He was going to get little support here but hopefully he wouldn't need it.

'So you see,' he implored, 'my crew's gone and that bastard's still out there. I just need to borrow some crew, until I can get new lads in. Otherwise my manor's going to be vulnerable. And this bloke, this Blaklok bloke, he still needs some payback.'

The Montserrat hadn't moved during Trol's oration. He waited, until he was sure Snapper had finished, then waved his hand lazily towards one of his huge guards.

Before Trol could move, one of them was on him, a huge hand lifting him and slamming him to the ground.

'Who said you could fucking sit?!' he bellowed right in Trol's face, spitting phlegm into his eyes.

Without pausing he grabbed Trol's suit jacket and wrenched him to his feet. Trol could hear the thread of his suit-lining tear as those huge hands pulled him from the ground, but tailoring was now the least of his cares. It appeared the Montserrat *was* pissed off with him after all.

'You know, Trol, I've always thought you were a bit of a cunt,' said the Montserrat. 'But this just proves it. Tell me, do you think I'm fucking stupid?'

'N-no. Of course not.' Trol could barely suppress his panic.

'Do I look like some fucking wino off the street, who doesn't know his arse from his tit?'

'No, boss, no—'

'Then why are you fucking treating me like one?'

Trol didn't have an answer.

'My eyes and ears are everywhere in this cesspit. I know you had trouble with some man named Blaklok. I also know he escaped you – twice – with nothing more than a flat cap wearing midget and some vomit. There were no hordes of ambushers nor any fucking demons. Trust me Snapper, you have no idea who you're dealing with. But luckily for both of us, I do.'

There was a sudden movement from behind, but Trol did not dare take his eyes off the Montserrat. To show such disrespect might mean his balls in a champagne flute – and he didn't have to guess who'd be drinking it down.

'It's time to bring out the big guns. You've made a complete hash of this, Snapper, but I know a few friends who are perfectly suited to resolving such piles of dog shit.'

Someone moved in closer, to stand almost at Trol's shoulder. There was a whirring, ticking sound, like they were carrying a huge grandfather clock. He couldn't resist anymore, he had to look. What he saw made him almost loose his bowels.

'Meet the Hounds, Snapper. I take it you've heard of them.'

Of course he had heard of them, who hadn't?

Standing beside him were the Hounds, the legendary mercenaries of the Cistern. They were rarely called upon to do their grisly work, and when they were, they were never seen. It was only in the direst circumstance that the Hounds were summoned, and it was only now that Trol Snapper realised what a mess he had made of things.

This Blaklok must be big trouble indeed if the Hounds had been called.

There were five of them, each very different in their own way, but they were all obviously of the same ilk. The closest was birdlike in look, his head twitching from side to side, the top half of his head covered in a metal cap with eye holes set in the side. His body was covered in sheaths housing an array of different knives.

To his right was a hulking brute, smaller than the Montserrat's bodyguards but twice as wide, his arms impossibly thick.

Behind him was the source of the ticking and whirring – a clockwork warrior, tall and straight, his head a long, thin funnel.

Next to him, a woman of unbelievable beauty but for the piercings and tattoos that covered every inch of her body.

And finally, smiling insanely – a smile that would never leave his face because he had no lips – was a slashed and haggard figure. Flense; the legendary leader of the Hounds and the man everyone in the Cistern feared, for when you saw him, it meant your doom.

'Say hello to the Hounds, Trol Snapper. And be grateful I don't fucking set them on you.'

Trol was very grateful. So grateful he made a little bit of water in his underpants.

CHAPTER
TWENTY-FIVE

THE RUN TO the Spires had taken a damn sight longer than his flight in an airship. Neither had it been as comfortable – Blaklok looked and felt out of place every step of the way. Despite trying to remain out of sight of prying eyes, he was still spotted by several of the well-to-do dwellers of the Spires district. People like Blaklok – hulking, bruised, menacing people – simply didn't walk their streets and it was inevitable he would draw attention. Luckily he managed to avoid the notice of the Judicature. They must have been far too busy looking for the rampant demon that was on the loose. Well, hopefully if they didn't get in his way, Blaklok would be able to halt the arrival of more demonic intruders... but only if he was quick about it.

He found the tower in question with ease, recognising it from the rendering in Julius's study. It was not the tallest or most resplendent of the vast skyward constructions of the Spires, but it did seem to stand out the most.

Its main body soared upward, like all of its neighbours, a red and black shaft rising up to the heavens. But towards the top it expanded outward, the sides curling round until its summit resembled the head of a vast toad. Large round windows ran around the perimeter, leering down hungrily, and great steel appendages jutted at random angles from the tower's head, like thorny spines set to deflect airborne predators.

Blaklok moved in. He had no plan of attack, no modus operandi for such an occasion. As usual he would develop his strategy on the hoof.

The base of the tower had a single door for entry, and it would undoubtedly be locked. He didn't fancy having to scale the sheer sides of the tower all the way to the top. It may not have been the highest tower in the Spires but, even so, Thaddeus was no bleeding spider.

He took the stairs up to the entrance three at a time, using the momentum of his approach to power his boot as it struck the door. Briefly he wondered if turning the handle might have worked just as well, but it mattered little as the door burst inward, surprising the two red-robed acolytes who were idling inside.

They both had carbines, but didn't seem overly confident in their usage. One of them fumbled his weapon, almost dropping it, and Blaklok decided he could wait. The other acolyte was much less clumsy, but nowhere near quick enough. A firm fist to the jaw and he was down, but the blow gave the second acolyte time to compose himself. He brought the carbine up, and Blaklok could see he was almost about to soil himself. With a lightning fast snatch Blaklok had grasped the carbine from the acolyte's grip before he had a chance to get a round off. The stunned cultist stared for a second, shock and fear rooting him to the spot, before Thaddeus gave him the butt of the carbine around the side of his head.

Easy enough!

As he made his way up the tower stairs he dropped the carbine. Blaklok was in no way averse to using a shooter when necessary, but in dealing with the occult he found it usually did more harm than good. Besides, he had a more effective plan of assault than a few rounds from a carbine.

He took the stairs quickly but carefully, always looking, always listening for that telltale shadow or that errant sound that would herald an attack, but it never came. Lax security would usually put him on edge; make him more wary of his approach, but the time for that was past. This was a situation that required speed above all else. There was no telling how far along this bunch were with their ritual. And one thing was for sure – with Julius at their head, they were already much more dangerous than Valac's mob. That being the case, the conflagration they were planning to inflict on the Manufactory would be much worse than a single president of the Pit.

Higher he went, round the circular staircase and ever upward until his lungs were straining for air, and then he started to hear it – that bloody sound, so familiar yet so alien at the same time. Chanting, but not the fell language of the ancients, this was so very different.

This was the language of the Pit itself.

The air seemed to grow thicker as he climbed higher, and nausea set in. The sound he was hearing was like no human voice, it was as though the sound was too paradoxical for mortal ears to hear. It was a cacophony and a whisper, a raging scream and a lover's scented sigh. The one thing about the chant that lacked contradiction was the wrongness of it. It stank of the forbidden, and Blaklok knew it had to stop.

Eventually the stairs led up to a wide, bare reception floor. Here it was plain why security had been so scant on the way up – there were almost a score of acolytes barring the way to a raised level above. Blaklok might be able to break through this bunch but he would be riddled with bullets by the time he reached the mezzanine, and then he would have no chance of stopping the ritual. Even now he could hear the chanting emanating from atop the raised level.

Blaklok retreated further down the staircase until he came to a huge clerestory window. Gritting his teeth against the inevitable sound he elbowed one of the panes as hard as he could manage. The glass gave, raining shards onto the ground far below. From above there came nothing but the sound of further chanting, and Thaddeus breathed a sigh of relief that he had not alerted anyone to his vandalism.

Strong winds blew in, whipping his face as he took a step out onto a thin ledge. To stop the ritual he would need the element of surprise – and what better surprise than to attack from above in a tower hundreds of feet in the air?

Thaddeus was not particularly scared of heights, but neither was he the kind of bonehead who would intentionally put himself in harm's way. As much as he tried to resist the temptation to look down as he climbed up the side of the building, the yearning to see how high he actually was overcame him. He instantly regretted it as he saw the teeming streets below. A primal fear gripped him, a fear that screamed at him, scolding him for his reckless actions but, as usual, Blaklok fought against his natural urges and stubbornly continued on his way.

It was a relief to find his missing digit was no longer paining him. If he survived this he would have to remember to thank the Apothecary for whatever nostrum he had used on the raw stump.

On he climbed, and several times the winds tried to pull him from the side of the building, but on each occasion Blaklok was defiant. Twice his fingers slipped on the smooth surface of the tower, and he felt the cold sweat of fear cloak him as he teetered on the brink of oblivion, but both times he managed to hang on. And all the while, shielded as he was by the hard stone walls of the tower's summit, he could still hear the fell sound of summonation from within and feel its aberrance seeping through the cracks in the mortar.

With bile rising in his throat, Blaklok finally made it to the tower's summit. A large airship pad stretched out for a hundred yards and Blaklok flopped onto its cold hard surface, panting for breath after the exertion of his climb.

Get up, he told himself, scolding with that bully's voice, the one he used to push his mind and body beyond the boundaries any normal man could endure. *This is no time for resting. This is the time for smashing heads!* And he stood on shaking limbs – limbs starved of oxygen, powered by muscles that were strained to their limit.

He ran to a stairwell that led to the ritual below, reaching into his pockets for the surprise he had in store for the Cult of Legion – a surprise he had been given by the Apothecary. That was something else he would have to give thanks for, if he survived.

He stole to the lip of the stair and peered over. The ritual was in full swing, and there was the high priest, Julius, the lying little shit. He would be the first to die.

Blaklok examined the device he held in his right hand. It was spherical, made of brass or some other alloy, studded for added grip and with a single bolt on the side. Blaklok unscrewed the bolt and pulled. Instantly he heard the hiss of a wick being ignited by flint. It was at this point he realised he should really have asked the Apothecary how long he would have before the wick burned down, but he supposed it was too late now.

With a flick of one powerful arm he sent the incendiary bomb flying down towards the mezzanine, and the chanting high priest. Though Julius now held the Key of Lunos in one hand, Thaddeus reckoned one small, fiery explosion wouldn't do it any harm. If it had survived on the surface of the Moon for untold aeons there was little chance of one piffling incendiary damaging it.

Before the device could go off, Blaklok was already unscrewing the bolt from the second. He looked down. The chanting was still droning on, but Julius had noticed the device as it had bounced noisily off the surface of the mezzanine at his feet. He took a tentative step forward and Blaklok almost laughed at his stupidity, bracing himself for the coming explosion.

There was a sudden flash of red, as something moved across the floor below like a meteor. It wore red robes, and parts of its bulky torso were visible through the cloth; leathery, spiky flesh protruding through the material.

Then the device went off, blowing the thing apart.

Bastard, Blaklok thought, one of the demon-touched acolytes had thrown itself on the incendiary.

Panic ensued as the cultists, no longer chanting their fell invocation, looked all about for the source of the incendiary. Julius had fallen back, shaken but uninjured by the muffled blast, though there was little left of his demonic follower.

Thaddeus didn't wait, flinging his second device down the stairwell, just as he was spotted by a screaming, pointing cultist. The rest barely had time to look up towards what their fellow was gesticulating at before the incendiary went off, showering them with molten fire. As the screams started to peel out, Blaklok was already making his way down the stairs. His priority was the Key. If he could retrieve it now in the confusion and make his escape, this summoning would be over.

The mezzanine was in flames, and several cultists were lying still, their red robes and the flesh within now charred black. Through the smoke, Thaddeus could just make out the prone form of Julius, his high priest's mask now skewed across his face. In two strides he was standing over him, instantly regretting his decision to discard the carbine. Never mind, there would be time aplenty to deal with Julius later.

Blaklok bent down, reaching for the Key at Julius's side, but before he could grasp it something smashed into him. It was like being hit by a steam engine; all the wind was instantly blown from him as he was bowled over the side of the mezzanine.

He fell down to the next level, his shoulder crunching against the granite floor. There was a weight atop him, something heavy and hard. Blaklok opened his eyes, and saw a familiar face staring at him with wicked intent.

Castor Cage's bestial features gazed down, his jaws open, drool dripping forth in expectation of a feeding frenzy.

'Wait!' shouted Julius, with a timely, albeit unexpected intervention. 'It's only fitting he should see this. Do you hear, Thaddeus? Your attempts at sabotage have been in vain.' Julius slowly descended the steps from the mezzanine level. 'It will take more than a thug with toy bombs to halt our becoming. You cannot stop the inevitable. Soon the Legion will walk this plane, and you, Thaddeus Blaklok, will have the honour of witnessing their arrival.'

With that, Blaklok was grasped by strong hands – hands with a strength borne of demonhood.

He gazed at Julius, whose wan features seemed more alive than he had ever seen them. 'Love the sound of your own voice, don't you, Julius?' he said, unable to stop a sly grin creeping across his face.

'Oh, we'll see how funny you find it when the Legion arrives,' Julius replied, his own grin creeping across his lips.

As much as he hated to admit it, Blaklok doubted he would find it even slightly funny.

CHAPTER
TWENTY-SIX

No MORTAL SHOULD have been able to speak the language of the Pit. It was an ancient and forbidden tongue, spewed forth by creatures that needed no vocal chords – not even mouths – to speak it. But here were the Cult of Legion, calling out to their abyssal lord in his own foul argot like they were natives of the Pit themselves.

It could only be the Key of Lunos that allowed them to shout across the planes, it was the only explanation.

As Lord Julius held the Key of Lunos in one tightly clenched fist, it glowed with a hellish light, black smoke effusing from its surface. He had discarded the mask now, and his face was twisted in rapture. Blaklok wanted to do something, anything, but he was held fast by the clawed hands of the two demoniac acolytes that flanked him. He could smell their fetid breath and the stench rising from their infected bodies, and it sickened him. The lengths they had gone to please their foul deity were loathsome in the extreme – they had allowed themselves to become energumen; infected by the evil of the Pit itself.

And less than ten feet away stood Castor Cage, staring at him with unbridled hatred. Had it not been for Julius's orders he knew Cage would have tried to rip him apart piece by bloody piece. Right now, Thaddeus only wanted him to try it.

The language of the Pit rose up as Lord Julius's voice seemed joined by a myriad others. But it was not the voices of his fellow cultists that raised the call to a crescendo. Something else was joining in the dirge… something infinitely more evil. These were Pit-spawned voices, and they came from the depths of Hell itself.

A pall began to fill the tower's summit, a black haze that started to coalesce. It pulled the light from the air, tainting it, twisting it into a corrupt blackness that manifested into a doorway. It was a doorway that Blaklok knew could only lead to one place.

Julius was smiling now.

'They hear the call, Blaklok,' he said, his maddened eyes growing wider as they stared at the black portal. 'They will be here soon. The Legion. It is coming.'

With that he pointed, and immediately Blaklok realised the true horror that was to be unleashed on the Manufactory. Julius was opening the way to the Seventh Gate. It was not to be a single demon that rose from the Pit. The Legion was indeed named well.

Through the gate, Thaddeus could see an army of twisted demonic shapes, running, flying, loping and slithering towards him. It was a frenzied horde, teeth gnashing in their corybantic rampage, each fell voice raised high in an infernal requiem. Blaklok felt the inevitable terror consuming him, but this was no time to succumb to it. Something had to be done.

Suddenly he could smell them, the musky stink of wet dog and rotten eggs filling the room with its overpowering aroma. A cry of pained terror went up from somewhere behind him, and Blaklok at first thought that one of the Cult of Legion had succumbed to the overwhelming aura of the Pit. It wasn't until a mutilated body was flung into the midst of the ritual that he realised the Legion of the Seventh Gate wasn't the only demonic presence that had decided to crash this vile party.

A roar filled the tower, and instantly the focus that had been on the hell gate was diverted to another fiendish presence. On the floor below the mezzanine Blaklok could see a confusing rush of red robes and the spatter of fresh body parts. Julius rushed to the lip of the raised platform and looked down agape.

'He has found us,' he spat, gesturing to two of his demonic cultists. 'Deal with it.'

The twisted creatures bounded forward and disappeared over the lip of the mezzanine, as Thaddeus strained to see what was going on. He was torn between the horror fast approaching through the gate and the battle going on below, which seemed to grow ever more fevered as the seconds passed.

Heralded by a gout of scarlet and torn guts, one half of a demonic cultist flopped onto the platform, still flailing as it desperately tried to stem the flow of its innards as they disgorged onto the marble floor.

Every fibre of Blaklok's being screamed at him to flee, but he was held fast in the powerful arms of two cultists. Even they were beginning to look uncertain, as something approached up the stairwell to the raised area.

Castor Cage rushed forward, fangs bared as he moved on all fours, but before he could reach the edge, a huge demonic visage rose into view.

President Valac had come.

Its face was twisted in fury, its jaws still moist from the cultists on whom it had so recently dined. As Cage moved forward it batted him off with one languid motion of its powerful arm.

'No!' Julius screamed. 'It must not be allowed to interfere!'

But Blaklok had a feeling it was not the Cult of Legion that Valac was here to interfere with. Its tiny baleful eyes swept across the collection of figures that stood on the mezzanine, its nostrils flaring as it picked up a familiar scent.

Then those eyes fell on Blaklok.

A flicker of recognition flashed across Valac's features as its visage turned from hunger to fury to hate in a single heartbeat.

Blaklok was helpless in the iron hold of the demonic cultists but he could feel their grip loosening as they saw the demon prince approaching.

Valac stormed forth onto the mezzanine, and all the while Julius bawled at his men to stop the creature as it approached. Castor Cage was the first to respond, bounding to his feet and leaping forward. The cultist holding Blaklok's right arm was quick to follow, releasing Thaddeus and leaping the ten feet to fight off the demon. To Blaklok's left, the other demonic figure stepped back and, with a theatrical sweep, two great wings suddenly unfurled from beneath the tattered robes at its back. Thaddeus felt a billowing of air as the cultist took to the wing and joined its fellows in the fray.

With snarling fury the demons set about one another, and Blaklok turned his attention back to the portal. The Legion was almost upon the gate, sweeping forward like an evil tide ready to submerge the mortal plane.

Blaklok leapt forward, hands stretched out and eager to wrest the Key of Lunos from the grip of Lord Julius. The high priest saw his intent but there was nowhere for him to go, and before Julius could utter a word Blaklok was on him. Julius fought with a surprising desperation as Blaklok gripped him – even a punch to the face did not persuade him to release the Key. As they grappled on the ground the demons at their side roared, the three smaller figures rending great swathes of flesh from the back of Valac. All the while, the President of Hell crawled ever closer to Blaklok, ignoring its assailants in favour of reaching him.

Grasping Julius by both arms, Blaklok bore down with the full weight of his body, smashing his forehead into the Lord's face. Immediately he went limp, releasing the Key of Lunos into Blaklok's waiting grasp.

Thaddeus stood, feeling the power of the Key and its inextricable link to the arcane portal that was even now in danger of being overwhelmed by the torrent of fiends that were bearing down on it.

He held the Key in both hands, allowing its secrets to fill him with their knowledge, allowing the link between Key and portal to reveal itself. He could suddenly see the intricate threads of arcane power that the Key held and with a single thought Thaddeus severed the connection as if he were shredding a single leaf of parchment. Before the first of the demons could reach the burgeoning portal, it began to fade, enervating back into a wispy cloud that no demon would ever cross.

There was a howl of fury, as though the hordes of Hell were screaming out in their entirety. Then, with a wink of dusty light, the portal was gone.

Heralded by a vile stench, a torrent of hellfire engulfed one of the twisted cultists. Valac had summoned forth another gout of its molten bile and its victim was even now bubbling and melting across the mezzanine, its surface liquefying beneath the unnatural ooze. The winged cultist retreated, desperately beating its wings to move out of range of the demon prince, and leaving a clear path straight to Blaklok.

As Valac took its chance and bounded towards him, Blaklok leapt, gripping the ancient Key between his teeth. Before the winged cultist could manoeuvre out of the way Blaklok had gripped the twisted being by the shoulders. The cultist thrashed in midair, gnashing its teeth and flailing its arms in a vain attempt to dislodge Blaklok, but he held fast to its back. Gripping one of the leathery wings at its shoulder Blaklok wrenched backwards, intending to guide the cultist's flight. Unfortunately his grasp of aerodynamics was rudimentary at best, and with a squeal the cultist was sent spinning straight through one of the tower's high windows.

In a shower of shattering glass, Blaklok and the winged cultist were flying into empty air. Again, Thaddeus could see hundreds of feet down to the stone-hard ground below and, despite the powerful leathery wings of the cultist, he was plummeting towards it. The creature beat its wings but they were not strong enough to power its body with Blaklok's additional weight.

Thaddeus gripped the Key in his teeth, holding onto the cultist for dear life as they fell, the sides of the toad-like tower shooting past them at a rate of knots. He could hear the cultist screaming, desperately beating its wings. Every now and again they would hit an updraft, halting their descent for a split second, but they were being inextricably pulled to the ground below.

With a sickening thud Blaklok hit the street.

He opened his eyes, tasting fresh blood, and realised he no longer gripped the Key in his mouth. He spat a tooth and slowly opened his eyes. Beneath him was the winged cultist, his body smashed and broken, having cushioned Thaddeus against the impact.

Blaklok staggered to his feet, scanning the ground for the Key of Lunos. Blood dripped from his mouth and it was likely he would need some extensive dental work, but at least he was alive.

He spied the Key, seemingly undamaged after the fall, and he took a tentative step towards it.

Suddenly the ground erupted as something heavy smashed into the earth, throwing Blaklok off his feet.

President Valac slowly stood, having flung himself from the tower hundreds of feet above. It appeared impervious to the fall, having created a crater in the ground where it landed.

Blaklok glared up at the infernal creature. It was relentless in its pursuit of him, and he realised that whatever he had done to offend the beast was about to be paid back in spades.

He struggled to his feet once more as Valac lurched forward, clawed hands flexing, razor claws extended to rend his flesh. Thaddeus barely had time to dodge aside as a great inhuman arm swept past where he had stood a second before.

Above all else, he had to get the Key – he could worry about escaping later, but as the thought passed through his mind he was struck a blow to the ribs and thrown to the ground. Though he had avoided being eviscerated by Valac's talons, his left side was numb from the pain.

He looked up from where he lay foundering on the ground. Valac was standing above him, leering down in victory, and as much as Blaklok wanted to stand and spit in the demon's face he couldn't. He was beaten, about to become so much torn and discarded flesh, and there was not a thing he could do about it.

CHAPTER
TWENTY-SEVEN

VALAC'S LEERING FACE bore down on him, and Blaklok could see deep into those eyes – eyes that reflected the depths of Hell itself. Razor teeth gaped open revealing a gore strewn throat coated in bile and the ichor of its recent victims. One of which Blaklok was about to become.

'Howdo!'

The statement was innocuous, spoken in a conversational manner, but it was bold enough to momentarily divert the attention of the President of Hell.

Valac paused, glancing around, looking for the source of the interruption, its brow suddenly furrowed in anger.

Blaklok was as confused as the demon, but grateful for his reprieve.

'I was just passing,' the voice continued, 'when I found this. Wondered if it belonged to anyone.'

Then Blaklok saw him, standing bold as brass in his grey raincoat and flat cap.

The diminutive figure was standing off to one side, holding up the Key in one tiny hand. As Valac saw him he reared, puffing himself up to full height in readiness to pounce on the troublesome figure – ready to rend Quickstep asunder for his audacity. As much as he wanted to berate Quickstep for his folly, Blaklok couldn't help but take advantage of the diversion, scrambling painfully to his feet and moving beyond the huge demon's reach.

'You are a big 'un aren't you?' Quickstep said, smiling from beneath the shadow of his cap. Valac paused, momentarily confused. Plainly the creature was used to those humans it encountered running and screaming in terror. Being engaged in conversation was doubtless a novel experience for it.

It leaned closer, fascinated by the curious figure, and Quickstep merely stared back, not a single notion of fear on his face. 'What's up? Lost your mummy, have you?' Valac tilted its head curiously. 'Well, we'll have to see what we can do about getting you back home again.'

At this, Valac raised its lip in a vile sneer. Its comprehension of Quickstep's suggestion was obvious and it clenched those wicked talons into fists.

'Quickstep!' Blaklok cried. 'What are you doing? Run!'

But Quickstep ignored him, still staring into those black eyes.

Then the demon roared.

Hissing spittle flew from its maw, splashing against Quickstep's coat and melting the dull material, but still the little man looked on, smiling happily. 'Ooh, I think maybe you're a bit tired. Not to worry.' Suddenly the Key of Lunos began to glow in his grip, wispy light peeling from its surface.

Valac roared again, heaving in a lungful of air, and Blaklok realised it was preparing to disgorge another eructation of hellfire.

But Quickstep was faster. Blaklok could see the little man's lips moving in silent incantation, and all the while the Key of Lunos glowed more intensely.

There was a rush, like a wind gushing down a narrow tunnel, and Blaklok thought that this was the last he would see of Quickstep before he was consumed by molten vomit.

But with a blinding flash of light all went quiet, and Quickstep was left standing alone.

Blaklok glanced around, unable to believe that Valac had gone, but the President of Hell was nowhere in sight.

Quickstep merely continued to smile from beneath the brim of his flat cap, the Key of Lunos held in one hand, looking no more important than an ordinary antique key.

'It's becoming a habit; saving your arse,' said Quickstep. 'Anyone would think you couldn't look after yourself.'

'Very funny,' Blaklok replied. 'Maybe you can give yourself a king size pat on the back when we've put some distance between us and the tower full of raving cultists.'

'Good idea.' Quickstep said, turning to leave, but Thaddeus placed a hand on his arm.

'That belongs to me,' he said, motioning to the Key of Lunos.

Quickstep glanced down at it, and there was a sudden spark of defiance across his face, but before he could argue, Blaklok snatched the object from his hand, and led them off through the Spires district.

They both tramped through the back streets as best they could, but it wasn't long before Blaklok found himself in unfamiliar territory. It had never been a district Thaddeus had much call to visit, and the unfamiliar streets were like a labyrinth. Without a word, Quickstep took the lead, guiding them down alleys and along walkways that Blaklok would not have even noticed. Eventually the streets became shabbier, and the characters that walked them less opulently dressed.

It was obvious they had left the austerity of the Spires well behind them.

Quickstep suddenly stopped as they entered a quiet plaza, elevated some feet above the bustling streets below. It was grimy and covered in filth that settled in piles at the plaza's edge.

'We need to talk,' said the little man, his cheery expression taking on a serious tone.

'Damn right we do,' Blaklok replied. 'For a start, how did you find me... no, for a start, how did you manage to get away from the Cult of Legion the last time we met? It's about time you started giving me ans–'

He stopped as Quickstep held up a hand to silence him. There was something weird about the little fellow; something that made Blaklok suddenly compliant. It surprised him somewhat, and he began to get an uneasy feeling that Quickstep was not all he appeared – as if rescuing him from a mob of criminals, surviving an attack by demonic cultists and banishing a President of Hell back to the Pit had not been clue enough that there was something odd about the man.

'No,' said Quickstep. 'We need to talk about that.' He motioned to the Key of Lunos in Blaklok's pocket.

'All right, let's talk about it.' Blaklok tensed, his hand reaching into his pocket and pulling it out. He grasped it firmly in one meaty fist, as though his life depended on it. There was something about Quickstep's interest in the Key he didn't like. There were too many people willing to go to great lengths for this thing, and if Quickstep was one of them, Blaklok would have to take him on. After seeing the little fellow in action, it would be foolish to underestimate him now.

'I've already told you the Fane of Zaphiel wants it, to keep it safe from prying hands. Well, now you know exactly which hands, and the lengths they're willing to go to. You've also seen the near misses we've had. It should be plain what you have to do.'

'By that you mean hand it over? How do I know you're any more responsible than the demon mentalists we've just escaped from?'

'Well,' Quickstep grinned, 'there's a lot to be said for trust, but I'm guessing you're all out of that.'

'Good fucking guess.'

'So let's just say we have plans – plans for the greater good – that the Key of Lunos is an integral part of.'

'Look,' Thaddeus began to back away. As much as Quickstep didn't look threatening at the moment he wasn't about to take any chances. 'I'd love to help you out, but this thing's already spoken for. I've got a job to do, and that's that.' He backed further away, ready to turn and run as fast as he could.

'Wait,' said Quickstep, concern suddenly crossing his features. 'Behind you!'

Blaklok laughed. 'Mate, that's the oldest one in the–'

Something hit him hard from behind, throwing him to the ground and knocking the Key from his grip.

There was a roar of triumph and, before he could start to rise, something grabbed him, grasping with vast meaty hands and lofting him high. Blaklok had time to glimpse a forearm as thick as a chimneystack before he was flung like a rag doll against the wall.

This time he was ready, and as he bounced off the wall to land on the ground, he managed to find his feet before his assailant could make another attack.

The brute was huge, wider than Blaklok was tall, with a face squashed and simian, heavy brows protruding over deep set eyes, and tiny pupils that stared out in rage. Its body was covered in curly black hair and it powered itself forward on short, thick legs.

Just before it reached him, Thaddeus braced a foot against the wall and pushed off, using the brute's head as a stepping stone to leap out of the way. He heard a thud as the gorilla man smashed into the wall, sending shards of brick and mortar flying.

Blaklok hit the ground running, his eyes desperately scanning the ground to try and locate the Key he had dropped, but he saw Quickstep was way ahead of him, already reaching out to grasp it. Before the diminutive man could grasp the object, more figures swept into view. Blaklok barely had time to duck as something cut the air inches from his face. It was heralded by an ear piercing shriek, like that of a wild hunting hawk, and as he saw the approaching figure he found the sound suited his attacker perfectly. The man – if he was a man – resembled a lithe bird. The helmet he wore was designed to resemble some kind of hawk head, and his body was adorned in short blades that resembled feathers. Already his swift hands, faster than

Blaklok's eyes could follow, were pulling more blades from the sheaths that covered his body and letting fly.

Thaddeus dived to the side, hearing the harsh clang as the metal blades struck the sidewalk beside him. He rolled and stood, finding himself beside Quickstep, with the Key of Lunos at both their feet. They glanced at one another, a second's repose, before they both leapt for it.

There was a harsh crack, and before either of them could lay a hand on the Key it was gone, whipped away by the end of a black leather lash.

Looking up, Blaklok saw the Key was now held in the grasp of an exotic looking woman. She was almost beautiful, but Blaklok thought her looks spoiled by a face covered in piercings, like a siren from some masochist's twisted erotic dream. Where her flesh wasn't covered by black leather and metal, it was tattooed with multicoloured sigils. She dangled the Key seductively in one hand, whilst casually holding a long, barbed whip in the other.

The hugely muscled brute and the bird-man were now standing impassively, watching the proceedings as Blaklok tried to plan his next move. He was about to speak to Quickstep, about to ask for some sort of advice, when he heard the sound of heavy clanging footfalls. From around a corner came another strange sight that made Blaklok think this bunch must have just escaped from the nearest circus freakshow.

A seven-foot sentinel of copper cogs and iron shanks was striding down the street towards them. Its arms seemed too long for its body, and were tipped with huge, thick, steel appendages that grasped and whirred as it walked on wide leaden feet.

'You're impressed, I can tell.' The voice was smooth and crooning, and as Thaddeus turned towards it he almost gasped at what he saw. Another circus freak stood waiting at one end of the plaza, and this one was the most hideous of all.

He was a man, but barely. Sinew and muscle was displayed moist and raw all over his body, and his face was a mess of scars and exposed tissue. He had no lips and his teeth shone in a perpetual grin.

'Let me guess,' said Blaklok, determined not to balk in the face of these hideous monsters. 'You're here for the Key as well?'

The flayed man laughed.

'No, Thaddeus Blaklok,' he replied. 'We're here for you!'

CHAPTER
TWENTY-EIGHT

'WE ARE THE Hounds,' said the skinless freak. 'Perhaps you've heard of us?'

'Sorry mate,' Blaklok replied, glancing around warily, trying to make sure none of them tried to take him unawares. 'I haven't been to the circus for ages.'

It was impossible to read any emotion on the flayed face, but Blaklok was pretty sure his comment didn't go down well.

That made him feel quite warm inside.

'Before we end your days, please allow me to introduce myself. I am Flense. Though not the leader of this picturesque party, I am what you might call the figurehead.'

Flense's lack of lips didn't seem to affect his speech and Blaklok was amazed by how he managed to pronounce hard consonants without them.

'The beautiful lady to your left is affectionately known as the Punctress. You'll be having a lot of fun with her, I assure you. My metallic friend here,' Flense gestured to the towering clockwork man at his side, 'is the Timekeeper, quite a modern marvel if I do say so. You've already met Gorbo there, he does so like to play with his food.' Blaklok glanced back at the hulking ball of muscle that had nearly crushed him, to see him grinning a wide, bovine smile. 'And Shriek here is–'

'All right, all right, cut the crap.' Blaklok had had more than enough of the introductions. 'I don't need to know who you are before I kick the shit out of you. If you want some, come on then.'

'Ooh, you are a coarse one!' The expression on Flense's face was probably the closest it could ever come to looking offended. 'Don't you even want to know why you're about to die? Are you not at all curious as to who has authorised your death warrant?'

'Go on then, if it makes you feel better,' replied Blaklok, his patience running thin.

'You have provoked the ire of the Lord of the Underworld himself. The Montserrat, master of the Cistern and commander of the Chambers, has sanctioned your demise, Thaddeus Blaklok. Now, I would be happy to listen to any pleas for mercy you might have.'

Blaklok glanced at Quickstep, who gave an almost imperceptible shrug. Before Flense could bore him any further he leapt at the Punctress, who still held the Key of Lunos in one tattooed hand. Blaklok had to hand it to her, she was fast. At his sudden approach, she took a step back, flailing the whip behind her in readiness to strike. The thick studded leather swept through the air, cutting towards Blaklok with lethal velocity, but he managed to raise an arm as it swept towards him. He could feel it sting his flesh as it wrapped around his forearm, but it wasn't the worst pain he had felt in recent days. As the whip curled around his arm he grasped it, pulling tight and forcing the Punctress closer. His other arm was raised in a fist that smashed into her suddenly surprised face.

Blood and nose rings sprayed across the plaza. The Punctress went down easily, losing her grip on her whip and the Key of Lunos. He could hear the sound of the other Hounds charging in as he reached for the Key, but all that mattered was that he retrieved the artefact – he could worry about the pain and bruises later.

Blaklok grasped the Key and tensed his body in preparation for the coming blow. It was Gorbo, the hulking brute, who was first to reach him. The ape-like figure shoulder barged him, and Blaklok was thrown through the air. The wind was almost punched out of him as he soared across the plaza, right into the path of the clockwork figure of the Timekeeper. One solid metal arm swept down as Blaklok landed, threatening to transfix him where he lay, but he managed to roll just in time as the steel appendage smashed into the ground, shattering the paving stone beneath.

As Blaklok got to his feet he saw that Quickstep was still present, and had not taken the opportunity to flee.

He must have wanted the Key more than Blaklok realised.

Even now he was bravely facing up to a torrent of throwing blades as Shriek the birdman unleashed a razor sharp deluge towards him. Strangely, most of the blades fell wide of their mark, and the ones that hit simply bounced harmlessly off Quickstep's drab overcoat. But Blaklok had little time to wonder what strange powers were at work before the Timekeeper swept in with another mighty swing of its arm.

Gears cranked and cogs whirred as the metal automaton attacked, puffing steam from vents on its back and moving like some gigantic engine, bent on smashing Blaklok to pieces.

It raised its arm high, expelling a gout of steam from a pipe at its neck as though blowing out a gaseous breath of air. Blaklok waited, picking his moment, hoping his next move would pay off. As he heard Gorbo galloping towards him once more he moved, dashing aside as the Timekeeper's arm swept down towards where, a second before, he had been standing. But Blaklok was not there, instead, the thick-necked form of Gorbo had rushed in, intent on smashing into his foe. The Timekeeper's arm crashed into Gorbo's head, just as the apeman smashed into the Timekeeper's metal chassis, and both of them plunged over the edge of the plaza to the ground below.

Blaklok could hear the sickening thud of Gorbo and the clanging crash of the Timekeeper as they hit the ground, but he had no time to gloat.

'You're a wily one, Thaddeus Blaklok.' Flense was standing right beside him, two wicked looking blades in his hands, their edges a forest of serrated teeth. 'But let's put an end to it. No more running, no more fighting. Today is the da—'

'Are you going to fucking cut me or talk me to death?' said Blaklok, taking a step towards the flayed man and offering him an easy target.

'Oh, please. Show some dignity in the face of oblivion, Thaddeus. There's no need for profanities.'

'Cunt,' Blaklok replied, and spat a gob of phlegm through pursed lips.

'Very well,' replied Flense, sweeping his blades in swift, almost invisible arcs. 'Have it your way.'

There was a screech, ear piercing enough to make Blaklok wince, and before Flense could stripe him with those wicked blades, something flew through the air and smashed into the flayed freak. Both figures went down in a heap and Blaklok could see it was Shriek who lay on top of Flense in a tangle of arms and legs.

Blaklok looked to the side and saw Quickstep grinning from beneath the shadow of his flat cap.

'Now,' he said, the grin suddenly evaporating. 'The Key, if you please.'

Thaddeus held up the Key. 'Sorry mate. If you want it, you'll have to take it.'

Quickstep gave a resigned nod of his head. 'That's what I thought.' He took a step towards Blaklok.

A strange feeling overcame Thaddeus as the diminutive figure of Quickstep moved closer. It was obvious there was something unnatural about the man – the way he managed to resist any and all attempts to kill him was one – but now there was an aura about him, one that Blaklok felt was familiar. He didn't glow or give off a strange sound or smell, it was something deeper than that, something more primal. Blaklok had felt it before, but for the life of him he couldn't place the exact time or place, or even the individuals in question. It all added up to Quickstep being something altogether more frightening than even President Valac or the horde of rampaging demons the Cult of Legion was determined to inflict on the Manufactory.

Searing pain enveloped Blaklok's hand and he found the Key of Lunos suddenly spinning from his grip. At first he thought it was something Quickstep had done – some foul magick he had conjured – but instantly he realised it was something much more mundane. As the Key went spinning away, Blaklok saw his hand was held fast by the end of a whip, the other end held in the grip of the Punctress. She snatched the spinning Key from the air and leered at him, her nose and mouth fat and bleeding.

'You must enjoy pain,' Blaklok said as he resisted her insistent tugging and pulled her towards his clenched fist.

'You have no idea,' she replied, licking the blood from the side of her mouth.

Blaklok threw his punch but this time it was the Punctress who was the faster, kicking out with one pointed, thigh high boot and catching Blaklok in the jewels.

He grunted, dropping to his knees, and felt the unique pain that only a kick in the balls can inflict.

'This is where the fun really starts,' said the Punctress, placing the Key of Lunos between her lips lasciviously and pulling out a flat baton with a studded head from her belt. For all the world it looked like some kind of twisted love toy, but Blaklok had a feeling it was far more suited to inflicting pain than pleasure.

Behind him he could hear groaning as Flense and Shriek began to stir, rising to their unsteady feet. There was an ominous clank of metal legs as the Timekeeper made his way up to the plaza.

Quickstep didn't seem ready to help him this time – the little fucker was trying to make himself as indiscreet as possible, pacing towards the rim of the plaza ready to make his escape.

It was time for Blaklok to make his escape too; the Key would have to wait. As much as it pained him to leave it in the care of these circus freaks, there was no way he could take them all on alone.

Blocking out the dull pain that went from his balls all the way to his throat, Thaddeus lurched towards the edge of the plaza, desperate to dive beyond it and run to safety. The Punctress pulled hard, trying to stop him, but Thaddeus was not about to let some masochistic bitch get in his way. He dragged her with him, her heels scraping along the concrete as he strode towards the edge. The whip untangled from his grip and the Punctress went sprawling, just as a shining metal blade flew past Blaklok's head.

'That's it, Thaddeus,' said Flense, rising to his feet. 'Run! They always do.'

Another blade flew at him but this one hit its mark, piercing the thick muscle of Blaklok's shoulder. Shriek and Flense moved like lightning, closing the gap between them and Thaddeus but before they could stop him, he flung himself over the plaza's edge, without checking to see just how high they were.

It was a short plunge, but high enough to do serious damage if he didn't land right. Luckily there was a large and bulky form laying prone on the ground ready to cushion his landing. Gorbo was just rising to all fours, shaking his head from his own fall, when Blaklok landed on top of him, flattening him back to the tarmac beneath. The bulky ape squealed as the air was punched out of his lungs, and Blaklok bounced off him and hit the ground.

He didn't wait to survey the damage, or for anyone else to land by his side and try to cut his head off. He just ran for his life.

Blaklok let the streets take him, racing through them like a madman suddenly freed from the asylum. People stopped and stared as he raced past, but they were faceless to him, inconsequential. He didn't know how long he ran for but it was long enough for his lungs to feel like they were two sandbags in his chest and his legs wooden blocks.

He didn't know where he was or how long he had been running, but eventually he had to stop. He leaned a hand against a grimy wall and bent over, sucking air into shrivelled-feeling lungs.

The ground at Blaklok's feet suddenly erupted in splinters, the telltale report of carbine fire exploding all around. Shards of brickwork were blown away beside him and he crouched down, raising his hands defensively. Figures surrounded him, weapons levelled, faces masked by the grim helms of the Judicature.

'Hello again, Mr Blaklok. You do remember me, don't you? I'd be ever so upset if you'd forgotten me already.'

He did fucking remember her – more's the pity.

Blaklok turned and there she was, the stern features on that youthful face softening as she smiled in triumph.

'It's Indagator Amelia, in case you'd forgotten,' she said. 'Shall we?' She motioned for him to follow.

Blaklok glanced around at the firepower arrayed against him, a score of guns all aimed right at his head.

'I guess we shall,' he said.

CHAPTER
TWENTY-NINE

ANOTHER DAY, ANOTHER interrogation cell. Thaddeus was beginning to feel quite at home here in the restraining pens of the Judicature.

Standing over him was Indagator Amelia. He had never quite appreciated how pretty she was – how innocent her features seemed, at least for a representative of the corrupt, totalitarian regime that watched over the rich of the city at the sufferance of the poor.

Her face was untarnished, not a blemish on that porcelain skin, and she seemed to have quite a regal bearing. From the look of her she had most likely attained her position through familial connections rather than hard footwork. Then again, Blaklok thought that a face like that and a well-to-do family might do more to hold someone back within the masculine precincts of the Judicature. Maybe she did deserve her position after all, maybe she had been compelled to put in twice the work for half the reward, merely due to her sex and her pretty face and daddy's money.

Most likely that meant she had something to prove.

It would certainly explain the stick up her arse.

Then again, Blaklok could only admire her for her tenacity. There weren't many who could claim to have got one over on Thaddeus Blaklok. Well, all right then, two over, but she had help both times, so it probably only counted as once.

There was only one goon with her now – the one with the carbine. She must have done some proper damage to the other one when she shot him.

Ruthless streak.

Blaklok was really starting to warm to this Amelia. Then again, that would most likely change when the actual interrogating began, but until then he would enjoy the silence.

'A colleague of mine said I should just follow the carnage,' she said.

This caught Blaklok off-guard, and he frowned, momentarily confused.

'To find you, that is. Of course my colleague's an imbecile, and on any other day I would disregard his advice. But on this occasion he happened to be correct, Mr Blaklok. Follow the sightings of demons, the reports of strange characters brawling in the streets, and there you are, waiting for me. I must say it was accommodating of you to run into us like that. Hodge and I found it most amusing, didn't we Hodge?'

She glanced towards her tipstaff, who gave a humourless nod in return.

Thaddeus turned to him, staring into those cold shark's eyes. 'Was it as amusing as when she shot your mate?' he asked, with a wink.

The tipstaff called Hodge stiffened slightly, his eyes narrowing with hatred. It was obvious he wanted to inflict some pain for that comment, but he wouldn't without Amelia's say so. That was good – discipline was always to be admired. And for one as young as this Amelia to have the respect and obedience of one so mindless and brutal was rare.

'What isn't amusing, Mr Blaklok,' cut in Amelia, 'is the devastation you leave behind wherever you go. Earl Beuphalus is a bloody corpse. The Repository of Unnatural History will never be the same again, so I'm told. Demonic manifestations and the theft of important arcane artefacts follow you like flies after a gangrenous dog. What is it about you that seems to attract so much wanton chaos?'

'Guess I'm just lucky.'

'Lucky? Indeed. As lucky as the family you butchered?'

Blaklok was silent.

'What? No smart answer for that one? Brings back memories, does it? Are they particularly pleasant, or is there a pang of remorse within that impregnable frame?'

'You don't know what you're talking about,' Blaklok replied.

It appeared that playtime was well and truly over.

'Do I not? Am I mistaken about the woman and her children? About the pursuit by the authorities in which you killed a number of judicial representatives? Come now, Mr Blaklok, mistaken? Then perhaps you'd care to enlighten me.'

He considered telling her where to go, or even taking a look into *her* psyche – ask about her parents, *her* past. Why such a prim and proper little madam would work for the Judicature. What was there in her history that made her want to prove herself in such an environment, when the obvious level of her education demonstrated a wealthy background and privilege that would mean she didn't have to work?

Instead, he decided to keep quiet.

'Well, there's not much I can do about that now,' she continued. 'It's a cold case, everyone involved is now dead and there's little evidence against you. However, what I do have is enough to see you swing. Theft, criminal damage, assault, evading apprehension, consorting with malodorous individuals, affray in a public place. By the way, was that the Hounds you were in a fracas with? Must say you do have brass ones, Mr Blaklok. They're never seen in the open, I only know who they are from their descriptions. Someone must want you very dead.'

'You know who they are? The Hounds?' Blaklok asked, suddenly interested by her endless diatribe.

'Of course I do. In the Judicature we know everything.'

'Well, just goes to show you shouldn't believe everything people tell you. The one with the bad complexion said they were never seen. Like shadows, he said. So you're telling me you could find them if you wanted?'

'What are you getting at?' Amelia leaned forward, her brow furrowing. It was obvious she suspected something and was determined not to be duped. Blaklok considered the best way to earn her trust was to be honest. It was a virtue he seldom resorted to, but the current situation pretty much made it unavoidable.

'If you want to see the Key of Lunos again, we'll need to find them,' he told her. Her eyes suddenly widened. 'That excite you, does it?'

Instantly she changed her expression, adopting a poker face. 'What do you mean *we*? You're not going anywhere. If the Key of Lunos is indeed in the keeping of the Hounds then I'll be the one to retrieve it.'

'So you know all about the Key's safeguards? You know how to make it pliant? You know how to stop it opening doors to places you'd never want to go in a million years? How do you think we ended up with a demon of the Eighth Tier on the loose? How do you think it was eventually banished? Could you have done that? No, didn't think so. Well I can, and if we don't find the Key soon it'll probably be too late. Some other fucker's going to open another door to the Pit and this time it might not just be one demon arsehole on the loose – it'll be an entire army!'

All right, so maybe he was embellishing the truth a bit there, but it never hurt to ice the cake when you wanted it sweeter. So what if he hadn't been the one to banish Valac? This Amelia wasn't going to know that.

'You're barking up the wrong tree here, Mr Blaklok. I don't give much credit to stories of demons and all that hocus pocus.'

Thaddeus heard her words, but he could tell she was as much trying to convince herself as him.

'You must be blind then,' he said. 'Got a rational explanation for everything, have you? Ten foot demons just a figment of mass hysteria? Have you been to the Repository of Unnatural History recently? Taken a look around? Half the exhibits are derived from malignant manifestations of the occult. No one believes in *nothing* anymore. Even the Sancrarium accepts that the Pit is fucking real. Open your eyes, love. There's an apocalypse waiting to consume the Manufactory and you can stop it. But you'll need me to do it.'

She stared at him and he could see her starting to cave. Her expression wasn't quite so stone-hard and her shoulders were starting to slump. Deep down she knew he was right, but she still didn't trust him.

'What guarantees do I have?' she asked.

'You don't have any,' he replied. Now it was becoming all too clear. She was a control freak, needed to be in charge every step of the way and anything less simply would not do. 'But I'll tell you what. You and Slow'n'Dim here can have loaded carbines at my head every step of the way. If I make a wrong move or if it looks like I've bullshitted any of this, feel free to blow my fucking head off.'

A smile crept slowly up one side of her mouth.

'Oh, don't worry, Mr Blaklok. That's already a given.'

HE SAT ALONE in one of the less salubrious drinking dens of the Cistern – and that was saying something. His suit was dishevelled, and it almost made Blaklok smile to see him fallen so far.

'Hello, Snapper,' Amelia said.

Trol Snapper's buck-toothed face was crestfallen as he looked up to regard her. 'You can do all you want to me,' he said, looking extremely sorry for himself. 'I'm ruined anyway.'

'We might just do that,' she replied. Blaklok could barely hear her from his place in the shadows, but he knew he would be most effective if he made a proper entrance. 'But I'm hoping you'll cooperate. We want some information, that's all. We don't want to hurt you or your men. Not that there appears to be any of them left to hurt.'

'I don't have a crew,' said Snapper, woefully. 'I'm a laughing stock. I can't even afford the good stuff anymore,' he said brandishing a shot glass full of thick liquor in one limp hand. 'Look what I've been reduced to.'

'You can still be useful, Trol. The Hounds were unleashed earlier today. They made a mess on the streets above. It's not often they do that.'

'It's that fucking Blaklok you're after,' said Snapper suddenly, a venom returning to his eyes. 'He's the cause of it all.'

'I know that,' said Amelia. 'But the Hounds have something important, something they took from Blaklok.'

'Ah, you mean the Key.' It seemed to have suddenly dawned on Snapper what Amelia was after and he nodded knowingly. 'Yes, well, it's gone now. Doubtful you'll see that thing again.'

'And why's that?'

'Oh, you're clever,' said Snapper, smiling. 'Draw me in, get me to talk. You'll get nothing else out of me, I'm not fucking stupid.'

It was a grim, insouciant smile. One that said Snapper didn't care anymore. One that said *you can do what you want to me, but the consequences of me telling you would be a thousand times worse.*

It was time for Blaklok to play his hand.

'Where's the Key, tusk-teeth? And don't fuck me about.' Blaklok stepped from the shadows, staring his mad stare.

At first Snapper looked like he was about to shit himself, but he quickly regained his composure.

'You don't scare me,' he said. 'Not anymore. What are you going to do to me? Eh? You can't hurt me anymore than you already have. I know what you can do, I've seen it. You hold no mysteries, Thaddeus Blaklok.'

By now, the drinking hole's other patrons had melted away into the shadows – even the barman had left on some hidden errand. It was time for Blaklok to resort to something other than standard methods of intimidation.

'The Hounds have it, you little fucker.' He moved closer, tensing his muscles and invoking the tiny tattooed sigil at the base of his spine. It burst into life, burning Blaklok's skin like a brand. 'Tell me where they are.'

The air went crisp as though a fire had just been put out. The burning sensation at the base of Blaklok's back began to move, running up his spine and into the back of his neck. It was intense, and Blaklok began to use the pain, focusing it on Snapper. Consequently, Trol began to waver, his bottom lip quivering as he stared into those eyes, now ringed with eerie black shadows.

'They don't have it anymore,' Snapper whimpered.

'Who fucking does?' demanded Blaklok, now focusing all the brand's hate and fury at his victim.

Snapper sobbed. 'They delivered it to the Montserrat. But it's no use. You'll never get close to him.' Trol suddenly slipped off his stool and fell to the floor in a heap, trying his best to stifle a whimper.

'I'm sure we'll manage with you there to make the introductions,' said Blaklok, the menace in his voice more than palpable.

Snapper nodded, not daring to look up.

'Well, that was easy enough,' said Blaklok, looking to Amelia and her tipstaff bodyguard. The arcane fury he had manifested was now dissipating like a snuffed candle, but he was still an imposing sight to behold. He wasn't surprised to see they had retreated to the far end of the bar. 'What's wrong, cat got your tongue?'

Neither of them answered.

CHAPTER
THIRTY

BY THE TIME Trol Snapper had led Blaklok, Amelia and her tipstaff into the bowels of the Cistern, the man was a quivering wreck.

'It's just up ahead,' he whimpered. 'Beyond that door.' Trol gestured down the tunnel and Blaklok could see a massive metal portal, guarded by two thick-necked brutes. 'They won't let you in, I tried to warn you.'

'We'll see about that,' said Amelia, striding forward and putting on her best authoritative air. Blaklok had to hand it to her, it was quite effective. He remained at her shoulder though, just in case.

'We're here on official business,' she said, walking proudly. 'I demand this door be opened immediately.'

She was forced to stop in front of the two broad sentinels who refused to move at her behest. They merely stared, eyes dull with their lack of comprehension. It was obvious they were unsure how to handle the situation.

Blaklok decided he'd best give them a hint.

They were big, bigger than Blaklok at any rate, and he had to put them down quick before they could defend themselves. Fastest way to do that was to smash a bloke in the neck as hard as you could. There was lots of theory behind it, Thaddeus had learned it a million years before, when he'd been taught all the complicated jargon and shown the precise techniques. But what it basically meant was he could knock the guy out with a single blow no matter how big he was.

Blaklok had to leap to get the right angle, swiping his forearm down on the first guard's trapezius. He connected against the rock-hard muscle of a neck as thick as most men's waists, but instantly the guard went down.

It was doubtful he even knew what hit him.

The second guard was more problematic; he was moving now, hand reaching for a weapon, body tensed and ready. This one would be much more difficult to drop.

Amelia moved in the periphery of Blaklok's vision, out of his focus like a spectre in a haunted house. There was a baton in her hand, something tiny and metallic, much smaller than the banded club her tipstaff carried. She hit the guard five times before Blaklok realised what she was doing. At first, the hulking sentinel didn't move. Then slowly, like a toppling tree, he fell onto the prone form of his fellow sentry.

'Mr Blaklok, I can't stress enough the need for subtlety here.' Amelia looked annoyed, or at least as annoyed as she would allow herself to appear. She still bore the cold mask of self control.

'There's a time for subtlety, and a time for smashing heads,' Blaklok replied, relying on an old and well-used adage.

'Yes, well. Might I suggest we proceed with caution?'

'Suggest what you like, love.' He gestured for her to lead the way.

Her tipstaff was already opening the vast steel door that led on to yet more subterranean shadows, so with Snapper whimpering to himself in the dark, they carried on.

After several minutes of twisting, turning tunnels, Blaklok could see light up ahead. He raised an arm for the others to stop, something that must have hurt Amelia's sense that she was in command, but she didn't complain.

He stalked forward, keeping within the shadowed confines of the tunnel, and peered out into the light. It was a wide reception hall filled with more brutal looking guards. Blaklok counted eight of them in various stages of repose.

This wouldn't be easy, but then it never bloody was, was it.

'We've got trouble ahead,' he said, after returning to Amelia's side. 'But I think we can get through. I just need a knife.'

Amelia looked at him uncertainly, then nodded to her tipstaff who duly produced a short blade.

'Can I go yet?' said Snapper suddenly, his voice sounding more pitiful than ever. 'I've done what you asked. Please?' The last word was said through a strangled sob.

'Go on then,' said Blaklok, not even bothering to look at Trol's tear-streaked face. 'But if I ever see you again–'

Trol was moving before Thaddeus had a chance to finish his sentence.

'So, what do you plan to do with that little pig sticker, Mr Blaklok?'

'I could tell you,' he said with a sly grin. 'But then I'd have to induct you into my cult.'

From her face, it was obvious Amelia didn't see the funny side.

SHE FOLLOWED BLAKLOK to the edge of the tunnel, and realised what he meant by 'trouble'. The room was lined with towering guards, each one bigger than the two they had brought down earlier. What he was going to do with a tiny knife was beyond her.

He stood at the threshold of the room, breathing deeply but silently and gripping the knife in a white-knuckled fist. Then he lifted his left arm, palm upwards. She could see a tattoo covered most of his flesh, but she couldn't quite make out the design in the dimness.

Blaklok ceremoniously lifted the knife and stabbed it into his upturned forearm. Amelia lifted a hand to her mouth to stifle the sound of her disgust. He dug the blade into his flesh and slowly, ever so slowly, ran it down towards his wrist. The flesh parted and blood began to pool in a black line along the length of the wound.

Amelia was assailed with a sense of nausea, her eyes watering as she watched. But it was something more than simple horror at Blaklok's self mutilation. This was something altogether sinister. As she watched, the blood from Blaklok's wound began to move, curling into the air like the tendrils of some creeping vine. The blood diffused, dissipating and spreading into the room, creating a slithering shadow that seemed to hunger for the light.

Her eyes were wide in horror as she watched and it was all she could do to stifle her screams. This Blaklok, this thug, this footpad and criminal, was some kind of warlock? It was beyond reason. Those who consorted with magic and demons were wizened old men with pointed beards and claw-like fingernails, dressed in sparkling robes. This Blaklok was a common criminal.

But as she watched it was clear he was so much more.

The black tendrils that sprouted from Blaklok's arm began to consume the light, coating lamps and candles and dimming the scant illumination in the reception room, right before the eyes of the thugs who guarded it. But none of them seemed to notice, at least not until the room was bathed completely in inky darkness.

Panic ensued, gruff voices rising in alarm and calling to their fellows, heavy boots stomping around in the blackness, desperately trying to find a light source. It was then that Amelia realised Blaklok was no longer beside her.

She heard the sounds of violence; muffled cries and solid blows in the dark. A carbine went off in the corner of the room, briefly illuminating the black. Something was smashed in a brief scuffle, then came the sound of someone falling to the ground. Loud voices, more carbine fire, brief muzzle flashes flaring in the dark and revealing the carnage in the shadows, but Amelia could barely make out what was happening.

Then silence.

With a sigh, the shadows lifted, dissolving into a wispy fog to reveal the chaos left behind. Blaklok stood in the centre of the room, broken furniture and smashed ornaments lay all around. Surrounding him were the prone forms of eight hulking guards; each bloodied, none conscious.

Amelia moved forward, suddenly more afraid of this Blaklok than she had ever been. He heaved breath into his lungs and she noticed that the laceration he had inflicted on his arm seemed to have miraculously healed.

'Well?' said Blaklok, after regaining his breath. 'What now?'

'Remember what we said about proceeding with caution, Mr Blaklok? Well, this wasn't what I had in mind.'

'Going to talk your way in were you? Rely on that old Indagator charm? Because to be honest I don't think this bunch would have been much impressed with it.'

'No, but now everyone beyond that door will know we're here,' she motioned to the huge steel portal that barred their progress from the reception room. 'Do you have a key to open it, because I don't think they're just going to let—'

She stopped as the sound of bolts being released echoed from beyond the door. With a whine of heavy steel hinges the vast metal portal swung outward.

Another hulking thug stood barring the way and Amelia could sense Blaklok tensing, ready for another battle, eager to add more scars to that battered face and more victories to his tally. But the guard merely beckoned them through, moving back and allowing them access to the room beyond.

'What do you reckon to that?' asked Blaklok, his question posed with a smug half smile.

'I reckon we should stay on our guard,' Amelia replied, taking the lead and walking towards the door.

The room beyond was most out of character with the stinking subterranean tunnels of the Cistern. It was a hazy, scented chamber more akin to a colonial brothel or whore's boudoir than the lair of a Manufactory crime lord.

Amelia walked through the room, her feet soundless on the plush rugs that adorned the floor, and followed the heavy as he led them towards a diminutive figure behind a large desk.

She didn't know what she had been expecting. The Montserrat was infamous – a man seldom spoken of and never seen – but this strange dwarf was far from what she had envisioned.

'You've made quite a mess out there,' he said, smiling an easy smile. 'Could you not just have knocked?'

The Montserrat reclined in his chair. There was something about his tranquil manner that put Amelia at her ease, but she fought against it. It would be foolish to relax in here, despite the sweet aroma and the Montserrat's polite small talk.

'You must be Indagator Amelia. And this,' he said, gesturing towards the scarred, tattooed madman at her shoulder, 'must be the feared and respected Thaddeus Blaklok.'

'Feared and respected?' Blaklok replied. 'You don't know the half of it, mate. Where's the fucking Key?'

'Straight to business,' replied the Montserrat, his smile not straying from his lips. 'That surprises me, Indagator, allowing a known criminal to speak in your stead.'

Amelia would have preferred to do the negotiations herself, but Blaklok's blunt-hammer attitude to this whole affair had worked so far.

'Just answer the question, Montserrat,' she replied.

'Well, obviously I don't have it with me. But I know where it is, and I can get it for you – at a price.'

'This isn't happy hour at the second-hand bargain shop you little fucker.' Blaklok took a step forward, the thug standing near them reached for a weapon and Hodge was quick to draw his carbine.

The Montserrat raised a hand. 'Please, no funny business in here. I've just had it done.' He gestured to the hangings and fine ornaments that gaudily adorned the room. 'The fact is, I have something you want. Being a representative of the Judicature, you're in a position to provide me with certain goods and services in return. Whether you like it or not, that's how this will play out.'

He smiled from behind his desk, pleased with himself, but Blaklok didn't seem to be the bargaining type, taking another threatening step forward.

'Look, you little–'

Heavy footfalls suddenly echoed from the room behind them, like a stampede heading their way through the tight tunnels of the Cistern. With a nod of his head, the Montserrat gestured to his bodyguard and the man brandished his carbine and rushed to see what was approaching.

No sooner had he disappeared through the mist and hangings, than there was a sickening thud.

The hulking bodyguard came flying back through the room in a wisp of smoke, dragging fine silks and linen drapes with him. He landed in front of Amelia, his dead eyes staring towards the ceiling.

Figures moved from the back of the room; red-robed figures, their faces twisted in bestial fury. To their fore was a thin man, his face blackened and scarred as though he had just barely escaped from a burning building.

'Where's my Key?' he demanded.

Amelia looked to Blaklok, who had an expression of consternation across his hard features.

'Julius,' he breathed. 'Great swinging bollocks!'

CHAPTER
THIRTY-ONE

'YOU HAVE STOLEN from me, Thaddeus Blaklok. You have hampered the plans of Legion. On your ever-living soul, you had best atone for this or the consequences will be dire. Give me the Key of Lunos!'

Obviously Lord Julius was annoyed.

'I'm afraid I don't have it,' Blaklok replied conversationally. 'But I know a man who does.' He turned, motioning beyond the large desk that stood behind him, only to stop in disbelief.

The Montserrat had done a runner.

'Don't play games with me, Blaklok. Trust me, your merry quips will do you little good now.'

At Julius's shoulder, Blaklok could see the remaining twisted acolytes; feral faces baring sharp fangs. Among them was Castor Cage, his clothes and face rent and torn by the numerous battles he had endured recently. It was obvious he was only too eager to be unleashed on Blaklok.

'I know you,' said Amelia. She struck an authoritative figure, despite the numbers arrayed against them, and Blaklok found himself further impressed by her strength of character. 'You're Lord Julius. I've been to your mansion! Are you telling me you're behind all this?'

'And I remember you, hell sow! You butchered my dogs!'

'Yes... well,' Amelia replied, suddenly on the back foot. 'That may have been a misunderstanding. What's more important is why you're dressed like that, and who these...

people are.' She motioned to the demonic acolytes at Julius's heel.

'I don't think you're in a position to be asking questions.'

'I am an Indagator of the Manufactory's Judicature. I'll ask any question I like. I have the authority–'

'Please, spare me. What authority do you think you have? Is it any higher than the authority of the nobles? Do you think it will do them any good when the Legion rises to claim this city… this world? We will cut out its heart and feed it to our masters, and there is no 'authority' that can stand against us.'

'Cut out its heart?' said Amelia, her smooth brow suddenly furrowing.

'Indeed, like we have with so many others.'

'It was you!' she said, her finger raised in sudden accusation. 'You killed Earl Beuphalus!'

'I wielded the knife. But the sacrifice was made by us all. For we are Legion.' Julius opened his arms wide to encompass his followers as they hovered around him.

'Right, I've had enough of this endless nattering,' said Blaklok, fast losing patience. 'Are we going to get on with the fighting or not?'

'So keen to meet your end.' A wicked grin stretched across Julius's face. 'Very well. Cage, if you'd like to do the honours.'

Without need of further encouragement, Castor Cage bounded forward, but this time Blaklok was ready for him. He had been taken unawares once, he would not let that happen again. He had seen this beast in action and knew its inhuman strengths.

But Thaddeus Blaklok had strengths all of his own.

Every mark and sigil that had been sliced, cut, pricked and stained onto his flesh had a purpose. Some were aesthetic, others looked like they had been scrawled by a blind and thumbless crone using a stick and a pot of septic ink. But each had a purpose. Dwelling in the pits of Hell were a myriad different demons, some great, some small, all diabolical.

Unfortunately for Castor Cage, he was not even as potent as the weakest of these.

The tiny marks stained into each of Blaklok's knuckles flared, their hatred for demonkind burning in a fulgurating rage. As his fist hit the half-demon full in the face, it unleashed a power of Hell that even the greatest demon would have flinched at. Cage didn't even have time to yelp before he was flung the length of the room, blood spurting from his smashed snout and spraying the drapes that hung limp from the ceiling.

Blaklok stood, a mad grin marring his face, eyes aflame.

'Right, you fuckers! Who's next!?'

With a collective howl of rage the rest were upon him.

THE MONTSERRAT FLED for his life. He was not a particularly brave man, having spent most of his days surrounding himself with loyal bodyguards and thick walls. But with all that gone to shit it was time to make a hasty exit.

He felt in his pocket for the Key and was conscious of it warming his thigh. He had no idea what it was for or why everyone wanted it so badly but he would be damned if he would let it go. At least not without receiving considerable recompense.

Somehow he had managed to keep his nerve when Blaklok and the Indagator had burst in. Managed to string them along by pretending he did not have the Key about his person, then fled down his escape tunnel when no one was looking. But that was the Montserrat's strength – subterfuge, smoke and mirrors, cloaks and daggers – whatever dried cliché you wanted to put on it, that was his power. People believed the Montserrat was an overlord, a ruthless kingpin. In reality he spent most of his time scared, cowering behind the backs of stronger men. He knew though, that as long as no one suspected his craven nature he was safe in this venal, ruthless environment.

Money talked just as loudly as the blaring of a carbine and from an early age the Montserrat had spent his time amassing men and wealth and, with them, power. He was not about to let that go now just because of one stray Indagator and a back street thug.

His feet slowly came to a stop as they slopped along the damp, narrow tunnel. Up ahead, the Montserrat could see that someone was barring his way, but that was impossible. This was his personal, secret escape tunnel. It led out onto a separate higher level of the Cistern, just below the Manufactory's surface. No one even knew it existed.

In his pocket the strange Key began to burn with a growing intensity. It became more and more uncomfortable with each passing second until it was almost too much to bear, but before the Montserrat could remove it a voice peeled out from up ahead.

'Ey up.'

The Montserrat squinted in the stygian dark, trying his best to discern the character's features.

'Who are you?' he asked, trying his best to disguise his fear.

'Name's Quickstep,' came the reply, and the figure walked forward into the dim lanternlight of the corridor, revealing himself as a short, nondescript individual in a flat cap and raincoat.

The Montserrat almost laughed at his caution. This was a nobody, some vagrant off the street who had strayed into his secret tunnel by mistake. It was rare that the Montserrat was brave but he was sure even he could handle this fool.

'Out of my way,' he said, 'I have pressing business. You'd do well to make yourself scarce, this is a private tunnel. On any other day I'd have you battered shitless for your intrusion, but you're lucky I'm in a rush.'

'That's not a problem,' said Quickstep, not making to move from the Montserrat's path. 'But there's just one thing – I'd like the Key before you go. There's a good chap.'

The Montserrat felt a cold chill run up his spine. How did this joker know about the Key? Something wasn't right here, but there wasn't time to fart around with some delusional interloper. The Montserrat pulled his snub revolver from the tiny holster at his side. It only fired two shots, but they'd be enough to see this cheeky tramp off.

'I don't have time for this,' he said, brandishing the weapon. 'Now move, or you're dead.'

'I see, pressed for time are you? Well, so am I. This is your last chance. Give me the Key or I'll have to take it from you.'

Two thunderclap shots rang out in the confines of the tunnel, echoing down the long darkness and bouncing off the walls, louder than sin. Smoke billowed from the revolver's barrel and the Montserrat's ears began to ring. When the smoke cleared, he saw that Quickstep was still standing there, not a mark on him.

'I've had enough of this,' he said from beneath his flat cap, seeming to pull himself up to full height. The Montserrat could see his eyes begin to glow with an inner fire, the flesh of his face becoming translucent. 'I have sought the Key long enough. Now, I'm afraid Zaphiel is coming.'

'Wait!' cried the Montserrat, panic gripping him deep down, an inner terror threatening to churn from within his bowels. 'You can have it. I was only kidding.'

'I'm afraid it's too late for that,' Quickstep replied as something large and feathery began to sprout from his back. 'There's nothing I can do to halt it now. Once he gets mad I just can't stop him.'

Blinding light struck the Montserrat, illuminating the tunnel as though it were aflame. Then he felt it, radiating forth, scorching and burning – a relentless aura of purity; the beneficence of the divine. It burned like nothing the Montserrat had ever felt before, and he screamed for as long as he could pull air into his lungs.

RED-ROBED BODIES lay in a heap, demonic and human alike, piled in a mass of pounded flesh. Atop them was Blaklok, a face of twisted rage, body covered in claret, but little of it his.

'I've told you fuckers before,' he screamed. 'But you just don't fucking listen, do you!'

His ire was directed at those of the Cult of Legion that still stood on their feet, but mostly it was aimed at Julius, who stood to their fore, his face arrogant no longer. Now all he showed was fear.

A sudden ear-piercing scream rang out from beyond the Montserrat's huge desk, distracting Blaklok from his work. The smell of cooking flesh billowed forth in a stinking cloud, and Amelia rushed to see what the source was.

'There's a tunnel behind here,' she said, holding a handkerchief to her nose. 'The Montserrat is the only one who knows where the Key is. If he's dead the trail ends with him.'

Blaklok leaped from the pile of dead and wounded, his vendetta with the Cult of Legion momentarily forgotten. All that mattered was the Key, and it smelt like their one link to it had somehow been turned into cinders.

Steeling himself against the smoky vapour, Blaklok headed into the tunnel. The heat was intense, and he began to sweat heavily in the tunnel's stinking confines. But there was something else here, something more than a burning tunnel – he could feel it in his bones. It was the antithesis of demonic – it was the touch of the celestial, the host, the divine, but it only served to fill Blaklok with equal dread. As far as he was concerned the heavens meant just as much shit as the hells.

He saw something moving up ahead, something big. It turned in the passage, churning the wispy smoke and wafting it towards Blaklok. As the pall began to clear, he caught sight of white wings, and felt the tug of awe pulling like a chord from his heart to his bollocks.

With a rising sense of dread Thaddeus pursued it, crouching low in the tunnel, his legs pounding down the distance to his quarry. But all the while his head told him that the last thing he wanted to do was catch it.

Then he was out in the open air of a vast cavern, lit from above by slanted sunlight. He breathed deeply, suddenly glad to be free of the cloying passage, but what he saw almost dragged the breath from his lungs.

There, gleaming with a light so pure it hurt Thaddeus's eyes, was the unmistakeable form of a seraph. Its white wings were spread wide, its naked body flawless from the tip of its blonde head to those perfectly formed toes.

Blaklok looked on the face of the divine and there was a sudden spark of recognition. At first he doubted himself, surely this couldn't be... Quickstep? But somehow he knew it was, somehow the features of this angel of unspoiled beauty were the same as the diminutive scruffbag who had saved him on more than one occasion.

Well, this certainly explained a lot.

As the seraph beat its wings and glided into the air, Blaklok caught a glimpse of the object he had been seeking for so long – the Key of Lunos was held within the grip of the angel as it soared skyward.

Amelia was suddenly at his shoulder and he heard her gasp as she caught sight of the celestial being.

'That's it. We've had it,' whispered Blaklok, realising there was nothing even he could do now to retrieve the Key.

'That's not like you, Thaddeus.' Blaklok turned to see Lord Julius staring at him no longer with hate, but with a smug air of self-confidence. 'We can get the Key back,' he said, 'but it won't be easy.'

'What do you mean *we*?' Blaklok replied, readying himself for another fight.

'Well, I have an idea where that seraph is heading, and you, quite obviously, don't. So if you want to see the Key again, you'll have to work with me.'

'How do you know?'

'How do I know?' Julius laughed. 'That was Zaphiel, the Lord of Thrones himself, I'd recognise him anywhere. Now, ask yourself, if anyone knows where the secret hermitage of the Fane of Zaphiel lies, wouldn't it be me?' Julius beamed once again.

Blaklok thought hard, trying his best to come up with an alternative that didn't end with him torturing Julius for the information. It was a shame, but he simply didn't have time for that.

'All right,' he replied. 'You've got yourself a deal.'

CHAPTER
THIRTY-TWO

As THEY MADE their way to the surface, Blaklok found it increasingly difficult to resist unleashing hell on Julius and his acolytes once again.

They stood for everything he hated; they were willing to let the world burn for their own aims, but he was bound to them now whether he liked it or not. Julius was more knowledgeable about the occult *and* the divine than anyone else in the Manufactory, and if anyone knew where Zaphiel was headed it was him. The only problem would be intercepting the seraph before he did something drastic with the Key of Lunos – catching an angel on the wing wouldn't be easy.

Luckily, Julius had ample resources.

As they reached the stinking, heaving surface of the Manufactory, Blaklok saw that their transport awaited. The huge bloated form of an airship hovered at a low mooring, its engines already humming in expectation of flight.

They moved towards it, and Blaklok felt Amelia at his shoulder once more.

'Can we trust these people?' she asked, trying to keep her voice low enough not to be heard by anyone else. 'They're murderers. What's to stop them flinging us to the ground from a great height?'

'Nothing, but Julius knows he needs me as much as I need him. He's not about to take on an errant seraph without me, even with his acolytes to back him.'

Amelia was suddenly looking at Blaklok with a strange expression. 'Who are you?' she asked, seeming wary of the answer he might give.

Blaklok merely gave a humourless grin. 'Hope you never find out.'

They boarded the airship and smoke billowed from the black engines, adding to the perpetual smog that hung over the vast metropolis. The mooring ropes were untied and with Blaklok and Amelia standing beside a group of battered and bruised cultists, the airship lurched skyward.

'Never thought I'd see this day,' said Julius. Blaklok saw he was staring at him with a maniacal grin. 'I go to war beside the infamous Thaddeus Blaklok.'

'You've changed your tune,' Blaklok replied. 'What happened to making me atone with my ever living soul?'

'Perhaps you already are, Thaddeus. Did you think of that?'

'Look!' Blaklok took a threatening step forward, and this time none of Julius's acolytes, not even his demonic brood, seemed willing to defend him. 'The only reason I'm here is to get the Key. This is a temporary arrangement. As far as I'm concerned you're still as much of a danger as the seraph.'

'Surely we can come to some accord? Perhaps we could share our prize?'

'I know you only want the Key, Julius. I know you're only bringing me along to help you take it from Zaphiel. I know a double cross is imminent.'

'And yet you've still come along. How tenacious of you.'

'You'd better believe it.'

'Oh, I do,' Julius smiled. 'Indeed I do.'

THE BASILICA STOOD in the centre of a derelict wasteland. All around the ground was blasted and torn, rubble interspersed with twisted metal struts and smashed window frames. There had been a disaster here years before – the result of an experiment long forgotten in the annals of the Lexiconium. What was for sure was that no one lived here now.

What the place was called before the great disaster was not a point of record. Nowadays they called it the Blasted Estate, nothing but rubble and toxic air for three miles in any direction. The only thing that stood on this patch of blighted earth was the Basilica.

It was a seeming oasis in a crumbling desert of smashed brick. On any other street it would have been an unremarkable sight – a simple church like any other. But in this place of devastation it stood more majestic than the highest cathedral. Its spires brushed the pall of smog that hung over it, and its grubby stained glass windows gleamed through the soot that caked them.

Zaphiel's feet gently touched the ground before the great wooden doors to the Basilica, his wings beating once and unsettling the dust and grime around him. He smiled at the sight: the Basilica... his Basilica. This was it, this was the place where the Thrones would rise. They would surge forth, a relentless host of holy warriors, and bathe this city in the light of their divinity. Zaphiel smiled at the prospect.

With a wave of one porcelain-white arm, the great doors to the Basilica swung wide and the seraph stepped forth. Where he walked, the ground seemed to churn and writhe, flourishing with life. Where his feet fell, flowering weeds sprang up from the dust, entwining the barren rock and mapping where the divine being had trod.

He entered the shadowed confines of the Basilica and a sudden light bathed its interior, shining like the heavens and illuminating the long crumbling friezes and faded murals. Dust and grime fell from the blackened pillars and a thousand dead candles suddenly sprang to life, bright flame guttering from their wicks.

In response to the proximity of such a place of consecrated worship, the Key of Lunos began to shine white with anticipation. Zaphiel lifted the basalt trinket, casting his divine gaze across its seemingly jejune surface.

'Soon,' he whispered, and the word was like a sudden symphony, filling the Basilica all the way to its stone wrought ceiling. 'Soon they will come. Soon we will take hold of this place – embrace this city to our bosom and make of it a realm of beauty. Soon my brothers will soar betwixt the adulteration of this seething metropolis and make of it a thing of righteousness.'

And, bathed in the light of the divine, the Key of Lunos purred its satisfaction, only too eager to commit to the bidding of the seraph.

BLAKLOK HAD SEEN some shit tips in the Manufactory but this place beat the lot of them. It was like some vast behemoth had decided to stamp down with one huge, scaled foot and crush the heaving streets beneath until they were flat as a fart.

'The Blasted Estate,' Amelia yelled over the buzzing din of the airship's engines. 'No one's been here for years. Word is the air is toxic. We must be flying above the poisonous fumes.'

'Well, I reckon the price of land must be cheap down there then. I might think of investing, at least you'll never have a problem with nosy fucking neighbours.'

'And what would you do about the poisonous air?'

'That's a myth!'

Blaklok turned suddenly at the new voice to see Julius standing right behind them. He smiled knowingly.

'What do you mean?' asked Amelia. 'It's common knowledge the place is tainted. Nothing lives down there.'

'Oh, you'll find the Judicature doesn't know everything.' Julius seemed to revel in his superior knowledge. 'The toxic air is merely a ruse propagated by the Fane of Zaphiel. It's to keep people away from their most holy place.' He gestured out of the open gantryway of the airship. 'The Basilica!'

Blaklok looked down, straining his eyes through the thick green pall, and he could just make out a single edifice standing in the midst of the destruction. At first its outline was obscured, but the airship began to dip, piercing the smog and descending ever closer to the building.

It was a church, at first seeming unremarkable in the extreme, but then Blaklok noticed the bright light streaming through its blackened windows, seemingly fighting against the dark smears with nothing but the purity of its illumination.

'It appears we may be too late,' said Julius. 'We have to hurry.' He turned to the massed ranks of his red-robed acolytes, raising his arms high. 'For the glory of Legion!' he cried.

'For Legion!' answered the cultists, religious ardour suddenly springing to their features.

Blaklok felt his loathing return. When this was all over, if he survived, there would have to be a reckoning with these fanatics. It was too dangerous to let them remain loose amongst the Manufactory.

'More speed!' Julius bellowed above the growling engines. The pilot glanced over one shoulder, a wide grin on his face as he gave a feverish nod of approval.

The airship bucked as the pilot wrenched forward on the throttle, urging the engines to greater effort.

Blaklok could see that the prow of the ship was aimed straight towards the front of the Basilica, directly at the great stained windows.

'Hold onto something,' Blaklok said, grasping a handrail. Amelia immediately obeyed, nodding to her tipstaff who braced himself against the side of the ship.

Blaklok could see that none of the acolytes seemed concerned about the imminent impact, so busy were they in boiling themselves up to a fervour of violence. The few demonic cultists that remained, Castor Cage included, began howling and snarling, stamping their clawed feet in preparation for battle.

With a last sputter of black smoke, the airship engines pushed themselves to the limit, propelling the huge flying behemoth towards the tattered monument standing amidst the desolate field of broken stone.

The great stained glass window shattered inward as the airship struck. With a tremendous grinding and the screech of smashing glass, the ship jolted to a halt, buffeting its passengers as though they were beans in a child's rattle.

Blaklok tensed his arms as they were almost pulled from their sockets, but he managed to hold on, clamping his eyes shut and trying his best to block out the sounds of screaming and rending metal. Brick dust billowed, blinding him momentarily, and his eardrums rang as they were assailed by the din of the crash.

Then there was silence.

Blaklok opened his eyes, trying his best to see through the pall of dense smoke and cloying dust. Something was lying on top of him and he pushed it away before realising it was a shattered body in red robes.

As he made to rise he felt hands grasp his arm, pulling him to his feet. He was about to react, and violently, when he realised it was Amelia, her pretty face smeared with soot and dirt, her eyes smudged and teary.

'Let's get to work, Mr Blaklok,' she said, her strength impressive in the circumstances. Behind her, the one remaining tipstaff at her beck and call was staggering to his feet, and Blaklok nodded.

'Yes, let's,' he said, pushing his way out of the smashed airship.

The dust was beginning to settle, and Thaddeus could see the airship had come to rest half-in and half-out of the Basilica. One wall of the building had collapsed, filling the rest with ancient rotted dust from the shattered stones. Blaklok's boots crunched through debris and smashed glass as he made his way forward, hoping he could find the seraph and retrieve the Key before it was too late.

Richard Ford

There was a sudden billowing of great white wings, and Zaphiel soared above the settling filth. His face was beautiful to behold, but the high majestic brow was furrowed in anger. It struck a primal fear in Blaklok, a fear much worse than any demon could imbue, but again, as he had so many times before, he fought against his better nature and faced the seraph down.

'Sacrilege,' said the angel, and his voice was like the blaring of a score of trumpets. 'You would seek to defile the Basilica of the Fane of Zaphiel?'

'I've come for the Key,' Blaklok replied, striding out of the dust cloud. 'And I'm not leaving without it.'

The frown atop the seraph's brow suddenly faded, and a beaming smile covered his face, which in turn transformed into a laugh like a thousand church bells.

'The Key?' he said, holding the object aloft in one great fist. 'So that you may halt the coming of the Thrones?'

Blaklok didn't move or speak. He knew that whatever was coming would be bad.

'I'm afraid, Thaddeus Blaklok, that you're already too late.'

Zaphiel waved languorously with one perfect arm and Blaklok followed the gesture with his gaze. As more of the brick dust settled in the smashed Basilica he could see a beaming light emanating from between two great pillars. It was as though a doorway had been set between the colonnades, which led to a perfect vista of pastureland in the foreground and mountains behind, topped with a perfect blue sky. And from within that landscape, sweeping forth on white-feathered wings, flocked a host like nothing Blaklok had ever seen.

'Behold,' said Zaphiel, that sonorous voice filling Thaddeus with heart-stopping dread. 'The Thrones are here!'

CHAPTER
THIRTY-THREE

'YOU'RE INSANE,' BLAKLOK raged, anger overcoming his terror. 'Do you think your gaffer's going to approve of this?'

Zaphiel laughed. 'My 'gaffer', as you so eloquently put it, has no sway here. He is a paper tiger, a gale force wind on an empty plain. The Thrones will be the new power now. We will hold sway over this rock and all will venerate us as the gods we are.'

'I can't allow that,' said Blaklok taking another step forward. He wished his resolve was as rock steady on the inside as it seemed on the out, but he had little choice. This seraph had to be stopped.

'What will you do, little man? I am immortal, I have seen the start of things and I will see their end. You are as an insect before me. An insignificant mishap on my journey to becoming.'

'You reckon, do you?' said Blaklok, already choosing his invocation.

It was time to play his final hand.

The cultists of Legion who had been imbued with the power of the demonic were twisted, foul things – puppets of powers they knew little about. Their bodies were tainted for a cause beyond their ken, though they saw it as a gift of the most beneficent kind. But for this task, Blaklok knew he would have to emulate their sacrifice – it was the only way.

He was a tool, he knew that, a weapon much like the misguided cultists, only there was a difference. Blaklok knew what awaited him on the other side, he knew the price for such power, and he was more than willing to pay it.

As he began the invocations, feeling the demonic power of the Nine Hells running through his bones, he could taste what waited for him in the deep dark.

His flesh hardened, a molten line of magma appearing along the needle thin tattoos that were etched on his arms, legs and torso. His bones began to grind and twist, the pain almost unbearable, but Blaklok made no sound. His eyes – reddening with a baleful glow – were locked on Zaphiel, the focus of his animus.

A flicker of doubt crossed the seraph's indefectible features, but it was gone as soon as it appeared, replaced by a lopsided smile of disdain.

'Call upon whatever foul magicks you wish, Thaddeus Blaklok. You know not the power you face.'

'Do you reckon? Let's fucking find out, shall we?' Blaklok replied, his voice a deep and monstrous growl.

With that he leapt forward and Zaphiel met his charge head on, sweeping forth on those powerful wings.

With twin roars of defiance, the titans clashed.

WHO ARE YOU? she had asked.

Hope you never find out.

Well, she was looking now, and the answer to her question was terrifying indeed.

Blaklok had transformed. He was no longer a man, no longer mortal. Where before he had been a hulking brute, hard and resilient in every way, now he seemed to be a literal embodiment of his own tenacity and fortitude, pushed to the extreme. He seemed almost as remarkable as the thing he faced – the angel, the *seraph* they had called it. At first, Amelia had thought this simply a name Blaklok put on the one they pursued, but no, it seemed this creature, this being that filled her with such awe, was indeed one of the heavenly host. And Blaklok – now transformed into a savage beast, his muscles bulging, his flesh hardened, his bones thickened and protruding from his extremities like weapons – was about to face it in mortal combat.

She needed a weapon if she was going to make any contribution to these events. Looking to her right she could see that a portal had appeared between two colonnades – a portal towards which a host of these divine creatures was fast approaching. Whatever these things were they were about to spew forth into the Manufactory.

All she knew was they had to be stopped.

'Weapon!' she cried, turning to Hodge. He simply shrugged, holding his hands up to reveal he had lost his carbine in the airship crash.

She turned back to the wreck of the ship, scrambling over the debris and bodies, desperately searching for anything she could use as a weapon.

The inside of the airship was thick with dust and it was difficult to see through the haze. Then her foot stubbed against something hard, and she forced back a cry of pain as she looked down. What she saw there, lying discarded and forgotten by some insane cultist, brought a smile to her lips.

ZAPHIEL HIT BLAKLOK hard, the seraph's huge granite fist smashing into his jaw. Blood spewed from his mouth and he fell sideways, momentarily dazed. The inside of his mouth was cut, his cheek lacerated by the sharpened teeth that had sprouted from his hardened gums. Had he not taken on the transformation, had he not manifested his powers before this fight began, it was likely that Zaphiel's blow would have taken his head clean off. Instead, the solid punch merely served to clarify things: the seraph was about to give no quarter, so none should be offered.

Thaddeus shook his huge head, hearing the vast thews in his neck crack and creak in response. Then he bowled forward, his arms held ready to block the seraph's strike while his head did all the work. His stone-hard forehead connected with Zaphiel's porcelain nose and rocked the seraph's head violently back, but the delicate features were misleading. It felt like head-butting a wall.

Nevertheless, the seraph staggered, the delicate features flattening under the blow, but he did not bleed or bruise.

With the buffeting of those huge wings, Zaphiel halted his fall, sweeping up into the air before his opponent. A smile crept across his perfect lips.

'Do you think you can defeat me? Even in your fell guise?'

'I'm willing to have a go,' replied Blaklok, using the brief hiatus to regain his strength. 'Do you think you can change the world with a bunch of angels?' he countered, gesturing to the Thrones, who were now almost at the portal.

'Of course. Our reign will be a magnificent one, in which the stain of defilement will be washed from these turgid streets. Why stand in our way? Surely we both have the same aim, else you would not fight your demons so vehemently.'

'You're just as bad as the demons – no, worse! At least with demons you know what you're getting, but you lot... you're all demons in disguise. You want the same thing, to control, to rule, but you'll take everything and won't stop until everyone is under your heel.'

'And what makes us different from the demons?'

'Because with a demon you can compromise. With demons you can bargain and on occasion you can control them. But you, you're relentless. No compromise, no dealing, no release. And above all, you don't have the right. Anyone controlled by a demon does so under a covenant of his own making, but you're willing to *take* without giving anyone a choice. That's why you have to be stopped.'

'So you would exchange your celestial masters for the demonic?'

'I don't have a fucking master!' Blaklok bellowed, his muscles tensing, sinew and veins standing proud on his arms. 'I kneel before no fucker. Here, let me show you.'

And they were at it again, powerful blows raining on one another, blows that would have smashed any normal man to bits, gnashing teeth and rending grasps and all.

Again the seraph managed to wrest himself from Blaklok's grip, this time holding his arm aloft, the arm that firmly held the Key of Lunos.

'You cannot stop me now,' he sang, 'you cannot hold back the inevitable.'

Thaddeus glanced over his shoulder, seeing the Thrones, the heavenly host, ready to soar through onto his own plane.

They would be unstoppable, unrelenting, things would never be the same, and for a second Blaklok wondered if that would be a bad thing. Then he shook his head against the doubt – of course it would. An eternity in thrall to the divine power of seraphs was every bit as nightmarish as servitude to arse-fucking demons.

But what could he do to stop it?

There was a sudden growl, a feral cry of rage, and a red streak leapt at Zaphiel from the dirt and bricks. Blaklok caught a glimpse of razor fangs as they clamped around the seraph's wrist, could see those teeth break as they bit down on the solid appendage, but they did their job. As the demonic acolyte of Legion attacked, Zaphiel dropped the Key.

Enraged, the seraph grasped the demon cultist and Blaklok could see who it was... Castor Cage. But before Cage could even cry out, Zaphiel tore him in two, pulling hard and spilling guts and organs to the floor.

Blaklok eyed the ground as Zaphiel discarded the torn body. All he could see was the Key of Lunos, all he could see was a way to stop all this, and instinctively he threw himself forward.

Instantly, Zaphiel was on him, pulling him back, beating his wings and dragging him from the Key, up and up towards the decrepit roof of the Basilica.

Thaddeus cried out in frustration, unable to reach the only thing that would stop the celestial onslaught, and he could only watch in defeat as the Thrones reached the portal and began to step through.

AMELIA STRUGGLED WITH her burden, lugging it as best she could while stepping through the detritus that littered the floor. The dust-filled air had all but cleared now, revealing the full extent of the carnage. Blaklok was high up in the lofty confines of the Basilica's roof, rending and tearing at his foe, who in turn beat his wings desperately, holding Blaklok aloft. And, as she scanned the rest of the Basilica, Amelia saw that the Thrones had finally reached the gate, their cherubic faces wracked with glee, their flawless bodies now stepping out from the utopian scene beyond the portal to the carnage of the Basilica.

This was not right. Despite their smiling faces, their perfect demeanours, despite everything her heart told her about these divine beings, her head cried out that this was wrong. Blaklok had told the truth; these things had no right to be here, no right to walk among the men and women of the Manufactory.

She hefted the weapon that rested on her hip, the Clarke & Wooster Super Heavy Carbine, Devastator Class. It was almost too heavy to carry, the bandolier of ammunition weighing as much as the weapon itself, but she could just about manage it. Besides, it would get light enough as soon as she started firing.

Amelia's thumb pressed down hard on the trigger and she was shocked by the deluge that was unleashed. It was as though a horde of drummers were beating a thousand metal dustbins all at once, using hatchets for drumsticks, right next to her head. The weapon bucked, showering hot rounds all across the Basilica, but she soon managed to wrestle control, directing the relentless stream of fire towards the portal.

A burning shower of shells screamed into the Thrones, smashing into their bodies and blasting chunks of bloodless

Richard Ford

flesh from their extremities. They howled in pain and fury, sounding like the distant peeling of a hundred church bells as they were pushed back beyond the limits of the portal.

'No!' bellowed Zaphiel, flinging Blaklok aside in fury, where he landed in a pile of collapsed stone. 'You will pay with your soul, hell-whore!'

With that he swooped towards her, displacing air and dust in his wake.

Amelia tried to remain calm, swinging the Devastator to bear on the charging seraph. Her finger pressed down on the trigger once more, but this time there was only a dull click. She glanced down, cold panic beginning to creep up her spine, and noticed that the overheating rod had slipped into place, stopping the bandolier feed from distributing any more shells lest they explode in the white hot breach.

She glanced up, seeing Zaphiel looming over her, the fury in his eyes more terrifying than any demon could have borne.

'Yyyeeesss!!!' came a scream that filled the Basilica all the way up to its collapsing roof.

Amelia glanced to the side, and even Zaphiel was momentarily distracted from his murderous advance.

Julius stood amongst the wreckage, his arm held aloft, the Key of Lunos within his slender grasp, triumph writ large across his battered and bleeding face.

'I have it,' he blurted, his face gleeful and maddened all at once. 'You cannot stop me now, seraph. Not you or your Thrones. We are here. We are one. We are Legion!'

With that, blackness swirled between the two pillars opposite the portal from whence the Thrones had come. Zaphiel reached out a hand, his mouth opening to command the maddened priest of Legion to stop, but he was too late.

From within the blackness of the new portal a taloned hand emerged, followed by another, and another.

'Behold,' said Julius, victorious at last. 'The Legion is come!'

CHAPTER
THIRTY-FOUR

FOR AEONS THE Host and the Horde had been at war, fighting their battles in the open, knee-deep in the primordial ooze, right up until apes learned to walk and began to dominate the earth. They had carried on their war for millions of years, casualties on both sides uncountable, the heroics and horrors of that conflict lost in the annals of time. On and on they had fought until the reasons for their conflict were long forgotten and the only motivation they needed to go to battle was their congenital hatred of one another.

With the eventual appearance of man, new recruits to their eternal war could be enlisted, and with the hearts and minds of mankind ripe for the plucking came another battlefield on which the immortals could ply their wits against one another, and their perpetual struggle for dominance took on a new guise. Now they could work insidiously, bringing mankind to their cause, working in secret through their minions and stretching out the never-ending hostilities for all eternity. The demons started their coteries and cults, working underground, whispering their promises and levying their honorarium when and where they could. More overt were the celestials, building their cathedrals and raising their fanes so that all could see and hear and flock to their cause.

Now, in the ancient Basilica, on a blasted patch of wasted earth, a conflict of eons was about to come to a head. As the Legion came forth, and the Thrones renewed their efforts to spring from their divine plane, this titanic battle of the ages was played out on a tiny stage. But the size of the battle was no reflection of the ferocity borne by each side. In all the battles fought between these two sides, neither had ever faced a foe with such utter hatred, such quintessential adversity... such rage.

Demons roared from twin mouths lined with razor fangs, spikes and talons standing erect on their backs, tails lashing with hooked appendages. Unflawed faces creased in hatred, spears held aloft, wings buffeting, thrashing in an onslaught of divine retribution.

The two sides met in the centre of the Basilica and shook the holy ground to its very foundations. Arms were torn from bodies, spilling hot, sizzling blood to the desecrated ground. Faces of utter perfection were bitten off, leaving skinless skulls to scream in pain and fury. Spears impaled armoured demon chests, unable to halt the fiendish assault, and such was the determination of the Host and the Horde to destroy one another that they would still rend and tear beyond the limits of their immortal lives.

The noise that filled the tall building was deafening as the velvet voices of the Thrones and the foul bleating of the demonic wave met in a dirge of relentless discord. Gurgling, spitting faces bellowed into the pure and untarnished visages of the Host, their contrasting sounds not countering one another, but only serving to make the din that much more terrifying.

Thaddeus Blaklok lifted his head from the pile of rubble where he lay, and listened for a second to the sound of Hell on Earth. His body was no longer imbued with the strength of the demonic – that cantation had passed – and now he would have to rely on his own innate strength and his wits to finish this. Well, he'd done a bang up job so far!

He rose, still crouching on the pile of smashed brick, keeping his head low and trying to avoid the attentions of the battling immortals. That wouldn't be too difficult, the Host and Horde were so preoccupied with rending each other asunder they would have little time for a single mortal.

Thaddeus scanned the carnage and soon spotted his prey. Lord Julius was standing to one side of the fray, gripping the Key of Lunos. His eyes were wide as he surveyed the devastation he had contributed to causing.

Picking his moment, Blaklok sprinted across the floor of the Basilica, dodging fallen bodies and smashed rubble. He ducked as one of the Thrones soared overhead, intent on its foe. The screaming angel piled into a mass of seething scaled bodies, sweeping its massive spear left and right, severing arms and heads and legs. But there seemed an endless array of demonic flesh that battled back, tearing at the flawless flesh of the divine with equal fierceness.

As Blaklok neared his prey, Julius saw him and his eyes widened, looking as though they would pop right out of his head. He glanced left and right looking for an escape route but there was none; he was surrounded by ripping, tearing beasts, and would surely be caught in the skirmish if he tried to move – Julius had backed himself in a corner and there was nowhere for him to run.

Blaklok allowed himself a smile as he ran forward. He was almost upon Julius, anticipating the thrill of inflicting pain on the conceited, foolish prig, when something smashed into him. Pain jarred him as he hit the ground hard, sharp rubble splitting his flesh, and he looked up in time to stare into the foul maw of a demon of Legion, its serpentine head dipping to attack with lightning speed. Blaklok instinctively raised his arms to fend off the blow, though he knew it would be useless, when a silver tipped spear lanced forward, transfixing the loathsome creature where it stood.

There was no time to wait and watch the repugnant spectacle as a seraph tore the demon apart. Leaping to his feet, Blaklok made to cover the last few feet to his prey, but Julius had found his escape route; a miniscule gap in the vicious battle. There was daylight peaking through a tear in the Basilica's wall and the leader of the Cult of Legion was headed straight for it.

Thaddeus stumbled forward, his legs feeling weak after their recent exertions, but he would not allow Julius to escape. There was no way he would let such a man walk free after what he had unleashed, and besides, he had a mission to complete.

But it seemed Blaklok was not the only one who coveted the Key.

A huge white figure slammed down, blocking Julius's escape route. The high priest of Legion stumbled back, crying out in panic as Zaphiel stood barring his way.

'Do you realise what you have done?' spoke the seraph, his voice no longer pleasant to the ear. Now it sounded like a funeral bell, the strength of it blasting Julius back on his rump. 'They must be stopped. The gate to the Pit must be sealed.'

Julius whimpered, holding up the Key of Lunos toward the irrepressible seraph, surrendering it in the face of the angel's divine will.

But Blaklok was quicker.

He stretched forward, snatching the Key from Julius's grip and staring up at Zaphiel.

The seraph smiled.

'Defiant to the last,' the angel said. 'You, at least, are a worthy adversary. But the time for games is at an end. The demons have to be stopped, you of all people must realise this.'

'The demons aren't the only ones,' Blaklok replied, closing his grip around the Key and feeling its power teasing his mind, trying to sway him to its will.

The Key of Lunos wanted this conflict – it was a tool for opening the forbidden gates and its purpose was being carried out to the utmost. Now it only wanted more, to tear open the portals between Heaven and Hell and allow the warring factions to spew forth and use the mortal realm as their battleground.

Blaklok forced the Key to bend to his will, though it resisted, fighting back with a fury. The Key glowed white hot in his hand, burning his flesh, the sound of its defiance shrill in his ears. Perspiration began to bead on his face as his mind struggled to break the Key's bond with the portals, and he felt the power that opposed him falter. The doors began to flicker in and out of existence, their link to the plane of men weakening.

Something hit Blaklok hard, throwing him back where he crashed to the ground, but he still managed to grip onto the burning Key of Lunos. He opened his eyes, feeling the Key regain its hold on the portals, allowing yet more demons and angels to spew forth, to fight and maim and rend each other asunder.

Above him stood Zaphiel, his golden breastplate glowing in the light, his face a mask of fury. Thaddeus wanted to rise, wanted to face the seraph down, wanted to meet his end with as much spit and fire as he could muster, but his ribs were broken and he could hardly breathe. It would not take much for the seraph to end him now.

'It will be a shame to cast you down, Thaddeus Blaklok,' said Zaphiel. 'You could have been an instrument for righteousness, but instead you elect to throw in your lot with demons and witches.'

'Go to hell,' spat Blaklok, flecks of blood spilling from his mouth.

'No, Thaddeus. It is not I who will go to hell.'

The seraph raised a massive arm, an arm of white marble that would finally smash the life from Blaklok.

White-hot blasts suddenly rained against Zaphiel's golden breastplate. Chips of the divine armour sparked away and the seraph was thrown back under the deluge. Before he could compose himself, another relentless blast hit him, shredding one wing and knocking him further back.

Blaklok forced himself to stand, watching as the seraph was blasted towards the gaping black portal by a rain of devastating fire. Zaphiel screamed in fury, staring defiantly at the source of the fire, and Blaklok saw that it was Amelia, holding the biggest carbine he had ever seen, pressing the ignition switch hard, gritting her pretty features as the weapon rocked and bucked in her grip. With a scream of rage, Amelia kept the carbine trained on the errant seraph, pushing him back beyond the boundary of the diabolical portal and into the gaping maw of Hell itself.

Thaddeus knew he had no time to waste, and gripped the Key tighter, smelling his burning flesh as it fought against him. But the power of his will was beyond question. Even now the Key's light was diminishing as it strained against him, losing its battle with this defiant, powerful human. And, as the light of the Key of Lunos ebbed away, so did the shimmering boundaries of each portal, their link with the mortal realm breaking, becoming ever less corporeal with each passing second.

Amelia's deluge of fire halted, the bandolier of inch long rounds having run out. Blaklok looked up, seeing Zaphiel's shattered chest and face – but these wounds were not enough to stop the seraph. He screamed, a divine cry of rage that gusted forth like a discordant wind, shattering the remaining windows of the Basilica. Zaphiel charged forth on shattered wings, but he would never be fast enough.

Before the seraph could reach the portal it quickly winked out, leaving nothing of him but the echo of his final cry.

CHAPTER
THIRTY-FIVE

SHE DROPPED THE massive weapon to the floor with a dull clank, its payload spent. The horror of the twin portals was now gone, but the battling creatures that flooded the Basilica were still writhing and biting and slaying one another more furiously than ever.

Hodge crouched to one side of the carnage, trying his best to avoid impalement on a ten foot spear or spiked talon, and Amelia frantically beckoned him forward.

'We have to leave,' she shouted above the din of battle.

From the look on Hodge's face she knew he was not about to argue.

Navigating the rubble-strewn floor of the church, Amelia and Hodge made their way towards Blaklok. He leaned heavily against the last remaining pillar of the Basilica that had not been smashed to pieces by the warring immortals. His face was ashen, his body bleeding and broken but still he gripped the Key of Lunos in one meaty fist, as though prepared to defend it to the last.

'Give me the Key and let's get out of here,' she said, looking into his heavy-lidded eyes. He grinned, glancing down at the Key in his hand, then back up at her.

'Take it if you can,' he said, his voice weak.

Without pausing, Amelia reached forward and snatched the Key from Blaklok's grip, feeling it cold against her palm.

Blaklok grinned, then slumped down onto his haunches, his

back still leaning against the pillar. 'I wasn't expecting that,' he said with a wry grin.

'We'll get you out,' said Amelia, moving forward to help him, but he suddenly rose, using the last vestiges of his strength, and shoved her backwards. In that instant two creatures, one hellish to behold, the other perfect in every way, smashed into the ground where she had been standing.

The creatures thrashed and wrestled, rending and tearing at one another, and Amelia was relieved to feel Hodge's strong hands grasp her and pull her away to safety. In the confusion she lost sight of Blaklok, so eager was she to avoid being caught in the melee of two immortal beings, and when she finally composed herself, Blaklok was nowhere in sight.

She paused, glancing desperately around the Basilica, but she could not see him – only the battling creatures from beyond the realms of man, now set on destroying each other absolutely.

Part of the roof suddenly collapsed beside them, and Amelia realised that as much as she wanted to stay and find Blaklok – whether to reward or imprison him, she was not sure which – she knew escape was the only sane option.

Light encroached on the Basilica from a breach in the wall, and Amelia immediately headed for it, Hodge close at her shoulder. Still in her hand was the Key of Lunos. What Amelia had expected from the much-coveted item she wasn't sure, but it seemed to be a wholly unspectacular object. It did not fill her with dread nor burn her flesh. Neither was she assailed by a psychic wave as the thing tried to control her thoughts or compel her to actions aberrant to her nature. It seemed almost impossible to think that so many had been prepared to kill for such a seemingly insignificant trinket.

Out in the open, the air was thick and miasmic with billowing dust from the assailed Basilica mixing with the polluted atmosphere of the Blasted Estate. Amelia took no time to pause, stumbling forward and trying to put as much distance between her and the warring legions as she could.

Through the pall up ahead she could make out other figures fleeing the scene – red-robed acolytes of Legion who had somehow survived the crash of their airship and were eager to save themselves from the carnage they were partly responsible for. How Amelia would have loved to wreak retribution on them, how she would have loved to unleash her tipstaffs on each and every one, but for now it would have to wait. She had to get the Key back to the Judicature, to have it examined properly by one of their scryators and kept safe within the vaults.

Then her eye fell on one of the fleeing cultists, and she knew that she could at least satisfy herself with just one small portion of retribution.

Julius crawled along, thick sobs racking his body as he dragged himself painfully across the sharp rubble of the Blasted Estate. Amelia stopped behind him, Hodge by her side, waiting for him to look around and see who it was that cast a shadow over his pitiful, fleeing figure.

Julius slowly turned his head, horror writ in his eyes. Relief washed over him; it was obvious he had been expecting some immortal form to descend on him, to cast its divine judgment on the man who had tried to destroy an entire city – perhaps even the world.

He smiled, spittle dripping from the side of his mouth. 'It wasn't supposed to be like this,' he said, holding up a grazed and withered hand.

Amelia felt her fist clench within one thin, leather glove… then smashed it into Lord Julius's face.

He squealed, holding up his arms in a pathetic defence.

'Get used to that,' said Amelia. 'There's much more waiting for you where you're going.'

Hodge grasped hold of the mewling noble and, as the Basilica still raged with the warring factions behind them, they fled across the Blasted Estate to the relative safety of the Manufactory. From a distance, Amelia could see the final throes of the building as it relented under the onslaught of demons and angels. Whichever side was winning she could not tell, but with any luck they would destroy themselves absolutely; countering light for dark so that nothing remained.

Only time would tell what consequences the Manufactory would have to suffer from the survivors of that ferocious conflict.

SHE STRODE INTO the Ministry of the Judicature with as much dignity as she could muster. Her fellow Indagators stared with a mixture of disgust and amazement at her ripped and torn attire, and more than a few administrants peered over their half moon spectacles at the strange sight.

Behind her, Hodge dragged the whining figure of Lord Julius, his demented eyes now glaring wide. He had defecated himself twice on the way to the Ministry of the Judicature, and the burly tipstaff was holding him at arm's length.

'I need to see the Grand Overseer immediately,' Amelia demanded, relieved that she still managed to retain some modicum of strength and command in her voice.

Fantassins and Indagators looked at one another in confusion – it was a demand that was never made, the Grand Overseer only ever saw his underlings by written appointment and seldom granted an audience even then, let alone responded to a summons. The silence was telling, and Amelia began to wonder if she might have overstepped her remit.

There was sudden movement, and down one of the antiseptic corridors strode a procession of heavily armoured fantassins. As they drew closer Amelia could see that they bore the clenched fist sigil of the Grand Overseer's personal entourage.

Amelia smiled at the gawping administrants who had, a moment before, thought her mad. Obviously her arrival had been expected – this would show them.

She strode forward, gripping Julius by the collar of his tattered robe, eager to apprise the fantassins of what was happening in the Blasted Estate, but their commander took a step forward, his aggressive manner silencing her before she could even begin.

'The Key,' he demanded. 'You will relinquish it into our care.'

Amelia stopped for a second. How could they have known? She glanced down into her open palm where the Key of Lunos rested; the simple stone key that had been the cause of so much strife.

'Hand it over. Now.' The threat in the commander's voice was thinly veiled. Something inside Amelia made her want to resist, to keep the Key from him, to keep it protected, but this man was part of the Grand Overseer's entourage, an elite custodian of justice and order within the Manufactory. What could she do against that?

Nothing.

She placed the Key of Lunos into his outstretched hand.

With no word of thanks, the commander turned on his heel and marched back down the corridor, closely followed by his heavily armoured subordinates.

All Amelia could do was watch them leave.

Instantly, as though a sudden flame had been lit beneath them, the administrants, fantassins and Indagators went about their business as if nothing had happened. They swept past Amelia as though she wasn't there, and it suddenly seemed that all she had achieved and gone through over the past few days had been for naught.

But at least she had Julius. She would have to satisfy herself with venting her frustrations on him. But then, looking at the pitiful figure before her, she doubted it would even be worth the effort.

'Where is it?' came a fluting voice. Amelia turned to see a tall, well-dressed figure flaunt into the entrance hall of the Ministry, surrounded by a scurrying collection of man-servants bedecked in ties and tails. 'I demand to know where my property is. I want it back,' squealed the man, bold as brass. He was roundly ignored by the staff of the Judicature, who appeared to have better things to do all of a sudden.

'It belongs to me. I demand to speak with the Grand Overseer.'

Amelia stepped back, trying to make herself inconspicuous lest she come under any scrutiny from this man and his demands.

'I think Duke Darian Hopplite will have even less chance of seeing the Overseer than you did,' whispered an oleaginous voice.

Amelia turned, seeing the leering face of Surrey regarding her with that scurrilous look. Somehow though, she did not feel as repulsed as she normally did. Today she was too tired to bat off his unwelcome attentions. She had done enough fighting for one day.

'No,' she replied. 'But then you can't always get what you want.'

'That's certainly true.'

'Sometimes you have to take what pleasures you can.'

At this, Surrey raised a suggestive eyebrow.

'Would you like to help me interrogate a prisoner?' she asked.

Surrey glanced down at the pitiful figure of Lord Julius. 'It would be my pleasure.'

Amelia nodded her assent, and together they dragged Julius, kicking and screaming, towards the vaults.

It might not be much of a release, but it was better than nothing.

HE LAY ON the familiar bed, staring up at the cracks in the ceiling. The pungent smell of disinfectant was ripe in his nostrils and brought tears to his eyes. Or were they tears of pain? Or tears of woe?

No, it was the disinfectant – definitely.

Somewhere in the room the Apothecary was pottering around, rifling through shelves packed with tinctures and gauze. He had, as usual, done a fine job of patching Thaddeus up, but it still hurt like hell. Neither was the pain helped by the knowledge that he had failed in his mission.

Yes, he had stopped an apocalyptic invasion of angels and demons. But the fact that he did not have the Key of Lunos hurt more than any of the bruises, or his broken ribs, missing finger, cracked knuckles and lacerations.

To add to his misery, it was likely he would hurt a lot more when he had to report his failure. But that one he would face when he came to it.

The light dimmed and Blaklok painfully moved his head to the side, seeing the bearded face of the Apothecary staring down at him. The old man's face was marred with amusement more than concern, but it mattered little to Blaklok.

'When will this all end, Thaddeus? When will it be time for your crusade to finish, and your life to begin again?'

It wasn't much of a question, but Blaklok took a moment to ponder his reply. The more he thought about it, the less he felt he could answer.

'For as long as the holy demand it,' he replied. It was a poor answer, and doubtless untrue, but it was the only one he could muster.

The Apothecary laughed, his thick moustache quivering as he exuded a series of sharp guffaws. 'You don't do what others demand, Thaddeus. Not unless you're sure it's to your advantage. There's something you're not telling me. What's in this for you?'

Blaklok stared into the Apothecary's eyes, wondering if his interest was purely altruistic. Thing was, you could never tell in this city – the Manufactory was a hive of suspicion and rightly so – it was a place rife with scum willing to stab you in the back. Blaklok had learned that the hard way.

'You might find out one day,' he replied, closing his eyes.

The Apothecary walked away, shuffling off to another part of his rooms.

Blaklok hated himself for not being able to confide in the old man, but it was the only way.

There *was* something in it for him, and the things he had put himself through *were* ultimately for his advantage, but the Apothecary had been wrong about one thing.

Blaklok *was* beholden to someone. And until he did for them what they asked he would remain so. But then, when all the tasks were finished, or when he was spent, he would get what he wanted.

Then there would be a reckoning.

Then the crusade would be over.

EPILOGUE

BLOOD RED CURTAINS hung from a high ceiling, brushing the dark oak floorboards; teasing them like a maiden caressing her lover's neck with a crimson feather. A fire roared in one corner, filling the room with an oppressive heat that only served to make the stench of rot all the more pungent.

He stood in front of a large portrait, his lambent robes made from satin, silk, ermine, velvet and taffeta. As he gazed into the portrait it was like staring into a mirror, the figure that stared back was dressed identically, the face bearing the same ebon hair and troubled brow. It pleased him that such an accurate likeness had been rendered. It was fitting that when he eventually ascended there should be an apt representation left behind for all to see. He had commended the artist heartily for his work. Then he had arranged for the man to be eliminated, so such perfect labour could never be repeated for anyone else. Well, it was only right and proper that the Hierophant of the First Fane of the Sancrarium should have no rivals of any sort, not even in image.

Absently, the Hierophant raised his hand and gazed languidly upon what it contained. The Key of Lunos sat innocently in his palm, cold and sleeping. But the Hierophant knew what it could do – what it yearned to do.

All in good time, he thought to himself, though he did not speak it. He would not want his guest to hear of his ambitions.

'Thaddeus Blaklok failed. What would you have us do about it?' said the voice from behind him.

The Hierophant turned to regard his guest as it squatted on the floor, ichor dripping and mist rising from its newly summoned body.

'What would you suggest?' he replied, raising an eyebrow in expectation.

'We think Blaklok should be given to us, so that we may convey him back to our plane. So that we may punish him for all his sins.'

The Hierophant smiled at the predictable response. 'You would so readily squander such a valuable asset? So typical of your kind. Despite his failure, Blaklok has proven himself resourceful, strong, and above all, loyal to our cause. As long as we have what he wants he will do our bidding. This,' the Hierophant held up the Key, turning it in his opulently ringed fingers, 'was little more than a test. I could have taken it at any time. As it was, circumstances meant it was delivered to the Judicature. And I own the Judicature. So in a way, Blaklok did not fail at all. But there will be more chances for him to prove his worth.'

'But he has allowed the Host and the Horde to be unleashed on the city. What are we to do about that?'

'That is of little interest to me. There are enough demons wandering the streets of the Manufactory already. What matter are a few more?'

'Your lack of concern in this matter is most—'

'My only concern is to keep the First Fane's involvement in all this a secret. And you would do well to remember with whom you speak. Remember whom you serve. We have the Key, we are above suspicion and that is all that matters. Now, to further business. When Blaklok recovers, there is another task I would have you give him...'

Rankpuddle squatted down, ready to listen as the Hierophant of the First Fane of the Sancrarium, wielder of the

Manufactory's faith, and moral compass by which all righteous men were judged, related his instructions.

And the demon was powerless to do anything but his bidding. For now...

About the Author

Richard Ford originally hails from Leeds in the heartland of Yorkshire, but now resides in the Wiltshire countryside, where he can be found frolicking by the Thames, drinking cider and singing songs about combine harvesters.
For more information on what he's up to check out
www.richard4ord.wordpress.com.

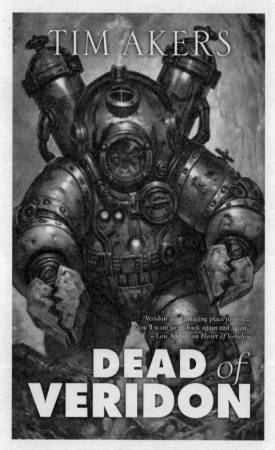

UK ISBN: 978 1 907519 47 5 • US ISBN: 978 1 907519 48 2 • £7.99/$7.99

Trouble finds Jacob Burn: kicked out of his house, out of his comfortable life – out of everything that is familiar – even turned away from his circle of criminal friends and colorful enemies. Two years after he saved an ungrateful city from a mad angel, thwarting the plans of every powerful faction in Veridon, Jacob is still trying to pull his life together.

And still trouble finds him. A bad job goes worse, and soon old enemies present themselves as allies, and former friends set themselves against Jacob as he tries to put the dead to rest and the living to justice. Things gets even harder when he's appointed by the Council to investigate the clockwork-powered rise of the dead, while some hold him personally accountable, and others in the city work to use the chaos to their advantage.

 WWW.SOLARISBOOKS.COM

Follow us on Twitter! www.twitter.com/solarisbooks